Greyladies

EMILY DENI

Dorothy Emily Stevenson, born in Edinburgh in 1892, was very proud of her family tradition of engineering and writing; her great-grandfather, Robert Stevenson, designed the famous Bell Rock Lighthouse and many others around the Scottish coast, and her father was a first cousin of Robert Louis Stevenson. She herself started writing stories as a small child,

Her first novel, *Peter West,* was published in 1929, but she did not find fame until 1932 with the publication of *Mrs. Tim of the Regiment* based on her own experience as an army wife with her husband Captain James Peploe, whom she had married in 1916. She went on to write a total of 45 (published) novels, which sold over seven million copies and brought her worldwide fame.

The extent of her early writing is becoming more evident with the recent discovery of some boxes of unpublished manuscripts, including *The Fair Miss Fortune* and *Emily Dennistoun,* in her granddaughter's attic.

The family moved to Moffat in the Scottish Borders in 1940, where she wrote her books in longhand, reclining on a sofa looking out over the Dumfriesshire hills.

She died in 1973.

BY THE SAME AUTHOR
and published by
Greyladies

The Fair Miss Fortune

EMILY DENNISTOUN

D. E. STEVENSON

Greyladies

Published by
Greyladies
an imprint of The Old Children's Bookshelf
175 Canongate, Edinburgh EH8 8BN

This edition first published 2011
Text © the Estate of D. E. Stevenson 2011
Preface © Penny Kent 2011
Design and layout © Shirley Neilson 2011
Image courtesy of The Advertising Archives © IPC Media

ISBN 978-1-907503-12-2

All rights reserved. No part of this publication may be reproduced, stored in or introduced into a retrieval system, or transmitted, in any form or by any means (electronic, mechanical, photocopying, recording or otherwise) without the prior written permission of the above copyright owners and the above publisher of this book.

Set in Sylfaen / Perpetua
Printed and bound by the MPG Books Group,
Bodmin and Kings Lynn.

Finding Emily

MY MOTHER would have called it a 'dreich' day, a damp, dreary, drizzly day when there is nothing one can do outside and very little one feels like doing inside. On this particular dull day, I decided to attack the attic and perform an almost impossible tidying task that I had been evading for a long time. When I reached the door, I realised that it would take me days to sort out the files, letters and cases piled high to the ceiling. I was just beginning to shrink from the idea and thinking that I would definitely be wise to leave it for another day when I spotted the three huge boxes that I had inherited from my uncle a couple of months earlier. I had completely forgotten about them. I had stored them right in the corner, under some old curtains and with two large old favourite teddy-bears, Fluffy and Big Man, guarding on top! The boxes were scarcely visible – I was terrified that my space-conscious husband would say that we had no room for them and take them to the dump. But did I notice Fluffy's piercing brown button-eyes willing me to stay and just urging me to have a look? Did he know something I did not?! And here my story begins:

My uncle, John, the youngest of my grandmother's children, inherited all the D. E. Stevenson manuscripts, lectures and memorabilia from my other uncle, Robin. Robin had dealt with all the D. E. Stevenson matters since my grandmother died in 1973, then he became ill and handed over the DES publications to John. A few years later, whilst John was tidying his attic in Oxfordshire, he thought that he would pass 'some DES stuff' to me, and I had a telephone message to say that 'some boxes' would be delivered to my house. I found three enormous boxes on my verandah which I immediately stored up in my attic, presuming that they contained manuscripts of my grandmother's that had already been published.

Where shall I start? I had no idea that it was going to be like being in Aladdin's cave for the next three days in my attic! The first box contained contracts and files of letters to Granny's agent and publishers – all very interesting but nothing unexpected. The next box included a wealth of treasures – a wonderful album full of newspaper articles, magazine articles, books of poems, lectures, family photographs and notebooks with reminiscences, together with manuscripts of books that had been published.

Now the third box was the one that was unbelievably exciting because it was packed to the top with manuscripts – some full length novels, some unfinished tales, some plays and some short stories – all with titles that I did not recognise. And then right at the bottom were two large manuscripts which looked fascinating – *The Fair Miss Fortune* and *Emily Dennistoun.* I was mystified because no one had ever mentioned the possibility of any unpublished DES works. It was actually a heart-stopping moment! I had an amazing time reading and collating them and trying to think when and where they were written.

I think that it was rather appropriate that I found these books in my attic as, interestingly, my grandmother wrote her early stories concealed in her secret hideaway of her attic. At first her family enjoyed her stories and then they said that it was 'ruining her handwriting'! That is when she took herself off secretly. I felt a comforting affinity to Granny as I lay sprawled on my dusty floor with all her notebooks scattered around me, only inquisitive spidery friends and dangly cobwebs for company!

Emily has had a long and tortuous journey to Greyladies. It was possibly written in the 1930s in Bearsden, Scotland, in my grandmother's beautifully rounded longhand, lying on her comfortable sofa puffing gently on her cigarette in its elegant, long black holder. I am not sure if *Emily* was ever sent away for publication and if not, was it because World War II was about to start or was it because her eldest child, Patsy tragically died at only 11 years old – it is unlikely that we will ever know. I know that my grandmother would be absolutely thrilled that *The Fair Miss Fortune* and *Emily Dennistoun* are now being published.

I was, and still am, immensely proud of my grandmother and I was fortunate to have known her for 20 years of my life. We called her Granny Bunge because she had such beautifully soft skin and when you kissed her cheek it was like melting into delicious sponge! She had a mischievous sense of humour and, suddenly thinking something was amusing, her eyebrows would arch up together and she would laugh infectiously. She had beautiful white shiny hair when I knew her and very sparkly deep blue eyes. But she had been a real beauty in her youth, as I have seen in many photographs.

Every Easter Holiday we went up to Scotland to see Granny in her house, North Park in Moffat, setting off at 4 o'clock in the morning and taking a whole day to travel up on the old A1, having breakfast in Newark and lunch at Scotch Corner. We stayed in Ebenholme, one of the Staff houses of Burnbraes School, because Granny could not accommodate our family of 7!

We went round to North Park every day, and as a child I had a morbid fascination with my great grandfather's trophies of sad-looking stuffed otters and beavers, staring down at us in the dark-brown wooden-panelled hallway. Papa Otter-Beaver, as he was aptly named, was not only a great hunter – highly-acceptable in those days – but also, he had a shaggy, whiskery beard!

My mother, Rosemary, has many delightful stories of her childhood, with her brothers, first-cousin Mary and highly-adored grandmother, Gaggie. But she generally had to find entertainment herself, under the impression that 'everyone's mother wrote books' but occasionally, she went out to tea with Granny in her holidays.

Family life was very different in those days – they did not seem to talk to children as we do today. When Patsy died, they did not tell my mother and one day she said 'I dreamed that Patsy was with the angels' at which there was a deathly hush. When John was born they said 'You have a little brother!' My mother, aged seven, carried on washing her dollies' clothes because she did not understand what it meant. She was sent away to boarding school, St Leonard's School, and enjoyed the camaraderie there. She didn't know her brothers well because they were also sent away to school; there was no real warmth or affection.

Granny suffered from very painful osteo-arthritis so rather 'hirpled' along with her two sticks. She had a hip operation which was not at all successful, being in the very early days of that type of surgery when the artificial ball and socket joints were made of porcelain.

She was always writing when we went into the drawing-room – a beautifully positioned room looking out over the lush rolling hills, sheep-dappled in Spring, heather-clad in late Summer, with, generally, the palest of grey clouds gathering ominously together to soak the valley as if in revenge for such an impressive natural countryside. She would put down her pen and welcome us happily, whether she was in the middle of a novel, or mulling over a crossword, or writing a letter in reply to a fan. She had a lift to get upstairs in her latter years – which was terribly inviting to us children but strictly out-of-bounds.

She loved to sit in the sloping garden to sort out her heather bed next to the garden shed, named 'Mickey'! Granny loved tea parties best, whether they were outside in the garden (picnics being an especial delight), tea in her house or out to tea with friends.

She was able to drive around Moffat, owning a grey Wolseley car which seemed to have quite a few bumps in the paintwork! In fact, one of the highlights of our holiday was to go shopping with Granny. Emmie, my younger sister and I, would speedily clamber into the depths of the back seat, no seat belts in those days, Granny would push her walking sticks across the seat and squeeze herself slowly sideways into the car. Her 'driving' position was very far down in the seat, and by gripping the top of the steering wheel and leaning forward she could just manage to peer out of the windscreen. I can still remember the lovely leathery smell of the seats and the feeling of excitement as the old car trundled down the road. We were treated like royalty in the shops – no Self-Service then, a proper Grocer's shop, packets of tea leaves, brown paper bags of fruit and everything weighed out with great ceremony on unwieldy scales. 'Will that be all, Mrs Peploe?' asked the polite shopkeeper in a soft Scottish burr. And then walking out of the shop regally, no shopping bags – they would be delivered; no money exchanged hands – that would go on the account. Sometimes we went shopping without Granny. 'Could you put it on Mrs Peploe's account, please?' we enquired, almost confidently. That is the nearest I will ever get to feeling famous!

As children, we played 'Pooh Sticks' in the burn at the bottom of the garden. We raced about playing hide-and seek. We crept up to Tank Wood (which, looking back, was also out-of-bounds) a very scary experience. We went to The Crook Inn and had tea by the Tweed. If it was hot weather we went swimming in the Tweed or the Belshie Pool – a truly bracing experience!

When we were older, we were allowed to proof-read, which made me feel very important! And we could walk to the Tennis Club in Ball Play – an aptly named road! Granny would play card games with us and I remember we often played Bezique, Rummy and Canasta. Her cards were stored in a gorgeous wooden box with little drawers and shell counters. She had a magnificent musical box which we would wind up and sing along with! I remember particularly 'There was a soldier, A Scottish soldier, Who wandered far away . . . '

I just adored having meals at North Park because the

dining room was furnished rather like a lighthouse. There was the special Bell Rock box which had originally been housed in the Beacon or Barrack whilst the Bell was being built and had always had biscuits and water in it for shipwrecked sailors or marooned workers. Robert Stevenson, my grandmother's great grandfather, was the Chief Engineer of that, the most famous, rock lighthouse. There was the amazing Turner painting of The Bell Rock being battered by high seas. And the poem 'Pharos Loquitor' written by Sir Walter Scott in the Visitors' Album framed and placed beneath a wood-carving by Jane Stevenson. But more importantly to me, because I was too young to understand the importance of the Lighthouse Dynasty, was the food, cooked by the delightful Jean, deliciously different – like haggis and neeps and black pudding! Even better than that was the piping hot chocolate sauce which we poured over ice cream leading to it instantly solidifying, like a choc ice!

In those days, there was no fridge and Grandpa was in charge of putting muslin covers over the milk bottles in the pantry beyond the kitchen. He was very deaf, having been badly wounded in the trenches at Mons and left for dead. Very fortunately, he was seen to move slightly and stretchered in to safety. He had great trouble adjusting his hearing-aid, the controls of which dangled precariously round his neck. It often whistled uncontrollably and emitted a high-pitched screech. He fumblingly failed to correct it and so generally resorted to turning it off! He loved pottering around in the garden, generally wearing plus four tweed trousers and a jacket. I did not know him very well because it was so difficult for him to hear us and any communication with him was virtually impossible but he seemed to like us, the grandchildren, and smiled congenially at us.

No wonder we thought that Moffat was magical – our holidays there had always been idyllic and times to treasure. Granny was so very special to us all.

I would like to thank all the following people, without whom this book would never have been published:

Geraldine Hogg, for helping all along the way with any DESsie queries, and for putting me in touch with Greyladies. I am deeply indebted to her.

My mother, for all her stories of her childhood and memories of Granny – there are many more!

Greyladies, for publishing *Emily Dennistoun* and *The Fair Miss Fortune*. I have thoroughly enjoyed my e-mails and telephone calls with Shirley and the trips to Edinburgh involved with the publication of these books. It was an emotional moment signing the contacts.

My sister, Wendy, who helped as a reader and accompanied me on DES business.

Uncle John, for sending me the 'treasure chest' of boxes!

I think it is absolutely thrilling that these delightful books that my grandmother wrote over 70 years ago will now be enjoyed by all her dedicated followers.

She would be amazed to know that her books are still read by so many people and that these two books have finally been published. Actually, I have a feeling that she does know.

Penny Kent 2011

PROLOGUE

Mr. Dennistoun's Seventy-Fifth Birthday

AT NINE-THIRTY every morning Mr. Dennistoun opened his front door and stepped out into the porch. By that hour he had breakfasted, and so, warmed and comforted, he could face what elements had to be faced with serenity. From his porch he could look over the sea in three directions, for Port Andrew stood on a small rocky promontory and Borriston Hall, of which he was the owner, was above the small town. If he looked straight down, the cluster of red and grey roofs were visible shining in the morning sunshine, while in the bay to the left of the harbour the small fishing fleet was steering seawards—a pretty sight.

Borriston Hall was a square Georgian building which looked roomy and comfortable and had been built to live in rather than to be looked at. It was of grey stone with a grey slate roof which had no eaves to catch the winds or to attract swallows set on nest-making.

Mr. Dennistoun held up his head and surveyed the heavens with the air of a connoisseur; he then walked down the three steps on to the gravelled carriage-drive and consulted his thermometer and rain-gauge. He had tapped his barometer before leaving the house so he now knew all that science could tell him about the atmospheric conditions. Mr. Dennistoun had done the same things at the same hour for the last thirty-five years—nearly half his lifetime—for he was seventy-five on this March morning upon which my story opens.

It was such a fine day that Mr. Dennistoun lingered a little before returning to his study to read the paper. He felt the need to share the satisfaction which possessed him with somebody else. (Not everybody arrived at the mature age of seventy-five with his five senses unimpaired and his digestion in perfect order.)

Purdie, the gardener, who was working in the potting-shed, would do as well as another. Mr. Dennistoun walked down the drive in the early spring sunshine and meditated on the essential fitness of things in general.

"Purdie," he said, with such unusual amiability that the gardener was quite startled and suspicious. "Purdie, it's a fine morning."

"It is that," replied the man without enthusiasm.

"Spring is early this year," continued Mr. Dennistoun.

"Ah'm no trustin' it," the gardener returned, eyeing the pale blue heavens with a frown. "Ah would'na' be surprised if we wus tae hae a rare storm."

Mr. Dennistoun's small store of patience gave out entirely—what a clod the man was. He had no business to damp his employer's birthday morning by prophesying storms without any scientific data to work upon. The barometer had been perfectly steady in response to Mr. Dennistoun's light tap so he felt justified in snubbing Purdie thoroughly. This was a very pleasing occupation but it did not open a way for the subject which was nearest to Mr. Dennistoun's heart. You could hardly squash a man completely and then expect him to congratulate you upon your birthday.

Mr. Dennistoun sighed as he turned away, he felt

mulcted of his just due. It is true that Emily had observed the occasion at breakfast that morning, but Emily did not count—never had counted—in her father's scheme of things. She had been inconsiderate enough to arrive in the world some four years after her parents' marriage when both her father's and mother's hearts were set on a son to inherit Borriston Hall and their not inconsiderable possessions. She was not even an attractive baby but a puling, crying scrap of womanhood and her mother was fond of observing to her chosen friends that she did not know what she had done to deserve it, she really didn't.

So Emily was banished to an attic-room with bars (which had the appearance more of a prison than a nursery) where her infant wails could not inconvenience her mother's nerves or her father's temper.

Years after, when Emily was a thin lanky slip of girlhood with a pale face and mouse-like manners, the quiet of Borriston Hall was again broken by the cries of a newborn infant—this time the son and heir so fervently desired by his parents.

If Borriston Hall could have spoken it would not have had much to tell of the years that followed. Without, a little growth of trees and shrubs in spite of the racketing wind which swept the garden from nearly every point of the compass; within, two young lives struggling to maturity in the stagnant atmosphere of a house ruled by a querulous and exacting invalid.

Mrs. Dennistoun paid a heavy toll for the birth of her son; she never walked again, and the atmosphere of the house took its tone from the atmosphere of the sick-room.

Mrs. Dennistoun feared her husband with the unreasoning fear of a weak, deceitful mind. She deceived him in small matters up to the day of her death and she soon taught her small son to deceive him also. He was his mother's pet, and constant attendant—spoiled and cuffed by turns according to her uneven temper.

Charles' birth brought one good thing to Borriston Hall and that incalculably good thing was Miss Roe. She was chosen as a governess for Emily out of a dozen applicants for the post, for her severe appearance and slightly masculine manner. It was fortunate for the neglected child that beneath a slightly forbidding exterior Miss Roe had the heart of a mother. She was thirty-five years old when she first came to Borriston, small and spare with a keen pale face and grey eyes. She came into that house of petty jealousy and deceit like a fresh breeze from the sea. Emily's heart was hers in a few hours and will remain hers until the day of her death. Charles was a more difficult proposition, for no discipline was possible under the aegis of his devoted mother. He was a frank and amiable child when left to himself but that was seldom, for his mother could hardly bear him out of her sight. Miss Roe often thought that it was indeed fortunate for Emily that her parents neglected her.

When Charles went to school at nine years old, Mrs. Dennistoun took a chill and died. She made no great struggle to live; perhaps she knew that her son had gone from her forever (at least he could never come back to her as he had gone), perhaps she was tired of her life of petty deceit.

Mr. Dennistoun did not miss his wife very much; she had for long been an invalid and he did not care for the atmosphere of a sickroom. The housekeeping had been in Miss Roe's capable hands for some time past so that there was no change in that. Things went on much the same as before, but the air of the house was clearer as though some canker had been removed. Emily knew peace now; she blossomed in a mild way under the skilful touch of Miss Roe. She put up her hair and let down her frocks, for she was eighteen years old, and went to a few small parties at some neighbouring houses. It was only later when Miss Roe had left that Emily realised all that she owed this good friend, realised how she had fought her battles with Mr. Dennistoun and stood, a solid rampart, between them. For Mr. Dennistoun was slightly in awe of Miss Roe. She was so small and yet so determined and her straight clear gaze went through him and made his sarcasm and cynicism seem cheap and pointless. He comforted himself—when he felt more than usually annoyed with her—by reminding himself that he could dismiss her if he liked. That he did not do so was due to the fact that he liked comfort and Miss Roe was an extremely good housekeeper.

Perhaps Charles was the only one who felt the loss of his mother very deeply. To him she was more real, less shadowy. But school life was very enthralling and his few tears were soon dried. Charles sailed through his school life with credit to himself and to his family—but not too much credit to be normal.

He did not care for Borriston or the quiet life that went

on beneath that roof, and, even in his holidays his own family saw little of him. He had many friends and he found their homes more amusing than his own. "I would have you to Borriston like a shot," he said once to Tom Murdoch, a great crony of his, "but it's so jolly dull there, you'd be bored stiff. Walls, great high chaps with broken glass on the top, all round the bally garden—and wind always, even in the height of summer, howling round the place."

"But there's sand, isn't there?" said Tom, who was secretly rather keen to see this forbidding castle. "And the village, you told me, Dennistoun, we could go fishing perhaps."

"Father wouldn't let us," replied Charles shortly. He had no wish to spend his summer holidays beneath the eagle eyes of his parent, of whom for all his indulgence he was secretly in awe.

Miss Roe stayed at Borriston Hall for fifteen years. She left because Mr. Dennistoun considered that at twenty-five his daughter should be able to run the house to his satisfaction. In this he was right, for Emily was eminently capable of the charge but what he did not consider was the intense loneliness he was inflicting on his child by removing her one companion. Miss Roe knew, and she offered, in the inviolable secrecy of her employer's study, to stay on for nothing and take care of the motherless girl, but Mr. Dennistoun had determined that she should go—so she went, sorrowfully.

For a time Emily was too stricken by the loss of the only friend she had ever known to realise the loneliness of her position. But gradually the numb feeling passed. They corresponded regularly. Miss Roe was now independent with a small house and garden which had been left to her by a conveniently deceased aunt so there was no need for her to seek another position, and if life at Borriston became unbearable Emily had a line of retreat open. Like Napoleon this sure line of retreat gave her a feeling of courage and security so that she could face the daily battle of life with equanimity.

So the years passed away and Charles left school and went to Oxford. He was twenty-one on the morning of his father's seventy-fifth birthday.

Something of all this flashed through Mr. Dennistoun's mind as he paced up and down in front of the house, smoking his pipe and admiring his own smooth lawns and tidy shrubberies enclosed by the high walls to which Charles so strongly objected. The walls were Mr. Dennistoun's especial pride. They measured eight feet and were crusted with glass which sparkled wickedly in the pale March sunshine. They had been built to keep out the village boys and stray orchard thieves and they fulfilled their task. There was no foothold to be found on their smooth exterior by the most nimble boy in Port Andrew.

Mr. Dennistoun looked back complacently on his quiet life at Borriston. He was bound up in his business which had grown and prospered exceedingly. Three days in the week he went to Glasgow so that he might, so to speak, keep a finger on its pulse. There was hardly need for this, for the thing ran itself, but Mr. Dennistoun liked to be reminded of his wealth, and the silent carpeted offices with their swing doors and plate glass windows reminded him of it constantly and comfortingly. The war had by no means decreased his profits—indeed the war had meant very little to Borriston and its inmates, the echo of it had sounded but faintly within those high encircling walls. Charles had been too young for any active part in it and Emily's ideas of service had been quickly vetoed.

Yes, thought Mr. Dennistoun comfortably, everything had turned out for the best. Even his daughter's seniority had proved fortunate. Emily had her uses as a housekeeper, she never wanted to gad about, that was one comfort. This revolt of youth that one read about had left her untouched—she was too deeply embedded in the grooves of her monotonous life—since his dismissal of Miss Roe she had managed everything capably. He was bound to admit that fact to her credit.

Seventy-five today, and good for at least another ten years of active life. Mr. Dennistoun felt delighted at his own cleverness at this defiance of the Psalmist—threescore years and ten might be the span of other men's activities but Mr. Dennistoun was not as other men—hence his satisfaction with life. He was as hale and hearty as any man of sixty. He had taken care, that was all, and had led a normal, reasonable life. He decided to tell Charles that. Charles was coming tonight to spend the weekend beneath his paternal roof and his father rather suspected that this sudden access of filial affection indicated a need for ready cash. It would be a good lesson for that young man—a normal, reasonable life and a man might live to eighty-five and still retain the vigour of his prime.

Mr. Dennistoun gave a dry chuckle. It would be an exceedingly good lesson for Master Charles to learn, for he was too fond of a gay life and wild companions. Not that Mr. Dennistoun grudged his only son the princely allowance which he had managed to dissipate in the last two years—on the contrary it gave him a feeling of importance to know that his son could hold his own with the best. The boy would sow his wild oats and he would then be ready to settle down and take the junior partnership in the business which had been waiting for him all these years. He might stand for Parliament later on if he liked, it would be a good advertisement for the firm.

"Dennistoun, Custance & Dennistoun—" that had a good sound to it, thought the senior partner. Custance had had a son, a promising young fellow, but he had been killed at Ypres when Charles was still at school. How Mr. Dennistoun had envied Custance this son of his—a frank, strapping lad when Charles was merely an uninteresting baby—but now it was his turn to be envied. Charles would bring new vigour to the firm. "Dennistoun, Custance & Dennistoun—"

He went into the house and opened the paper at the financial and shipping news.

BOOK I

CHAPTER 1
Two Storms

IT WAS NIGHT. The foreshore to the south of Port Andrew was dark and sinister, wild ragged clouds coursed across the sky while above them the darker and more stately masses gathered ominously. The wind was high and rising stormily, whipping the tops from the big waves and hurling them shorewards in luminous spray.

It was a triumph of Nature, a wild orgy of strength and hatred, a clash of the warring elements of Earth and Sea. Emily stood watching it, absorbed in the wild scene, at one with the turmoil. The ever increasing clamour of wave and wind eased her heart, soothed her nerves and swept some of the bitterness from her rebel soul.

For a long time she stood, wrapped in her dark cloak buffeted by the driving rain which fell in short gusts from the swirling masses of cloud, then she began to tramp along the heavy sand. The soft wet mass clogged her light shoes, and she was so tired that each step was a struggle of mind against body. Yet the mere fact of motion seemed to calm some demon of restlessness which dwelt within.

Presently she came to the point for which she had been making; she was now on the edge of the bay—a perfect half circle—and from the farther point a lighthouse swung its beam across the lowering sky and made a shifting path of ruby light to Emily's feet. She sank down exhausted and leaned on a wet rock regardless of her evening gown which draggled from beneath her rain-cloak. Her mind was a blank for the moment—it was as if the wind had blown it clean and the rain had washed it.

To Emily this beam of light had come to mean hope in the dreary greyness of her life; hope of some cessation of her daily grind and hope of escape from Borriston. She often came out at night—slipped out when there was nobody to see—and came here to feed upon the cheering beam of light. It was Emily's daily bread without which she would have starved—for souls need food as well as bodies and if they are doomed to exist in a loveless atmosphere they must find some substitute for love.

These things were the substitutes which Emily had found for human love. The wild beating of the storm soothed and satisfied passion, the twinkling waves, as they lisped on the summer's shore stood for the prattle which she should have heard upon the lips of her children. These things she gathered to her, touched with the magic of her strong personality and put forth again in flowing words to charm the ears of the fastidious in prose and rhyme.

She lay there motionless as the stone upon which her arms and head rested—and as cold. The intermittent blatters of rain beat upon her unprotected hair, ran into her eyes and sought out the opening at the neck of her cloak to wet her through and through.

How long she lay there Emily did not know; she was roused at last by the report of a rocket. She struggled to her feet, stiff and cramped with her long vigil in the rain. Somehow or other her feet found the path which led back to Port Andrew and the harbour.

What could be the matter? The rocket, she knew, was the signal for the launching of the lifeboat. Emily soon realised that there were other people besides herself hastening to the little harbour to see what was afoot. It was very dark but she could glimpse figures hurrying in front of her and hear snatches of conversation fitful in the wind's harsh gusts.

When she reached the steep little street of the town itself she found it seething with life. Dark cloaked figures with hurricane lanterns ran past her, and women with flapping skirts peered out of lighted doorways and shrieked, "What's amiss? Wha's boat is it?" to any who would vouchsafe a reply.

"It's a ship," she heard someone say as she battled on down to the small harbour where the life-boat was stored. Another figure in gleaming oilskins paused to shout back, "A boat—one o' the fishin' boats—on the rocks."

The all enveloping darkness added to the confusion and when Emily reached the harbour and left the slight shelter of the small houses the wind tore at her like a mad thing, tore at her cloak and her hair, and the rain lashed her face as with whips. One could not believe that the wind was a natural phenomenon, there seemed to be a spirit of evil in its brutal strength.

She found herself next to a woman with a plaid shawl over her head, leaning on a frail railing which edged the pier.

"They'll never get the lifeboat launched in this," she shouted and the words were torn from her lips and scattered to the four corners of the heavens. The woman turned and looked at her with amazement.

"Save us, Miss Dennistoun—it's never you!" she said.

There was no time for more speech. The men were getting the lifeboat out and every eye was fixed upon the twelve heroes in oilskins and cork jackets. Emily marvelled at their unconcerned demeanour—how brave they were! Half a hundred hands helped to drag the boat down the shore, they pushed it into the sea in the teeth of the gale and the twelve scrambled in and bent to their oars. A cheer went up from the little crowd, a cheer which was half drowned by the roar of the breakers.

"It's gey soon tae cheer," a man said soberly. He was old but still hale, and the drops of rain glistened on his grizzled beard. "Ower soon—gowks—they've no got the boat beyond the breakers—"

He was right. Scarcely had he spoken when a monster wave caught up the frail craft as though it were made of paper and flung it back on the shore.

"Heaven help us," a woman shrieked.

Emily covered her eyes, she could not look. It seemed to her as if the big cruel monster which was the sea had refused to be baulked of its prey by the puny efforts of the rescuers—it had flung them back with a gesture of defiance.

When Emily found enough courage to look again at the battle which was being waged before her eyes, the boat had been righted and was well out beyond the white line of foam where the waves began to break. It looked very small and frail amongst the great green hollows —sometimes it disappeared altogether, and the crowd held its breath, but always it bobbed up again and always seemed a little nearer to the cruel ragged rocks, draped in spray. There, in the fitful gleams of the moon between the flying clouds the wrecked boat could be seen. A few splinters, that was all, and as the waves tore madly at their prey these too gradually disappeared from view.

For the most part the crowd was quiet, huddled together on the pier and the harbour rocks, clinging to each other, or to the rings where in calm weather the fishing boats were moored. But sometimes a woman would break into weeping, helpless as a child's, or another would lift her voice in simple prayer.

It was dreamlike to Emily, or, more truly, she felt as if all the rest of her life were a dream, and this only real. She tried to pray—as these prayed—but her God seemed a great way off—not near and real as He was to these people. Her mind entered fully into the distress of those around her. That it could do so was due to her gift of writing which led her to understand their sufferings with the sympathy of her emotions. But while she suffered with them she was able at the same time to view her own uneventful life running upon a grey level which missed both the heights and depths of human experience. "I am not even alive," Emily thought. "I am like a ghost among them."

These simple folk—the most of whom Emily knew quite well from everyday contact with them—had suddenly grown to heroic proportions in her eyes. She envied them. She even envied the dangers and anxieties which beset their path.

A voice beside her cried, "Oh why does God let the sea be so rough?" and looking down Emily found herself gazing into a pair of anguished brown eyes. They belonged to a child—as years count—but a woman's soul lurked in their depths.

Emily could not speak, she felt that she was inadequate, her thirty years had held no such agony as racked this slip of girlhood, and so she could have no part with those who knew the deep and troubled waters.

"God help them," was all that she could say, and a deep voice somewhere behind her in the crowd echoed, "Amen to that."

By this time the gallant little boat had reached the rocks where the wreck was stranded and all ashore strained their eyes to see what was being done. Would it be possible for the rescue party to go near enough to get the men off without being themselves stove in? This was the all absorbing topic of conversation amongst the watchers. Emily, herself, could see nothing, the wind whipped the rain in her face and blinded her unaccustomed eyes, while every now and then a wave, more gigantic than its fellows struck the pier with a nerve-shattering crash and covered the watchers with a shower of icy spray. The man behind her with the grizzled beard had a telescope which he rested on a buttress and kept those around him informed as to how things were going.

"They've got twa—an' noo they're comin' back."

"But there were three," someone shouted, and the words were taken by the wind and hurled away so that it sounded "ee-ee-ee" like the cry of a soaring gull, or the wail of some disembodied spirit.

"There was three o' them i' the boat."

"One gone."

A shiver of horror swept over the little group on the pier, and the child who had spoken to Emily leaned against her heavily as if the strength had ebbed out of her body at the words.

"One gone—which o' the lads is gone?" was whispered from mouth to mouth for there was scarcely a creature in the crowd who was not nearly connected with at least one of the three men who had put to sea so cheerfully in the little boat only that morning. And now one of then was "gone"— the sea had taken toll.

"Bear up, lass," someone said, addressing the girl with the brown eyes. "Bear up Kitty—it'll no' be Joe."

"He cu'd swim like a fush, cu'd Joe," said an old woman who leaned against the outer wall and was drenched with spray every time a wave came. She seemed quite oblivious of bodily discomfort and balanced herself easily in her dangerous position, shading her eyes with one wrinkled hand.

"Much use swimmin' is when the waves tak' ye and dash ye agin the stanes like a paper doll," grumbled a small wizened man with the dark complexion of a southerner.

"Wheesht, mon; dinna haver!"

Silence fell then—if silence it could be called when the waves beat deafeningly upon the masonry and the screech of the wind was a physical pain to the ears. All knew that the return journey was the more perilous for the waves overtook the small craft and broke upon it, filling it again and again with water. Presently as it neared the shore there was a recrudescence of talk.

"Can ye see what like the men are, Bob?" someone asked. The man with the telescope did not reply, it was too vital a question to risk making a mistake, and in the fitful light it was impossible to make out which of the three men was missing. The girl who had been called Kitty clung to Emily's arm and whispered agonisedly, "Oh God, don't let it be Joe!"

Just at that moment the boat swung into full view perched on the crest of a half broken billow. Emily leaned forward to look—it seemed to her unaccustomed eyes perilous beyond everything that had gone before. There was a cordon of sturdy men breast deep in the swirling waters linked together by a rope. They caught the boat as the wave fell, caught it and hesitated a moment struggling against the backwash which threatened to sweep them off their feet. There was a rattle of pebbles, like a volley of musketry and then with a cry of victory they dragged the boat out of the sea, well out of reach of the succeeding wave.

Emily saw no more. She was conscious suddenly of a limp weight on her arm and of someone saying pitifully, "Aye, it's Joe that's gane—puir lassie!"

"Tak' her hame, Bob," said another voice in peremptory tones.

The man addressed shut up his telescope and stowed it away in his pocket, then he bent down and gathered the unconscious girl in his arms and turned away from the scene of mingled pain and rejoicing.

For once the iron reserve of these people was broken—women clung to their husbands and mothers to their sons with loud tears and hysterical laughter. The hurricane lanterns shed a fitful light upon the scene and shone redly upon the streaming oilskins of the twelve heroes. Beyond, the sea roared and threatened like a monster bereft of its lawful prey.

Emily found herself following Bob down a small narrow street with houses at either side. She could not have said why she followed him save that she felt as if she had been chosen by the girl to be a sharer in her grief. The man went quickly, he looked back once or twice to see if she were following and when he saw that she was there he moderated his pace to suit hers. Presently he stopped at a small cottage which boasted a little tiled garden, and pushing the door open he carried in his burden.

Emily followed him into the house and found herself in a small parlour, spotlessly clean and tidy; a fire burned brightly in the shining grate and a lamp stood upon the round table ready for lighting. Bob laid the girl upon a sofa which was in one corner of the room.

"There's things tae be din, Miss," he said. "Ah maun gang back tae the harbour, an' gi'e them a han'," and so saying he disappeared apologetically. Emily found herself alone in the house with the bereaved girl. An hour ago she had not known of her existence; it was a strange experience.

A lump rose in her throat and nearly choked her, for the slight form which lay on the sofa seemed dazed with grief. There were no tears. The wide brown eyes were like those of a wild timid animal which knows not why it has been mortally wounded. For a moment Emily hesitated, bound by her shyness of emotion due to her narrow and loveless life. And then suddenly a gust of pity blew through her heart like a rushing wind and with a little cry of sympathy she kneeled down and gathered Kitty's slight body into her arms.

CHAPTER 2
Two Calms

THE STORM had spent its fury and a thin fine rain was falling when Emily at length groped her way home. It was so dark that even the familiar way seemed strange and terrifying and every stone in the path was magnified to gigantic proportions and moved to trip her hesitating feet.

A dark form was lurking behind the wrought iron gates, and ran to open them as Emily approached. She knew somehow that it was Charles even before he spoke, although she did not know that he was coming. Perhaps her senses were quickened by the strange emotional experiences of the night.

"You, Charles?" she whispered in amazement. "I didn't know you were coming, is anything wrong?"

He signed to her to be quiet and they let themselves into the house by the side door as silently as possible. Charles pushed her into the dining-room and closed the door, still with the utmost precaution against noise. The lamp stood upon the table and shed a circle of light in the gloomy room and the fire burned brightly in the grate. Emily leaned against the mantlepiece and tried ineffectually to dry her soaking shoes—they were ruined, she reflected idly. She was startled out of her trivial preoccupation by Charles' voice, husky with feeling.

"Where on earth have you been?" he demanded. It was amazing to think that Emily had been out in the storm like this. Judging from the condition of her cloak she must have been out in the open all night—what on earth had she been doing, wandering about by herself (at least he hoped it was by herself) on a night like this? Emily, of all people the most conventional, whose day was so ruled by the clock that it required imagination to think of her doing anything but going to bed at 10 o' clock! Charles had a queer feeling that this was not Emily at all but some strange woman who had sought refuge from the storm in Borriston Hall. There was something strange about her, a sort of suppressed excitement or passion very foreign to her usual calm demeanour. No, this was certainly not the rather colourless sister he knew so well—if he went upstairs he would find *her* asleep in bed—this woman was a stranger, and an interesting one at that.

"What do you want with me?" Emily said quietly, she felt tired and over-wrought and was longing for her bed.

"What do I want?" he echoed, gazing at her with astonishment. "I want some explanation of your extraordinary behaviour. I've been hanging about here for *hours* waiting for you. How could I go to bed not knowing where you were? Father had no idea that you weren't in bed—probably he wouldn't have cared if he *had* known, but *I* couldn't take your disappearance as a natural thing—on a night like this—Emily—where have you been?"

"Does it matter?" she wondered, not bitterly but just questioningly.

"Why of course it does," he replied eagerly. "Of course it matters to me. I've hunted for you everywhere—I've nearly been frantic about you. Maggie told me you had gone for 'a little walk', that you often did at night—*a little walk* on a night like this—"

"I like walking in the rain, I love the feeling of a storm," Emily said. "I didn't know you were coming tonight—"

"*He* knew," Charles interrupted.

"Possibly."

Charles thought about this for a moment. He had known, of course, that Emily was not properly treated at home (that was how he put it to himself) but this seemed a cruel and unnecessary slight to put upon her—petty too, and bad for her authority in the house, for the servants had been told of their young master's arrival—his bed had been aired and the fire lighted.

All this however was a side-show which could be thought of later, the burning question of the moment was "Where had Emily been?" He came across the room to her and stood beside her at the fire.

"You're soaking wet," he said concernedly.

The real trouble in his voice touched Emily and she suddenly felt that she could tell something of her feelings and the passionate desire for freedom which possessed her.

"I've been down at the harbour—there's been a wreck on the Craitn rocks—one of the fishing boats got caught in the storm. The lifeboat went out and saved two of the men—one was drowned. The courage of those men, the endurance of them! Oh, Charles, that is life. It has made me more than ever dissatisfied with my cotton wool existence. What good am I? I wish I had been born to a poor woman in the village, it would have been better for me—she might have loved me."

She was silent for a moment trying to steady her voice and to conquer the feeling of self-pity which had risen suddenly and threatened her composure, then she continued more quietly, "I was with a girl—quite a child—the wife of the man who was drowned. They had been married scarcely a month—and now he's gone. That's what they call it, 'gone'. Some of them are superstitious about it and think of the sea as a living monster who demands the sacrifice of a life—it does not seem fantastic when you are in the midst of it—that poor child, and yet somehow I envied her. She has lived, she has memories to feed on—"

"I never knew you felt like that," Charles murmured.

"You never knew I felt anything at all," she told him. "You hardly knew I existed."

It was so true that Charles could not deny it. He had not realised the existence of his sister until tonight when his anxiety over her disappearance had awakened him to the fact that she was a human being like himself.

"I was beside this girl when the lifeboat came in," Emily continued, "and when she saw that her husband was not there, she fainted in my arms. She had spoken to me before and I felt that she clung to me—she seemed rather apart from the other people, they were so fatalistic about it—she had chosen me, I felt, and so when a man carried her home I followed. I did what I could—not much, for I am a shadow in the world of men—not properly alive—"

She lay back in the deep leather chair with a sigh of exhaustion, her arms were over the sides of the chair, hanging limply, the end of her dress dripped on to the carpet, her shoes were soaked, her dark hair was plastered in wet streaks across her forehead. Yet for all that she looked somehow vital, a flame which burnt in spite of the dampness of the wood, and he realised that she was a rebel—even as he was—but with none of the sweets of rebellion, none of those aids to courage which were so dear to his own heart. She was alone in the world far more than the veriest orphan, and her courage was untouched. She was more courageous than he, bigger than he, yet for all her courage she needed comfort and sympathy just as he needed it.

"Emily," he said, "you're tired and wet—dead tired, I can see that. This experience has tried you more than you think. Your heart is not dead, my dear, or that girl would not have chosen you to comfort her."

"So you understand," said Emily slowly. She looked at him with new eyes, seeing him for the first time as a grown man, quite another being from the spoilt child of ten years ago (she had not seen him much in the interval). The thin face with the brown eyes was insignificant at first and the smooth brown hair was ordinary but as one looked more closely the face gained in power, for the mouth was firm and the chin determined and well shaped.

He bore her scrutiny amusedly for he had felt the same sudden awakening of interest in her. In his childhood she had seemed a great tall gawky creature who was always in disgrace. Later she had grown smaller—in proportion to himself—and had become merely a shadow, not a real person at all.

"Well," he said at last.

She flushed guiltily. "I never seemed to have realised before that you were—grown up," she told him.

"I'm afraid I've been a beast," he said quickly, "but I never realised what an awful life this was for you. We'll go away together someday and have a good time. You're not old," he added with endearing naivety. "You've still time to enjoy life—we'll have a good time together one of these days."

"I feel dreadfully old tonight, Charles," replied his sister, half laughing. She rose, and gathering up her wet garments led the way upstairs to bed.

When Charles came down to breakfast the following morning he found that his father had already finished and had gone down the garden to talk to Purdie and to see what damage had been done by the storm. Emily was waiting for her brother and as she poured out his coffee he tried and failed to discover signs of the passion and fire of the previous night. She was the same as she had always been, but Charles saw for the first time that she was a graceful woman, her pale narrow face was almond-shaped and her grey eyes set rather wide apart under their dark brows were soft and bright with intelligence. Emily suddenly became conscious of her brother's gaze and flushed to the roots of her thick brown hair. She was annoyed with herself to think that she had betrayed her feelings to Charles.

"Father is furious with you," she said, more to change the trend of thought than for any other reason.

"I know," replied Charles. "We had a fearful row last night—he's so unreasonable, fifty years behind the times. He would rather I wasted his money in having a good time at Oxford than tried to be a useful member of society —says he doesn't expect me to work hard. I've told him I haven't the *brain* for figures in the office and for Parliament. (Can you see me in Parliament, Emily?) I've neither the brain nor the inclination. I'm just wasting my time at Oxford for it is no good stuffing my brain full of things that aren't going to be any *use*."

"What do you want to do?" Emily asked him wonderingly.

"I want to do something with my *hands*," he replied, helping himself fiercely to kedgeree. "Old furniture is my hobby—I *know* about it. I want a shop where I can buy and sell the stuff and a workshop where it can be mended up properly by people who understand it."

"You want to have a shop?"

"Oh, what nonsense it is!" cried Charles. "As if the mere fact of buying and selling furniture made one unfit to associate with decent folk! All business is buying and selling if it comes to that. Some men do it with their brains, but I want to do it with my hands—*in a shop*. Oh Heavens! A shop—*how* ungentlemanly!"

"I never said it would make you unfit to associate with decent people," Emily said quietly. "I was thinking of Father—of his plans for you."

Charles looked at her in surprise, it was strange to him that she should care for her father's feelings—he had certainly never considered hers. What was she like *really*

31

—this Emily whom he did not know?

She had finished breakfast by this time and was standing by the window looking out at the garden, her hands clasped behind her back like a child's. There was an air of peace about her—or was it control—a curious contrast to the storm and stress of the previous night. Charles could not get over his surprise that the night's experience had left no trace upon her. Nature's storm of wind and rain had battered down the early shrubs and scored watercourses in the smooth yellow gravel but the inner storm had passed leaving no traces upon Emily's quiet face. She seemed apart from the stress of life, calm and secure as one who had some secret place for the refreshment of her soul.

Charles answered her last remark after a long silence.

"I think father can look after himself," he said with an attempt at lightness. "At all events he holds the key to the position."

"You mean—"

"I mean he is quite pleased to give me £500 whenever I want it to throw about and squander on riotous living," Charles laughed a trifle bitterly, "but when it comes to settling me in a good business for life—"

"He had other ideas for you," Emily reminded her brother.

"I know, I've told him I'm sorry. I *am* sorry but I don't recognise his right to ruin my life. Emily, I couldn't sit in that gorgeous office all day and sign my name to everything I was told—I just could not do it. I want to live an interesting life, a life full of incident—he has no right to bind me down—"

Emily pondered this for a few moments—she was slow to judge for she knew her limitations. Charles, though nine years younger than herself, had actually seen more of life. Put quite squarely it came to this—what did Charles owe his Father? And the question was hard to answer. For the mere accident of birth Charles owed him nothing—Emily was convinced of this. For training, companionship, affection—again nothing, for these things were non-existent in their relationship. It came then to be matter of board and lodging and as much money as he could spend—

"You needn't *laugh*, Emily," Charles said suddenly. "You are a strange unfeeling creature."

"I'm sorry," she replied. "I was not laughing at you, I was thinking of something funny—I wish I could help you, Charles."

Charles was mollified at once, he sprang up and crossing over to the window slipped his arm through Emily's. They stood there for a long time, wrapped in their thoughts and the resemblance between them was very strong.

"It's something to find you understand," Charles said at last. "Father is hopeless—it's no use beating my head against the wall—he can't understand. It's not his fault in a way, really, more his misfortune. He's never suffered, never even seen suffering—he's taken jolly good care not to. What does he know of the conditions of modern life? What does he know of the people who live at his gate in poverty and distress? He has put cotton wool in his ears and yellow tinted spectacles over his eyes so that he can't hear the wind howling or see the black clouds gathering in the sky. I tell you Emily, the day is coming when we will all have to take a share in the battle, or go down under foot and get trodden on by the mob."

He was eager and full of fire and enthusiasm but Emily could not share in his convictions, she felt that the foundation upon which her life was built was too firm to be whirled away by a few wild spirits. She knew the conditions of life in Port Andrew better than anybody—better even than the minister for she was familiar with all creeds and in her charitable errands made no difference between Catholic and Protestant. She knew that they were as far from any form of rebellion as any community in the world in spite of the fact that they had due cause for dissatisfaction. The fishing which from time immemorial had been their right and their only means of livelihood was now so poached and disturbed by trawlers that there was scarcely a shilling to be made out of it. It had been a winter of distress and hardship amongst the poorer and less thrifty folk in the village and although Emily had done what she could she knew that she had merely touched the edge of a great work by her timely help.

Emily could not see, however, what this had got to do with Charles' shop—unless it was that Charles felt acutely the uselessness of his life in the midst of all the economic troubles of the world? If so it was a theory which had made a rebel of him which she, womanlike, had required something visible and tragic to stir her emotions before her rebellion against fate could come to the surface.

His eagerness endeared him to her as nothing else could have done, and as she walked down to the harbour to see Kitty she wondered whether it would be possible for her to help him.

Kitty was asleep so Emily did not allow her to be disturbed. She spoke for a few moments to the woman who was looking after her—a neighbour who informed Emily that she had left four children at home to come and mind the house.

"We couldna' leave her, puir lassie," said the woman kindly, but somehow Emily could not help feeling that she was getting a good deal of satisfaction out of her mournful duty. Several people came to the door while Emily was there to enquire for Kitty and Emily could see that Mrs. Brown was considered an important person in Port Andrew by reason of her position in the house of mourning.

"It's tae be hoped they'll find the body," she said, as she came out on to the doorstep to see Miss Dennistoun away. "It'll be gey hard luck on Kitty if the body's no found—a berryin's aye a kin' o' comfort tae ye."

CHAPTER 3
Several Kinds of Magic

THAT AFTERNOON Charles and Emily walked over to Craitn, a village nestling in a fold of hills where the Water of Craitn ran into the sea. Nature had dowered the small valley with a prodigal hand for the red sandstone rocks were a treasure house of ferns and small plants—chiefly sea-pinks and cowslips and king-cups—which flourished in their different season and starred the bright rocks with coloured jewels. Fir trees twisted their roots into the crumbling soil and raised brave branches to the wind; below, the sand was white and full of small but beautiful shells and the Craitn ran into the sea between dark rocks covered with glistening seaweed, green and brown.

It was a fine afternoon for a walk, the storm of the previous night had cleared the air and washed the land. The tide was out, and the waves rolled contentedly and broke with a little abrupt "swish" upon the brown sands. These sands were a feature of Port Andrew, they stretched unbroken for several miles along the shore and they were marked with ripples from the strong undercurrents which vexed the bay. Far out Emily could see the rock where the boat was wrecked. It stood well out of the water today for the tide was low, a jagged spar showed that the sea had not yet finished its work of demolition and destruction. Beyond the sandstone rocks of Craitn stood the lighthouse, white and glistening yet insignificant by day compared with its importance in the darkness.

An older brother of Charles' school friend who was an artist had taken one of the small and recently built bungalows at Craitn and was living there with his wife. Charles had suddenly decided that it would be a good excuse for a walk to visit the couple and revive the friendship, he had insisted on Emily's accompanying him partly because he thought it would be nice for her to make the acquaintance of his friend, but chiefly because he wanted to talk to somebody about his latest scheme.

As they went along, Charles elaborated his idea of the furniture shop to his sister, bringing it down from the realms of the fantastic and absurd. He had his eye on a man who would be the "very chap for the job"—he had a wife, and was out of work having lost a leg in the war. His pension would obviate the necessity of high wages, and he would be quite willing to work for a very small pittance at first till the shop began to pay. His wife would keep the place clean—it was ideal. Emily began to see that this was not a mere boyish whim but a real purpose in what had hitherto been a purposeless life. She began to wonder whether her father or anyone else had a right to deny Charles his desire, which, after all, was quite a reasonable desire and which might prove to be the making of him. She was not however, sufficiently optimistic to believe that Mr. Dennistoun could be brought to see it in this light, and so, though her imagination accepted Charles' shop with all its accessories of show rooms, store rooms and workshop, her practical mind made her doubt its realization.

Charles was prone, both by nature and upbringing, to

look upon the bright side of things. He was angry with his father but he still believed that Mr. Dennistoun's opposition to his plan could be overcome. Charles had never been denied a request for money before, however unreasonable. There would be a mock argument and then Mr. Dennistoun would sit down and write a cheque. "Here you are," he would say with a dry chuckle. "Go to the devil in your own way." But there was no feinting about the argument this time. Charles still shuddered when he thought of it for Mr. Dennistoun had not minced matters when he found that his son's heart was set upon his insane scheme. Still he would "come round", Charles thought, this was merely a temporary check—annoying of course—for Charles with youthful impulsiveness was anxious to leave Oxford at once and start straight away to amass his treasures—but only temporary. Charles had warmed himself to a fine glow by his conversion of Emily, surely his father might also be won over.

The sun shone, and the distant sea sparkled happily, already the shop had taken concrete shape in his eager brain. There must be a top light in the workshop—he could *see* Pring's bench placed beneath the window and the patient face ennobled by suffering raised a moment from some delicate piece of work. Already in his vivid imagination the shop was filled with treasures of oak and mahogany, dear to his heart.

"It must come true—it must—it must," he said boyishly.

Charles and Emily had some trouble in finding *La*

Boiselle. It was tucked away amongst the sand dunes and none of the people whom they asked seemed to have any knowledge of the place. They were nearly turning homeward in despair when Emily had an inspiration and asked for "Mr. Murdoch's cottage."

"Oh, it's Murdoch's ye're wantin'," said a small boy with red hair and a supercilious manner. He pointed out a footpath across the common.

"It was evidently our pronunciation which was at fault," Emily said smiling, but Charles, who was tired and slightly out of temper, only mumbled something about "fool-name for a house anyway."

The Murdochs were just starting to have tea when their unexpected guests arrived. The bell was broken, so Charles knocked loudly upon the door with the handle of his walking-stick. It was opened almost immediately by a tall good-looking young man with fair wavy hair and a sunburnt complexion.

"By Jove," he said eagerly, "it's Dennistoun or I'm a Dutchman. How good of you to look us up like this. How d'ye do, Miss Dennistoun—come right in as the Yanks say. You're just in time for tea. Laura, here's Charles Dennistoun, he was at school with Tom. Miss Dennistoun, behold my wife! Now that's finished," added the young man laughing gaily. "Sailed through the introductions like a bally usher—I say, it *is* nice to see you!"

Emily had been dreading this visit. She saw so few people that she was terrified of strangers but nobody could feel nervous after such a warm and unceremonious welcome as this. It was most reassuring and she followed

Charles into the little house with renewed confidence. She found herself in a long lofty room which was lighted from the roof and which seemed to be the general living room and Mr. Murdoch's studio combined. The room ran the whole length of the small house for there was a window at the far end which looked out over Craitn Bay. In the inner wall were three doors leading to two bedrooms and the kitchen—this was the extent of the cottage.

Laura Murdoch came forward with a smile of welcome on her calm face. She was a tall fair woman with a slow easy grace of movement and a slow soft voice. Emily judged her as older than her husband—possibly about her own age—and was not far out. The third occupant of the bungalow was a Frenchwoman, short and dark, with the olive skin of meridional France. She was introduced to Emily as "Mademoiselle Jacquot".

The tea-table was set before a log fire which burnt cheerfully. It leapt with tongues of blue and red, rivalling the afternoon sunlight which fell in broad strips across the polished wooden floor.

Harry Murdoch, still talking vivaciously about nothing, pushed one of the crazy looking arm-chairs nearer to the fire.

"It's better than it looks," he assured Emily. "I know because I often sit in it myself."

Emily was not good in the interchange of social banalities, she sat down without answering and was surprised to find that it really was a comfortable chair.

"Laura, Laura," the Frenchwoman lamented, *"que faire?*

Il n'y a qu'une tasse."

"Never mind that, Ivette," said Harry Murdoch laughing. "I'll take mine in a tumbler—it's not often I get such a good excuse. What about you, Dennistoun?"

Charles laughed. "Tea, please," he said. "Give it to me in a jug or anything you like—it's all one to me."

For one moment Emily felt quite uncomfortable and very sorry for her hostess' predicament—it seemed so extraordinary not to have cups enough to go round—but the next, she realised that her sympathy was certainly not required. Nobody was the least disturbed by the deficiency, least of all Laura. Her hands moved about the tea-tray with slow deliberation and after one glance at her husband—who had retrieved a bottle of whisky from a side cupboard and was mixing himself a long drink—she took no further notice of him.

Emily decided that Laura Murdoch had a genius for silence; she could be silent without seeming unsympathetic and when her soft voice did make itself heard she said what she had to say in the fewest words possible.

Emily spoke to her about a water-colour which hung on the wall near the fire-place and she replied at once, turning to her visitor with a little smile which irradiated her rather heavy face with sudden light.

"I am glad you like that, Miss Dennistoun. It was done for me by a great friend of mine who is not really an artist —or at least does not call himself one. That is the only picture he has accomplished and Harry says it is full of faults, but it pleases me."

"It pleases me too," Emily said. "And I cannot imagine how anyone can say he is not an artist. The sunlight is so beautifully suggested and falls so softly through the dark branches of the pines."

Harry Murdoch had returned to the little group about the tea-table and was standing, glass in hand, surveying the little sketch with critical eyes.

"I have never said I don't like it," he said to Emily with an apologetic air. "It is a fairy glade, full of real sunshine, not just yellow paint. It has the power of evocation out of all proportion to its technical power—it's magic, sheer black magic. I like it, *malgré moi*, but the thing's a fluke."

"I like it," Mrs. Murdoch said softly.

"And have I not said that I also like it?" demanded her husband with a whimsical smile. "Only I think that Francis is too good a man to make a second-rate artist. His other talents are greater—"

The little Frenchwoman leaned forward eagerly. "It has been said that everybody can paint one picture, *n'est ce pas? Peut être que celui-ci est le seul tableau de Monsieur Hood.*"

"Not Francis Hood?" cried Charles excitedly. "You don't mean that Francis painted that—can it be the same—a great tall fellow with red hair—"

It was the same and the four people who knew Francis Hood began to talk about him delightedly. Emily noticed that Laura Murdoch did not say much but she leaned forward a little so that she could see the eager face of Charles as he spoke about his friend.

"Met him in Switzerland last Christmas," Charles was

saying. "He was doing tutor to Lee's small brother for the hols and I was with them. By Jove he is a corker, been all through the war—joined as a trooper to begin with."

"My father used to say that Francis was a born soldier," Laura put in.

"He is a born everything," cried Charles enthusiastically. "There's nothing Francis can't do if he's put to it but before everything he's a surgeon. He's studying in Edinburgh now and if I ever want my appendix cut out it'll be Francis that will do it."

A shout of laughter greeted this substantial tribute to the efficiency of the young doctor.

"I met him in the war," Laura said, when the merriment had subsided. "He was in my father's regiment."

Emily felt her attention wander, for there is nothing so uninteresting as the virtues of someone we have never seen. Their delinquencies may have piquant qualities but this man apparently had none.

She felt lazy and content, at rest in this queer atmosphere of Bohemia which demanded nothing—not even conversation—from its guests. The excitement and strain of the previous night were beginning to tell upon Emily, and in the reaction from the grim realities, she felt as if she were living in a dream, or had become an audience of one, seeing but not partaking in the action of a drama.

The pale afternoon sunlight fell in broad swathes of light on the bare floor and showed up a fine grey film of blown sand upon its polished surface. There was a gate-legged table of dark oak in the centre of the room; it was piled with books and held a blue Nankeen vase with sprays of willow buds. On this the dust lay thickly and in any other house it would have disgusted the housewifely instincts of Emily but here it seemed not right exactly but somehow unessential.

Mademoiselle Jacquot rose and vanished noiselessly into the little kitchen from whence came a clatter of pots denoting her activity.

This, then, was the setting of the little play. In the foreground were the two young men—disputing, agreeing and arguing about the attributes of their mutual friend; Charles serious and eager with a flush of excitement on his pale face, Harry Murdoch earnest too beneath his gay and debonair exterior. The woman sat listening to every word in that strange thoughtful silence which was her chief characteristic, showing her awareness only by the flickering smile which came and went about her straight mouth but did not reach her eyes.

The feeling of unreality was so persistent that Emily was only mildly surprised when she saw a man's face appear at the open window. It had appeared so suddenly and noiselessly that Emily could hardly believe her eyes. She rubbed them and looked again; the face was still there—an unusual face with high cheek-bones and deeply set grey eyes. Emily had just decided that he was the ugliest man she had ever seen when he laid a hand on the window sill, pushed the window wide open and vaulted lightly into the room.

"I got tired of ringing the bell," said the newcomer

apologetically.

"Francis!" cried the two men with one accord. They ran forward and dragged him over to the fire, protesting laughingly that he had come to rob the plate chest. There was a chorus of questions.

"Where have you come from?"

"Are you going to stay?" but Laura asked nothing. She rose and gave him her hands with a quiet look of pleasure which was more welcoming than words. Then she turned and introduced him to Emily; "Francis Hood —Miss Dennistoun."

The latter could now see that his hair was a queer dark red colour like old mahogany. His grey eyes met Emily's with a steady gaze that seemed to weigh her in the balance. Returning the gaze she saw that the man was tired. His eyes had a filmy look and there were little wrinkles about them which had no business to be there. He answered Harry's numerous questions a trifle wearily, explaining that he had got a fortnight's holiday quite unexpectedly and had thrown himself into the train without troubling himself to let them know. The train only brought him as far as Pennybrigg—from there he had walked.

Laura, who had gone for fresh tea came back and said in her gentle voice, "It will be lovely to have you for a fortnight, Francis. You can have a bed on the divan, it will be quite comfortable."

"You've slept in worse places than that, Francis!" cried Charles with a flash of hero-worship.

"Yes, I have—and tasted worse scones," replied Francis

Hood, helping himself from the plate which Laura had placed before him.

For all his light repartee Emily could not help feeling that the man was suffering in some way, either from over-fatigue or pain. He longed to be left in peace, why could they not understand?

"He's studying medicine," Harry whispered to her under cover of some exchange of banter among the others. "Studying in Edinburgh now—awfully clever chap, Francis—was all through the war without a scratch. Bad luck for Charles and me missing that show, wasn't it?"

"Some people might think it good luck," said Emily uneasily. She was still watching the red-haired man. Although he was no bigger than Harry he seemed immense; he dwarfed the others completely—even the studio looked smaller now that he was in it. Charles was leaning forward and listening to every word which fell from the lips of his idol—how was she going to get him away, she wondered. They had some way to go and it was getting late. The thought of her father whose dinner hour was sacred nerved her to an effort at departure.

"Charles," she said, a little shyly, and rose to her feet. The move was greeted with dismay.

"You're never going before supper," Harry cried. "Oh I say, it's too bad of you, Miss Dennistoun."

"Do stay," Laura said quietly.

"I'm afraid we must go, my father is alone," Emily murmured unhappily.

Francis Hood rose and lit a cigarette.

"I will walk home part of the way with you," he said in

a matter of fact voice. "It will be good for me after Laura's scones. I think you are wise to go now, it is clouding over and will probably rain later."

Emily felt a glow of thankfulness—she was rescued, but whether or not the Knight knew that he had rescued her she could not determine. His face was inscrutable as he turned towards the door.

"You go too, Harry," Laura said. "Ivette and I will get the supper ready."

Emily said goodbye to her hostess and promised to come again. She started off with Mr. Hood leaving the two younger men to follow. Charles always took hours to say goodbye and she was afraid they would be late for dinner—this would make Mr. Dennistoun even more angry than before. Charles was heedless.

"Well, he's very young!" said Francis Hood softly. Emily looked up in astonishment and saw that her companion's eyes were fixed upon her with the clear look that she had noticed before. "Your thoughts were very obvious, Miss Dennistoun," he explained quizzically. "Time was made for slaves and Charles is a free man—or thinks he is which comes to the same thing. He will either forego his evening shave or be late for dinner—I can't bear to think of it!"

"You are laughing at me," Emily said with a smile. "But really I am not so foolish as you think. Our father is very angry with Charles—about something—and if we are late for dinner it will not help matters."

The young man felt rather ashamed of himself—this strange girl or woman (he had not quite decided in which category she belonged) had taken his rather impertinent jibe in good part and by her simple reply had put him in the wrong. He was all the more ashamed because it was not his nature to be cynical—it was merely his jarred nerves which had got the upper hand of him. This was no excuse in his eyes—he ought to be able to control them. What business had he to be having "nerves", that last resort of the feeble-minded.

"You were right and I was wrong," he said impulsively.

There was silence between them after that but not a strained silence. The path which they were following led along the top of the sandhills where grey-green grass shivered in the breeze. A rabbit, sitting on the path, vanished suddenly with the flash of its white scut and they both laughed at its hurried disappearance.

"Have you known Laura for long?" he asked her at last.

"A few hours," she replied, smiling.

"But you like her."

"Yes—I think so." She was surprised to find what a clear impression the strange woman had left upon her. Laura Murdoch had barely spoken, yet her personality was indelibly printed in Emily's receptive mind. It showed how unimportant words really were in the intercourse of soul with soul.

"Laura needs a friend, Miss Dennistoun," said Francis Hood. He did not let her answer that, but began immediately to speak of Charles and his ambition with which he seemed conversant.

"It would be the best thing for Charles," he said earnestly. "Just now he is wasting his time—not slacking, for with an eager nature like his that would be impossible, but pursuing the wrong things, and pursuing them with an energy worthy of better objects. I hope you are in favour of this venture, Miss Dennistoun."

"I—don't count," Emily said, not bitterly but merely as one states a fact. "But—yes, I think I agree with you. Charles needs an object—something to strive for."

"We all need that," Francis said earnestly.

They were walking now by the sea's edge for the tide had come in over the flat brown sands while they were at tea. The sky had clouded over, and a cold wind, laden with moisture, blew in their faces.

"Don't come any further, Mr. Hood," Emily said suddenly. "Why should you when you are tired out?"

"How do you know I am tired?" he asked her brusquely. Emily did not answer, and after a moment's pause he added more gently, "I suppose I *am* fagged—it's been rather—strenuous lately."

"A fortnight's rest will do you good," said Emily quite simply and kindly. Her hand lay in his for a moment as they said goodbye and she noticed the long slender fingers and strong wrist of the born surgeon. Harry had been right when he said that this was too good a man to become a second-rate artist.

"I shall see you again," said Francis as he turned away.

Emily was enough of a woman to be almost disappointed that he had taken his dismissal so easily.

CHAPTER 4
The Red-Haired Man Again

FORTUNATELY for Charles, Dr. Dingwall was a guest at dinner. The good doctor was a regular visitor at Borriston Hall every Saturday night for both he and Mr. Dennistoun were keen chess-players, and in pawky skill they were evenly matched. Chess was their one point of contact, for the doctor was a bluff, kindly old man—simple as a child in many ways—while his host was a cynical worldling with scarcely a thought beyond his business and his dinner. The mere presence of Dr. Dingwall at the dinner-table shielded Charles from his father's displeasure for Mr. Dennistoun was not the man to launder in public and although he might—and did—think his son unfilial and a fool at that, he had no intention of betraying the fact to Port Andrew as represented by the doctor. A few sarcastic remarks which were incomprehensible to the stranger but did not fail to sting the rebellious Charles showed that Mr. Dennistoun had neither forgotten nor forgiven his son's amazing proposition.

Emily was even more silent than usual and the doctor began to wonder if she were ill. To his simplicity people were either ill or well—if the former they probably needed a tonic. Should he suggest iron and phosphates for her—the spring was often trying—yet she did not look ill, in fact her colour was better than usual. Not for the first time he reflected that it was no life for a young woman to be shut up year in and year out with a crusty old man. Since the departure of that nice Miss Roe, Emily had become more and more silent and reserved. She had a faraway look as if her spirit were withdrawn to some inner fastness.

Dr. Dingwall had never understood the reason for Miss Roe's sudden disappearance from Borriston; he had thought of her as a fixture for life, and then suddenly she was not. He leaned forward and said to Emily (under cover of one of Mr. Dennistoun's sarcastic speeches to Charles),

"Emily, d'ye ever hear of Miss Roe, these days?"

He had to repeat his question twice before his hostess heard him and answered,

"Yes, I hear regularly. She has a little cottage of her own near St. Mary's Brook in Devonshire—an aunt died and left it to her."

"I'm glad to hear that," he said kindly. "She's a fine woman that, and she would have found another place irksome to her after being here so long—fifteen years wasn't it? She was fond of ye, Emily. It was more like her home here."

Dr. Dingwall had to lean forward to hear the reply to this, which he had intended as a feeler, and he was not sure even then that he had heard aright for Emily said softly,

"She was my Mother," and Dr. Dingwall knew that to be untrue—who better since he had officiated at the speaker's birth?

There was no time to say more, for Emily rose, and Charles, thankful to escape, followed her out of the dining-room with a murmur of "letters to write."

The good doctor, somewhat perplexed, was left to keep his host company with a bottle of port.

Once free from the atmosphere of his father's cynical —if veiled—disapproval, Charles shook off the mask which he had worn all dinner time and showed his true feelings. He walked up and down the drawing-room excitedly waving his hands and anathematising his parent's stupidity and false pride.

"It's a shop, you see!" he cried. "If I'd wanted to go into the Army or the Navy, or even if I had announced my intention of loafing to the end of my days father would have been quite content but just because I want to become a useful member of society—"

Emily listened for a little as she bent over her sewing but presently Charles' voice died away and she was walking along the sands with Francis Hood. She could feel the salty taste of the damp mist upon her lips. After a lifetime of days wherein nothing happened the last twenty-four hours had been packed with incident. She was weary, not so much physically for she was a strong woman, but emotionally tired and disturbed under the veneer of her stillness. She was conscious of some change taking place in herself—some change which had begun last night when the storm began to whine in the chimney and which had gone on through all the strange happenings of the night and day until she was oppressed and frightened at the thought of it. Something was going to happen; this life which she knew so well and which was but a weary chain of days alike grey and uninteresting was not going on for ever as she had so often feared. Events had started to move which would alter the whole face of life to Emily. How she knew this it would be difficult to say, suffice to say that she did know it. She was in no hurry for events to move; she scarcely knew what direction she wished them to take. Patience had been taught her in a hard school and the lesson was well learnt.

Emily was startled out of her reverie by her brother's hand on her shoulder.

"Emily, what do you think of Francis? Isn't he splendid? Oh Emily, I do want you to like him!"

She felt nearer to Charles at that moment than she had ever felt. He was lovable and boyish in his hero-worship. It was true that he was apt to be selfish, and was too easily swayed by the passing breeze but these were defects of youth and upbringing—time would eradicate them and the real nature of the boy would shine out brighter than before. In spite of Emily's sympathy with Charles she did not feel able to answer his question—she did not know what she thought of Francis Hood. At first she had been disinclined to like him after hearing his praises sung too loudly by Charles and the Murdochs, and then he had arrived too dramatically for the fastidious "author-mind" of Emily to approve. But once in the studio he had dwarfed the others by his strong and virile personality, and his subsequent behaviour had pleased Emily—even his rudeness had a piquant charm all its own. It was obvious that he was very much attached to Laura Murdoch—and she to him. Emily recalled his voice—deep and slightly husky—as he asked her to befriend the lonely woman. She smiled as she reflected that Laura Murdoch was probably not half so lonely as *she* was. Laura had a husband and that nice Frenchwoman who lived with them and helped with the house—and then Emily frowned as a sudden thought struck her. Perhaps the red-haired man had sensed her own lack of friends and was trying to kill two birds with one stone. She knew he could be subtle when he chose but was he as deep as that and why should he trouble himself about Emily's loneliness?

It was a puzzle to which no answer could be found.

The following day being Sunday, Mr. Dennistoun's son and daughter occupied the Borriston pew in the gallery at the Established Kirk. Charles was still meditating on his grievance and it is to be feared that he did not follow the simple service very closely. The Anglo-Catholic movement in Oxford had found in the beauty-loving Charles an easily influenced and enthusiastic convert and he could not help comparing this simple homely form of worship with the elaborate rites to which he was accustomed. When the spirit of criticism enters by the door the spirit of worship flies out at the window and therefore the young man's devotions were perfunctory and lifeless.

Emily's case was different. She had been brought up in this church; it satisfied her and she knew no other. Today however the sight of a red-head below her in the body of the church disturbed her devotions. The first glance had convinced her of its identity—nay, before she had so much as seen it she had felt that Francis Hood was in the building, so strong a hold had his personality obtained on her unconscious mind.

He was alone in the pew, and the sunlight filtering in through a coloured glass window surrounded him with a halo of dusty light. Through it his figure loomed even more huge and portentous than she had remembered it.

Emily had known in her heart that she could not escape him, for he had said, "I shall see you again." No mere idle words of polite valediction these, but a definite statement which he intended to make true. Did she want to see him again? That was the question, and her wildly beating heart answered, "Not today please God, not today."

Francis Hood had stirred up something within her that Emily did not know existed, and the disturbance was all the more alarming because it was the first time in all her thirty-one years that it had taken place. She was puzzled, frightened and rather ashamed. If only she could escape when the service was over, if only she could avoid him until her unruly feelings had subsided and her natural poise and sense had re-asserted themselves.

Charles was wrapped in his own meditations and had not seen his hero, so there was just a chance of escape—if Francis had not seen them. Perhaps he would walk back to Craitn without waiting for them. When the service was over Emily dawdled as much as possible, collecting the books and stowing them away in the little cupboard beneath the book rest. She stopped to speak to the pew opener, and to one or two other old women who were recipients of her bounty during the hard times which had come to Port Andrew.

"Come *on* Emily," said Charles at last, and, as she could find no further excuse for tarrying, she followed him into the sunlight of the kirkyard with a fluttering heart.

The big man was waiting for them at the gate as if it were the most natural thing in the world.

"Why, there's old Francis!" cried Charles delightedly, and Emily felt the hand of Fate tighten.

After greeting them conventionally the young man suggested that they should walk along the Machers together. This is a stretch of common land along the top of the sandhills between Port Andrew and Craitn. It is inhabited by rabbits and moles with an occasional seagull to liven the monotony. Here the lark sings all the year round, and the peewit marks her nest undisturbed. Here in summer the borage plant tints the landscape with sea-colour, and the yellow tansy vies with the deeper gold of the flowering gorse. But in March these notes of colour were missing, only the grey-green bent grass waved in the fitful breeze or shimmered with spear-like leaves in the bright sunshine.

The two Dennistouns and Francis Hood walked along the sandy path enjoying the fine sea breeze and brilliant sunshine after the stuffy gloom of the Kirk. The young men had plunged deeply into a discussion upon religion, and the different methods of approaching the throne of God. Charles confessed that the service this morning had not appealed to him, he considered that it was not a "meet offering" to the Deity. It was wrong to confuse poverty and ugliness with meekness and piety. Francis—his grey eyes flashing with the joy of battle—tore these arguments to pieces and jumped on them. Sincerity was the keynote of the service in which they had just taken part and Francis acknowledged himself deeply impressed with it. He reminded Charles of the Covenanters—the forebears of these simple folk—and enlarged upon the privations and sufferings that they had undergone for their souls' sake and to purge their church from what they rightly or wrongly considered impurities. Everyone needed a slightly different way of approach to the Ultimate Good and at the end all paths converged towards the Throne.

"But if I consider my path better than theirs am I not justified in trying to convert them," Charles demanded.

"Who are you to judge them?" was the swift reply. "True you may need the fuller and more mystical interpretation of the Anglo-Catholic Church; their simple natures are satisfied with the simpler forms of religion." He quoted Buddha, "Love each other and live in peace," and Browning, "When the fight begins within himself a man's worth something."

"That's contradictory," Charles interrupted.

"Not a bit of it," cried Francis, thrashing at a thistle with his stick. "It's ourselves we've got to fight, not others. Each man captain of his own soul, steering his own course—

'In every man's career are certain points on which
he *dares not* be indifferent—

> Thus, he should wed the woman he loves most
> And—follow at the least sufficiently,
> The form of faith his conscience holds the best.'

That's what these people are doing, Charles, and not easily either. They've suffered for their freedom—fought for it. It's more than you've done. Freedom of thought is every man's right, that's the Buddhist belief and it's a damned good one. What right has anyone to meddle with a man's soul?"

Thus talking and arguing heatedly they reached a small hillock crowned with a crazy broken-down shed which had been used at one time for a bathing-hut but had now fallen into disrepair. It still offered a fine view of the sea and land and was a favourite haunt of Emily's. She was quite breathless—partly with the effort to keep pace with the strides of her companions which lengthened and quickened as the argument increased in vehemence, and partly with anxiety at the heat of the discussion which she quite expected would end in blows. She did not realise the intense joy of matching brain with brain—when both were equally gifted, in a subject worthy of a struggle. She did not understand that these two collegians could argue and wrestle in mental combat for hours, not only without rancour but with positive joy in the clarity and quickness of each other's brains.

Once the thought crossed her mind, "What a fool I was to fear *too much* attention from this man!"

The battle died away with the same suddenness with which it had begun. Francis flung himself on the close cropped grass in the lee of the deserted bathing but and cried,

"By Jove, the sun *is* warm today. You get the ultra violet rays *here* all right."

And Charles retorted ungracefully,

"Ultra violet fiddlesticks. Don't pretend to me that you are a doctor and a scientist. You're a sun worshipper that's what you are."

"Perhaps I am," replied Francis thoughtfully. "P'raps you would be too if you saw what I see every day of my life. Little kids, puny and miserable taken from the slums where they never see the sun and put on balconies where they get sunshine on their starved bodies—man, you can see them grow and—and flower."

"I hope you propitiate your deity," Charles replied whimsically. "Do you creep out here every morning at dawn and kill a wretched little bunny for a blood sacrifice or must it be a human life to satisfy the yellow Sun-god?"

"Idiot!" ejaculated Francis affectionately.

There was silence then between the three humans who had disturbed the deserted sandhills with their chatter, and the screaming of a seagull sounded very loud as it wheeled and dived into the blue-green water.

"There are the Murdochs," said Emily suddenly as two solitary figures appeared round the corner of a sandhill about a hundred yards from where they were sitting. She stood up and waved, but instead of coming nearer the couple hesitated a moment and then turned back.

"Shout to them, Charles, they can't have seen us," she added.

A quick look of comprehension passed between the two men.

"Murdoch has got one of his bad headaches today," said Francis easily. "I expect they would rather be left to themselves. Miss Dennistoun, I was to ask you from Laura if you could come to tea on Tuesday."

"I don't know that I shall be able to come," Emily said slowly. She had sat down again and was digging her thin fingers into the roots of the grass, loosening the sandy soil upon which it grew. Her face was turned away and only the fine curve of her cheek and neck was visible to Francis. At that moment she hated Francis Hood, she was filled with a blind unreasoning fury against him. She hated his thin ugly face that looked so white beneath the flaming colour of his hair, hated the deep voice with its infinite modulations, hated all his long slimness which lay stretched out beside her on the sandy turf.

"He is rude and horrid," she told herself with silent fury. "Rude and horrid—I never want to see him again."

Francis said no more then—perhaps with his almost uncanny sensitiveness he divined her anger—but as they walked back to Port Andrew across the uneven waste of sand dunes she found him by her side, and for long afterwards his whisper rung in her ears.

"You will forgive me, and come on Tuesday."

She had not answered that for she was still vexed with him, and tears of rage were not far off, but Francis evidently did not think his statement required an answer. He said goodbye to them outside the high walls of Borriston Hall and swung off down the hill whistling cheerfully.

"We might have asked him to lunch if father were not in such an unholy rage," said Charles, bitterly. But for once her parent's uncertain temper was a source of satisfaction to Emily.

CHAPTER 5
Silent Companionship

ON TUESDAY afternoon Emily left Borriston Hall early, carrying a roll of illustrated papers and a plum cake. Charles had travelled south the previous day and although she missed him very much, his departure was in a way a relief to her, so acute had the tension become between father and son. Mr. Dennistoun would neither discuss the matter of Charles' shop nor leave it alone, but by constant satirical references he kept the subject sore and open. Charles was too impulsive and too keen about his plan to take the ridicule in good part. He either sulked or answered heatedly and so laid himself open to more baiting.

Her helplessness appalled Emily, she knew the futility of interference and forced herself to be silent when every nerve in her body was aching with the desire to take Charles' part. She was not silent from any selfish motive, she knew well that her advocacy would actually harm the cause she had at heart.

"If you could only pretend that you did not mind," she adjured her brother.

"I can't," he replied hopelessly. "I'm not a cold fish like you are—I care terribly. He has no right to trample on my soul. Sometimes I think he's the devil himself."

"Oh, dear no," Emily said, passing over the insult to herself and answering the last sentence. "He's not the devil—just an old man with the cruel instincts of a little boy. Boys all enjoy torturing things weaker than themselves—pulling off flies' wings and maiming spiders and beetles—"

"I don't know how you can sit there and say nothing," Charles cried reproachfully.

"I don't know either," replied Emily, "except that I care more for the success of your plan than for my own temporary satisfaction."

Charles looked at her wonderingly, she made him feel like a petted child crying for the moon. She was so calm and wise. Sometimes a hint of bitterness crept into her words when the guard was down for a moment but it was a mere surface bitterness, it did not have roots in her soul.

"Oh Emily!" he said. "I don't know how you can bear it. When I get my shop you shall come and live with me—it's not right for you to be here—"

"Don't worry, Charles," Emily replied. "Life has its compensations and I'll tell you this—I can go to Helen Roe if things get unbearable. You'll marry, my dear, and you won't want your poor old sister to make a third in your house. Bless you all the same for the thought."

Emily thought over this little talk which she had had with her brother as she made her way down towards the harbour, with the plum cake and the illustrated papers tucked under her arm. She had decided to spend the afternoon with Kitty so that there would be no chance of meeting Francis. He was quite capable of coming to Borriston Hall to find her and escort her to Craitn by moral if not physical force. Charles' impulsive invitation had touched her heart. In spite of the fact that he had as yet no shop nor any prospect of having one his words were precious to her for they were sincere and affectionate.

Kitty was sewing by the window; she ran to open the door when she saw Miss Dennistoun coming down the street. Her little face was white and strained and there were blue shadows beneath her pretty eyes. Emily's heart went out to the girl as it had done before, she forgot to be shy and remembered only her sympathy for Kitty in her sorrow. They sat together for a long time, and gradually bit by bit the story of Kitty's life was unfolded to her new friend—there was not much to tell.

Mrs. Anderson had been dead some years and Kitty had kept house for her widowed father. She had only been married to Joe for a month—they had been so happy together in their new little home—so happy. Now it would have to be sold up for Kitty could not live here alone—she would get a pension from the Fishermen's Mutual Benefit Society, but it would not go far. All the things that she and Joe had chosen together with such happy hearts would be sold to strangers—it was hard to bear.

"You will go back to your father," Emily said gently, trying to show Kitty the brighter side of the picture. "He will be so glad to have you back with him."

"He is to be married," Kitty told her, wiping away the tears which *would* fall in spite of all her efforts to be brave. "Of course I can go back to him, but it won't be the same. Oh Miss Dennistoun, if only I could get away somewhere—"

Emily understood that desire for flight—to hide somewhere, that was the first need of a broken heart. She was silent for a few moments and then she said,

"I wonder what you will think of this plan, Kitty. It has just come into my mind and if you don't like it you must say so quite honestly. I have been looking for a sewing-maid and I think if you would care to come to me you would do very well. You can sew well and that is the main thing. You would soon pick up the other little things which would be part of your work."

"Oh Miss Dennistoun!" Kitty cried. "Do you think I could—oh, I would work so hard and do my very best—"

"Do you think you would be lonely away from your own people?" Emily asked her.

"I would be near you," replied the girl quickly. Tears rose in Emily's eyes. She had so little affection in her life that Kitty's impulsive words had touched her deeply.

Kitty was delighted when she found that Miss Dennistoun was prepared to stay to tea. She laid a snowy white cloth on the table and put out her best cups with deft hands. Emily, watching her, liked the efficient way she went about her work and began to think that Kitty would really be useful to her. She had not been entirely without misgiving when she suggested the scheme for she felt that Kitty was an unknown quantity and might consider herself above the other maids. But she had felt bound to give her a trial and Kitty's real good sense might make a success of her new life. I shall be able to help her, Emily reflected, and her heart warmed at the thought.

She stayed so long at the little cottage that it was getting dark when she started for home, and, after the lamp-lit room the street seemed somewhat sinister. She was not keyed up as she had been on the night of the storm and when a tall figure stepped forward and took up its position by her side she was extremely alarmed. Tales of robbery and even of murder flashed through her mind with a vividness born of terror.

Emily looked up—and was amazed to find that her companion was Francis Hood. He was looking down at her with a smile on his ugly face which softened the harsh contours incredibly.

"What on earth does this mean?" she asked sternly, for she had really been frightened and was annoyed with herself at her stupidity.

"I've been waiting for you," replied Francis as if that were a sufficient explanation of his conduct.

"How long?" she wanted to know but the red-haired man did not answer that, indeed he was very silent and scarcely spoke a word all the way home.

Strangely enough that silent walk did more to soothe Emily's anger than anything else could have done. Her thoughts pictured Francis waiting for hours in the little mean street which seemed to be inhabited only by cats and message boys with bicycles and baskets, waiting for the privilege of escorting her home. She was pleased with him because he did not upbraid her for not coming to Craitn, nor making any fuss about having found her. His rough tweedy sleeve smelt of Harris peat, it brushed against her shoulder protectingly, and once when they crossed a road he took her elbow in his firm capable hand. Emily told herself that she had been foolish to avoid this man, more foolish still to be frightened of him. She arranged to meet him one afternoon and walk over to *La Boiselle* for tea.

Emily found the Murdoch household exactly the same as on her previous visit. Laura was very friendly in her silent way and after tea the two women went out together to feed the ducks, leaving Mademoiselle Jacquot to clear away the tea and to entertain the two men. Emily decided that she was entirely capable of both these duties—her deft manipulation of the crockery was none the less efficient for the fact that a long cigarette stuck jauntily in the corner of her dark-red mouth. She shouted witticisms at Harry Murdoch while she washed the dishes in the kitchen sink. These witticisms were very French and quite untranslatable; they caused Harry inexpressible joy and even Francis was obliged to laugh.

Meanwhile Emily and Laura strolled down to a small burn which ran past the end of the garden. Laura carried a pail full of scraps for her ducks, her head was bare and her fair corn-coloured hair gleamed in the sunshine. The ducks came running and waddling directly they heard her voice; they looked very comical and ungainly and Emily could not help laughing at them. When they were all fed and shut up for the night Laura sat down on a fallen tree and made room for Emily to sit beside her.

"It is quiet here, and sheltered," said Laura in her quiet voice. "I often come here when I want to be alone."

Emily agreed that it was a pleasant place to rest; the burn ran by, gurgling over the stones and a few gnarled fir trees broke the wind. The garden of *La Boiselle* was a wilderness of long grass and brambled undergrowth. Harry had planted some crocus bulbs and a few early daffodils but his energy had soon evaporated when he found that the rabbits preferred them beyond everything for their early morning feed. On the whole, however, the wilderness was soothing, it was too wild to give the idea of untidiness.

Now that they were alone Laura found quite a lot to tell her new friend. She told Emily about her childhood which had been spent roving round the world with her father who was in the army. She had met Harry Murdoch in China where he had been sent by an illustrated paper to do a series of sketches.

"We loved each other at once," she said simply. "Of course he is younger than I am—but he needs me."

"Father was against our marriage," she continued after a little pause, "but when he saw that we were both determined upon it he gave in. Father is very fond of Francis and, I think, wanted me to marry him but we were too good friends for that. I have known Francis always; he is more like my brother. He has a great career before him, I am sure—everyone speaks well of his surgical skill. I think, don't you, that it must be a fine thing to be a doctor."

Emily agreed with her, and the conversation passed on to other things. She found herself telling Laura about Charles' ambition to have a shop and of her father's horror at the mere idea. Laura was sympathetic without being a mere echo. She had ideas of her own which were unconventional and interesting. Emily found her an inspiring companion and the time passed swiftly. Both women were sorry when they saw Francis approaching to put an end to their interchange of ideas.

It seemed natural to Emily that the red-haired man should walk home with her across the Machers. She had forgotten her fear of him and found that she could talk to him comfortably.

"Have you heard from Charles since he got back?" he asked at last, and the answer being negative he drew a letter out of his pocket and glanced over it quickly. "I got it just now. He—he has changed his mind about the shop."

"What *do* you mean?" Emily asked, looking up at him in amazement.

In spite of his earnestness Francis could not help smiling at his companion's astonishment.

"He has met the most wonderful girl in the world," he told her with a whimsical inflection in his voice. "They met in the train, I gather, and he offered to pull up the window for her. After that all was plain sailing—dear Charles, he is such an attractive beggar—"

"But the shop!" cried Emily.

Francis shook his head.

"I know Charles better than you do," he told her. "He's very young and eager but he has not got backbone. He hasn't found anything to stabilise him yet."

Emily could not take Charles' sudden change of purpose

with such equanimity—could not understand a character which could be so easily turned from what was practically an obsession. Even the letter which she received from him the following morning did not help her to understand his point of view. That Charles was impetuous nobody could deny but that the mere sight of a pretty face in the train could upset all his plans and turn him from his most serious purpose seemed to the sensible Emily almost incredible. The letter itself was sketchy and incomplete; it told Emily the exact colour of Alice's eyes, but not what her surname was. It informed her that the lady had "wavy hair, the colour of ripe corn," but gave no details of her mental attributes. Emily knew no more after she had read the letter than she did before except that Alice and her mother had a little house at Oxford and Charles saw her every day. He did not mention the shop and she came to the conclusion that Francis' letter must have been more detailed than her own.

Of course the infatuation might pass. Emily knew very little of the world and the ways of young men but she imagined that they often fell in love—it was not a deadly disease. Francis would know what the chances were, Francis would talk it over with her and that would be a comfort. Somehow or other she must see Francis soon.

She had no sooner settled that she must see him than she decided that it was quite impossible for her to do so. How could she go over to Craitn and seek him out? The thing was unthinkable. There was only one thing to be done—she must invite Francis to dinner. Kitty could take the note over to Craitn; the walk would do her good.

So Kitty put on her plain little hat which suited her much better than an elaborate one would have done, and proceeded to walk to Craitn with the letter addressed to F. Hood, Esq., in her pocket.

It was a pleasant afternoon for a walk and Kitty's pale cheeks were soon glowing like twin roses. She found it impossible to be sad today; her new life had lifted her out of her sorrow. Miss Dennistoun was so kind. Only sometimes the sorrow came back upon her with crushing force and she longed for Joe's strong arms about her with a terrible longing which was physical pain.

She had a strange longing—inextricably mixed with the other pain—to see Joe again, dead or alive. If she could have buried him it would have helped her to feel that that part of her life was done with—gone forever all the dear intimacy of their short married life. But even that small comfort was denied her, for the current must have washed Joe's body far away to some shore where he would not be known and where strangers who did not know his goodness and worth would lay him carelessly in the ground. Kitty could not think of this; she felt she would rather that the sea would keep him forever.

CHAPTER 6
A Dinner Party

EMILY surveyed herself in her mirror before she went downstairs to dinner. She saw a tall graceful figure in a black charmeuse gown. It had been made for her by the village dressmaker, more as a charity to the little struggling woman than for any other reason, and with Kitty's help and long discussions over fashion papers it had been stripped of its fussy trimmings and rendered more or less up-to-date.

"You look awfully nice," Kitty said shyly, and Miss Dennistoun had the grace to blush with pleasure at the innocent compliment. She went down the stairs with more confidence for Kitty's admiration.

But in the empty drawing-room her anxiety returned. What would happen? How would things go? There were so many unknown and disquieting factors about this dinner party which she had arranged so carefully. First of all her father's uncertainty of mood. If he disliked her guest he would take no trouble to hide the fact. What a fool she had been to ask Francis, to let him in for this possible unpleasantness! Fortunately, being Saturday night, Dr. Dingwall would be here to play the buffer. He was a good buffer—a fine friend to have. Emily smiled as she thought of the bottle of tonic which he had sent her. She had never felt better in her life but she was taking it regularly. There were so few ways in which she could repay the good doctor for his kindness and, whimsically, Emily felt that this was one. She thought of him affectionately every time she poured out her dose.

The second uncertain factor in tonight's proceedings was the red-haired man himself. She knew so little about him—how would he fit in with these surroundings so familiar to her, so strange to him—

Emily's forebodings were cut short by the arrival of Dr. Dingwall. Fate had been good to her in sending him first, she was able to explain her other guest and to smooth the path for his appearance.

"A young medical student, eh? That's very nice, Emily. Doesn't seem so many years since I was at College myself. Little I thought then that I would be stuck in a place like Port Andrew all my days—but there, I don't grumble. Somebody's got to do it, it's a useful life and a full life—what more can a man ask?"

"I think you're—indispensable," Emily replied warmly.

"That's nice of you, but it's not the case. We all like to think we are indispensable, but we soon find the world can wag along without us easily enough," said the doctor smiling.

Mr. Dennistoun could now be heard coming downstairs and Emily was suddenly filled with a sick fear that Francis would be late. It was hardly formulated when the bell rang and in a few moments Francis was shown into the drawing-room.

She had not seen him before in evening dress and the conventional garb suited him well. He looked every inch of a gentleman, and his quiet dignified manner sent her unworthy doubts flying to the ends of the earth. She saw at once that he could hold his own with Mr. Dennistoun very easily.

Emily's heart fluttered as she led the way to the dining-room but the cause of her agitation was not fear for her guest's comfort, it was much more complicated and deep-seated than that.

She had longed to see Francis in this setting of familiar things. Had she hoped that it would cure her of the disturbance (which he had caused) of her inmost being? If so it was a vain hope. In the circle of golden lamplight above the gleaming mahogany he looked perfectly at home and natural. Bohemia to him, as to her, must be merely a pleasant picnic, a holiday from conventions. His attitude at her father's table was not due to adaptability, for he was the least adaptable of men. He was always himself under every circumstance, dominating every gathering, not by much talk like Harry Murdoch, nor by sheer egoism like her father but simply by a natural dignity and the force of his strong personality.

These were Emily's thoughts as she looked across the dark table with its glittering glasses and saw the red-haired man sipping her father's port and discussing it with the air of a connoisseur. And whether she was right or wrong about Francis Hood remained to be seen,

The drawing-room was dark when Emily reached it. She lighted a lamp upon the piano and played a few soft chords. She was uplifted now by this strange feeling which had crept into her heart, changing the whole aspect of life. She did not definitely own to herself that this new and absorbing interest was love for Francis Hood, but she let the vague nebulous happiness of his presence near her drift over her and engulf her in rosy clouds.

When the two older men were safely engrossed in their chess, Francis sought the drawing-room, and standing in the shadows near the door, he caught his breath for the unearthly radiance of this woman's face.

Of what was she thinking? What dreams of heaven were hers? A phrase of hers flashed through his mind; "we all have something to make life liveable." What had she to make life not only livable but full of glory, the glory that was reflected on her quiet face? Was it a lover? He put the idea from him as somehow unworthy of that virginal dreaming look. Yet he must know, even at the risk of forfeiting some of her friendship, and so he went forward to the piano.

Emily began to play softly when she saw him and pointed to a song which lay open on the music rest.

"Sing it," she said. "It will suit your voice."

"How do you know I have a voice?"

She did not reply but played the introduction again.

"You sing to me, Emily," he said, risking for the first time the use of the old-fashioned name which seemed to suit her so well.

"I only sing to please myself," she told him. "I have never had lessons. Music to me is a means, not an end. That is heretical, I know. It opens the door—that's all."

"The door to what?" he urged, feeling that at last he was near the secret of her serenity.

For a moment she hesitated and then moved across the room to a desk which stood by the window. In spite of his feelings which verged on excitement, Francis noticed the graceful line of her figure. Her arms and neck were white and firm, her throat "like the ivory pillars of the temple". The expression came to him in a flash, it was eminently descriptive, it fitted the thought like a glove. Francis was not a poet, but tonight he felt the blood run through his veins like wine, nothing but poetry could describe what Emily had become to him—he knew that he loved her as he had never loved any woman before.

For a moment he held the cup to his lips—he would make her love him, he would wake passion in her virgin soul. They two would face the world—at the next he had dashed it to the ground. What had he to offer a woman such as this—a woman gently nurtured, reared in luxury? He did not flinch from the answer to the question but pressed it into his heart as if the pain of it could dull the other pain. And the answer was—"Not even a name."

All this had taken but a few moments to pass through Francis' brain. He found himself standing behind Emily as she reached to a book-case above the writing-table and took down a book. Her eyes met his half shyly as she placed it in his hands.

"That is mine," she said quietly. "I have written now for some time—*always,* more or less. It is nothing very wonderful but it satisfies something in me that needs satisfying—partly and temporarily. I'm only telling you this because I feel you understand, or at least you *want* to understand. That day we spoke about all needing something to strive for—you remember?"

"I remember," Francis said.

"Nobody knows that I do this—not even Charles—except a great friend of mine, Miss Roe. She manages all the business part of it for me."

They were still standing by the writing-table, Francis holding the book she had given him in his two hands. He had not looked at it yet, for it seemed to matter so little in comparison with the gentle face and the soft white hands that moved a trifle nervously in explanation. He was disturbed to his heart by these nervous movements of the small white hands which usually lay so still and placid. He wanted to take them in his and hold them tightly so that they would be still and safe. God, how he loved her! Could he go away and leave her knowing that she was his —if he chose he could win her, he knew that. He did not realise that already she was deeply in love with him.

Greater than the desire to clasp her hands in his was the desire to help her. She was frightened, timid as the sparrows which came to his window for crumbs. He dared not speak lest he should break the thread that held her words together, words which came slowly from the gnarled and secret depths of Emily's soul.

"Sometimes," the voice went on, "I feel as if this world were unreal and that other world the true one. I can escape so easily now from worries and vexations. Perhaps you will think it extravagant if I say that I could not endure life without this—this refuge. Yet we say we cannot endure and life goes on much the same. When Miss Roe left me I said to myself I could not bear it, but I have borne it and am outwardly the same."

"Your life is not easy," he was able to say.

"It is hard, sometimes," she replied simply. "You know 'Man cannot live by bread alone', but I think it is bad for a woman to live only on dreams. I lose myself sometimes," she added thoughtfully, "and I forget who is real and who exists only in my imagination."

"It is bad for you."

"I know," she nodded. "I have got a little girl now, a sewing-maid, and I am going to take an interest in her. She lost her husband the night of the great storm. It will be better for me than always living in dreams."

"Much better," he agreed.

There was now a pause while Francis looked at the book which he still held, somewhat reverently. He treated all books as if he loved and understood them, supporting the back of the volume with one hand and turning the pages lightly and quickly.

Emily watched him and saw *her* book lie in the palm of his facile hand with a strange stirring of the heart.

"I have read this book," Francis said at once, "and your previous one as well."

He did not realise any need to tell Emily that he liked her books—they were above liking—apart somehow from the general run of novels. She had written of what she knew; of the poor folk of cottage and hut, of the sea and its moods, all of which she had observed and transmuted. The result was a pattern complete and fine—beautiful as a needle-work picture where every stitch has its place and goes to make up the perfect whole. It was artistic, it was true and therefore it satisfied.

But somehow the discovery of this other side of the woman he loved was disturbing to Francis. He was by no means old-fashioned enough to want his woman to be a nonentity sitting at a sampler or caring for his house all day, but the fact that she had this gift, this other side to her brain, which she acknowledged was by far the most powerful interest in her life, made her for the moment a stranger to Francis. He felt shy with her, and presently with the excuse of a long walk before him he took an early departure.

It was not till he had gone that Emily remembered the reason she had asked him to dinner—she had forgotten Charles' love affair completely.

The lamp in the studio was still alight when Francis reached *La Boiselle.* He let himself in quietly and found Laura in her dressing-gown with two long yellow plaits of hair which fell below her waist.

"You are early, Fan," she said, turning from the fire where something bubbled in a saucepan. "Did you enjoy yourself?"

Francis did not answer—there was never any need to answer Laura unless one wanted to, and he did not know whether or not he had enjoyed his dinner party. He sat down by the table and leaned his elbows upon it dejectedly.

"Did Miss Dennistoun refuse you, Francis?" Laura asked with startling smoothness.

"Laura!" he cried rising to his feet and pacing up and

down the room. "Are you mad? Do you imagine that Miss Dennistoun would ever look at me?"

"Yes, I do," said the fair woman earnestly.

"What makes you think—"

Laura was thoughtful for a moment. It was always difficult for her to find words to express her exact meaning.

"You are a man," she said at last. "What more can a woman want?"

"She might want a name," he threw at her.

"Does a name matter so dreadfully much?" Laura wondered. "Aren't you morbid about it, Francis?"

He thought of that for a minute or two and then he said,

"It isn't the name that matters so much as the fact of not knowing who you are. That haunts me, Laura. Heredity does count—I see that more and more in my experience as a medical student. Take your own case, my dear. You know what you owe to that gallant gentleman who is your father."

Laura allowed that.

"Of course it's true," she said. "But why must you be so certain that your father was not everything that he should have been?"

"Because I know he was a villain."

"You don't know it," she countered. "And when I look at you I am sure that he was not. You can work heredity both ways, Francis."

"For all I know he was a gaol-bird," Francis replied bitterly.

"And for all you know he was a Duke," Laura told him. "Why Francis, if you could only know yourself—see yourself."

"I see myself every morning when I shave, thank you," said Francis laughing in spite of himself. "And it's almost enough to put me off my breakfast."

But Laura did not laugh.

"Oh Francis," she said sorrowfully, "and she's so nice."

"Nice!" cried Francis, aghast at this too faint praise of his perfect Emily. *"Nice."*

Laura had to laugh then. "Well I'm not a poet," she said as she poured out the milky food which she had been stirring and prepared a small tray to carry to her husband. "I'm only quite an ordinary person, but if you take my advice you'll marry Emily because, as I have already told you, she's nice."

"She doesn't love me," he replied in a low voice, "and even if she did what right have I to ask her to—to marry me?"

Laura paused at the door, tray in hand. "Every right," she told him mischievously, "because you see—you're nice too."

She disappeared in time to escape the pillow hurled in her direction, shutting the door gently behind her. How good she was, Francis thought as he retrieved his missile, how calm and sure. She made the best of her life and created an atmosphere of peace which those around her were able to share. Nobody seeing her as she went about her daily tasks could have guessed at the load of anxiety which she carried in her heart. "Nice!" echoed Francis as he climbed into his improvised bed on the divan. "By Jove, Laura has not got the gift of words." He lay for some time thinking of how *he* would describe Emily, until at last he fell asleep.

CHAPTER 7
Bearing Burdens

TO GIVE Alice her due she was very pretty and Charles was not the first young man who had fallen for her, as the saying goes. Fair fluffy hair and eyes of baby blue are very appealing. Charles found them irresistible and her only drawback in his eyes (if so perfect a creature could be said to have a drawback) was her extreme wealth. Charles would have liked her to be poor, in rags if possible, so that he could shower upon her everything that money could buy—the shower lost its point when the showered upon had more than enough of the good things of life already. But Alice could not help her father having made his fortune any more than she could help her mother's figure. That they were both on the large side was no fault of hers. Charles explained all this to Alice with his usual eagerness—omitting of course the reference to Mrs. Brunton's embonpoint which would not have been polite. He expatiated on what he would have done for her if he had found her starving in a garret, but Alice, so far from being suitably impressed by Charles' eloquence and devotion could do nothing but laugh. When, however, he added that in spite of her riches—which he considered a very serious disability—he intended to marry her, Alice stopped laughing and said, "Oh, Charles, you must ask mother," in the very proper manner in which girls are said to have behaved when they wore crinolines.

Charles walked on air for he had no qualms as to what the mother of his beloved would say, and in this he was proved right for Mrs. Brunton after being suitably surprised, gave in gracefully. She knew better than to cross her Alice who had ruled her with a steel bar, decently covered with velvet, ever since she was a few hours old. There were only two conditions made by Alice's mother and to both of these Charles, the devout lover, joyously agreed. The first was that Mr. Dennistoun's consent must be gained, the second that all thought of a "shop" must be given up. Alice could not marry into trade however high class or respectable! There was a dark secret in Mrs. Brunton's past which was not known even to Alice, and this dark secret consisted of the disgracing fact that Mrs. Brunton's father owned a shop in a small manufacturing town in the north of England. It was this which made her all the more determined that no such stigma should attach itself to her only child.

The shop was given up without one backward glance, for all Charles' mind and heart were full of Alice. Alice as his sweetheart, his wife, as the mother of his son. They were very beautiful thoughts and they had a marvellous effect upon Charles' character. He became gentler and more considerate not only of Alice but of all women. His eyes took on the bright sparkle of happiness and his mouth the full curve of perfect contentment. As regards Mr. Dennistoun's consent Charles was confident, for as he pointed out to mother and daughter, anybody who got Alice for a daughter-in-law was obviously the luckiest man alive—except of course her husband.

At this Alice gave a little scream and blushed divinely and the conversation became too foolish to chronicle.

Mr. Dennistoun was amazingly agreeable over the matter of his son's engagement. He had known Edgar Brunton in business as a wily man who knew how to butter his bread, and therefore he could guess at Alice's income. He stuck her photograph on his mantelpiece and remarked to Emily (there being nobody else handy) that she was a "good-looking girl" and that "of course he was too young to think of marriage—damn him—but he might have chosen worse, and perhaps this would settle him and chase some of those fool notions out of his silly head."

Emily did not answer, she was wading through eight pages of closely written script in which Charles used the word "adorable" no fewer than eleven times. At the end there was a postscript in a grotesquely large handwriting which announced that Alice had "never had a sister but was perfectly crazy to have one and could she come to Borriston in the Summer to make Emily's acquaintance."

That night Emily sat up very late writing to Helen Roe. Kitty looked in once or twice but the pen was still flying on untiringly and she dared not interrupt her beloved mistress; so the door was closed again very quietly and Kitty went back to bed. What was she writing, Kitty wondered and how did ideas come to her so quickly and clearly. As she lay in her little bed and watched the glow from the lighted room reflected on the dark garden she thought of many things. Of Joe and of her life with him, of Miss Dennistoun's goodness and cleverness. To Kitty she was "the height of admiration", and it was sheer happiness to serve her in any way that was possible. Emily soon began to find all sorts of small services rendered to her in an unostentatious manner. If she was going to dress the flowers she found the glasses all ready to hand—washed, polished and filled with fresh water. Ribbons were run in her garments, holes in her stockings disappeared and buttons were replaced silently as if by magic. None of this was Kitty's legitimate business but it was very pleasant to both people concerned, and Emily would have been less than human if she had failed to return the affection which prompted the little services.

As the days went past the affection between Emily and Kitty deepened and strengthened and the former came to depend more and more upon the girl-widow's sympathy. She was too reserved to confide in Kitty, but it was easy for the eyes of love to discover that Miss Dennistoun was far from happy and indeed Kitty had found out the cause of her sorrow without much difficulty. That she could not understand it need hardly be said for it seemed incredible to the simple girl that any man could be blind to her mistress' qualities. What did he want, she wondered miserably—would an angel straight from Heaven suit him better?

Emily was far from believing that the girl had divined her secret (she forgot that love is fundamentally the same in every woman's heart and Kitty's own sorrow made her perspicacious) but the unspoken sympathy helped her through a very dark time and drew them nearer and nearer together.

To bear one another's burdens does not only fulfil Christ's law but it also helps to lessen one's own. And the two women discovered, perhaps unconsciously, that the easiest way to bear sorrow is to share the sorrow of someone else.

Kitty thought of this in a vague, half understanding way as she waited for her mistress to stop the interminable writing and go to bed. And the pen still flew on covering sheet after sheet with hopes and fears for Charles and his future weal. "He's so young," was the burden of her letter, "really just a child. I fear terribly that he may not have chosen right, for someday he will surely grow up and it seems to me that he is bound to outgrow his childish fancy. You know I told you of the old furniture shop which he was so madly keen about? This has all gone by the board now, he never mentions it and has even consented to go into the office if father wants him to—a course which he abhors—or perhaps I should say abhorred. He seems absolutely infatuated with this girl. Oh Helen, write me one of your nice long letters and tell me if I am very stupid to be so fearful. I did not know Charles before—this sounds strange but it is an absolute fact—but just lately I have come to know him well. He is very young and impetuous, very eager about things, very lovable. I have come to know him through a man—a friend of his—"

Emily laid down her pen, and folding her hands, gazed across her bedroom to a little photograph which was tucked into a frame on the mantelpiece. It was an amateur snapshot of a group standing on the verandah at *La Boiselle,* and from where she was sitting it was hardly possible to recognise the three figures as Laura, Mademoiselle Jacquot and Francis Hood. But Emily had looked at it so often that she did not need her eyes to see it. The three figures to her were merely one, and that one was imprinted on her heart. Laura had given her the little picture with a deprecating smile and a remark to the effect that Harry's attempts at photography fell short of the artistic standard but no doubt it would serve to remind Emily of her friends.

"Francis Hood," she said slowly, "why can I never escape from you—from the thought of you?"

She rose then, and opening the window leaned far out and pressed her cold hands against her burning cheeks. A wild access of shame possessed her, that she, Emily Dennistoun, should think about a man "like that", so that the mere thought of his slim capable hands was enough to send the warm blood into her pale cheeks. "How can you?" she whispered to herself. "A man who showed you a little polite attention and then went away and forgot that you exist."

Emily had not seen the red-haired man since the night of her dinner-party. He had gone away the following day and left no message. She expected him to write and looked in vain for a letter. Until at last it was borne upon her that he was not going to write, he had vanished out of her life without a word. Emily felt humiliated in her own eyes

—fortunately there was nobody else to witness her humiliation—for she had been so certain that the man had returned her interest, had at least accepted her as a friend. It was difficult to believe that he had been amusing himself at her expense for the hypothesis failed to tally with what she knew of his character. He *had* felt drawn to her, she knew it certainly what then had changed him, what had come between them?

If in some unknown way she had offended him, it would have been fairer to tell her and give her a chance to defend herself The most desperate criminal is not condemned unheard. She could not believe that Francis could be unjust.

Laura Murdoch relieved Emily's mind of the fear that Francis might be ill. She apparently heard from him regularly for she had always the latest news about his doings. It was heartbreaking to Laura to see the havoc that Francis' pride was making of his own life and Emily's. The latter's courageous attitude did not deceive Laura, it merely made her more annoyed with Francis, for she recognised in Emily a soul whose power of endurance matched her own and who was in every way a fit mate for her old friend.

The game was too complicated—too ticklish altogether —for Laura to take a hand. She was too loyal to betray Emily's feelings to Francis, while his feelings were equally sacred in her eyes. All that woman could do to persuade Francis to reconsider his decision had been done, but she had not been able to move him from his determination to go away and try to forget Emily Dennistoun.

The sight of Emily in that quiet well-run house had frightened him—what was his position compared to hers? What could he offer the mistress of such a mansion? And then had come the discovery of her talent, assuring her an honourable position in the world of letters. This impressed him even more. Francis himself intended to fly high in his particular world, but the flying was all to do. He had no position to offer Emily socially or professionally.

And so it was that Laura's persuasions fell on deaf ears and Emily mourned the loss of a friend.

CHAPTER 8
The Golden Girl

CHARLES and Alice arrived at Borriston Hall one very hot evening at the beginning of July. Alice, having celebrated "Commemoration" in time-honoured fashion, was magnanimous enough to forego the pleasures of Henley, much to the disappointment of Mrs. Brunton, to whom the gay regatta was one of the chief delights of the year.

"You *are* selfish, it will be *no* fun without you," she moaned, to which her dutiful daughter retorted agreeably, "Don't go then, I'm sure *I* don't care."

Thus mother and daughter cheered and comforted each other in the privacy of their small but luxurious flat in Oxford High Street, and neither their dearest friends nor their most keen-sighted enemies so much as guessed their secret.

Borriston Hall had been in a fever of excitement and anticipation at the prospect of the lovers' arrival. The fever had even infected Mr. Dennistoun himself and he so far unbent as to order a bottle of his most cherished *Veuve Clicquot* to lend a sparkle to the dinner and to drink the health of the future Mrs. Charles Dennistoun. Nobody could help being pleased with the pretty creature who was Charles' choice, and Emily, who was prepared to be critical, was won by her artless pleasure in her surroundings. She laughed and chattered till even Mr. Dennistoun became human and Charles was more and more enamoured of his pearl among women.

It was late before a move was made to bed, and Emily lighted her future sister-in-law to her room.

"I hope you have everything you want," she said in the anxious manner peculiar to hostesses.

Alice was staring at the two candles upon her dressing-table with a sort of horror. To her eyes, used to the brilliance of electric light, they only served to make the darkness visible. What a prehistoric hole! she thought disdainfully. They must really get a plant and put in electric light. How on earth am I going to see my way to bed?

Aloud, she said, "Oh, it's all so *perfect*, so *restful*, dear Emily, I know we are going to be the *greatest* friends."

Emily's tenderness was quick to respond and the two girls bade each other a fond goodnight.

The morning after the arrival of Charles and Alice was very sunny and warm. Alice had her breakfast in bed but came down soon after, looking delightfully cool and pretty in a blue linen frock which matched her eyes. She was so exquisite that Charles felt he must show her off to somebody. He liked everyone about him to share his wonderful happiness.

"I know," he cried jumping up and throwing the paper into a corner of the room, "we'll walk over to Craitn this morning. It will be a fine walk along the sands—you'd like to, wouldn't you darling?"

Alice wanted to know where Craitn was and who lived there before she gave her unqualified consent, but when she heard it was an artist and his wife who were great friends of Charles' and were simply longing to see her—"Dearest, you are so pretty," Charles explained, "Murdoch will rave about you, he'll probably want to paint you or something,"—she agreed that it "would be simply too divine for words," and ran upstairs like a flying bird to get her hat.

They left Emily weeding the rockery and strolled off with happy faces. She looked after them, and her heart was filled with a motherly prayer for their happiness. She could not help feeling that their youth was a danger. Youth is so exiguous and intolerant—and they had too much money for Life to be a safe thing for them.

Emily finished her job and then rose to her feet feeling rather sick and dizzy with her labour in the hot sun. She paused for a moment in the cool dimness of the hall and then went upstairs to the sewing-room. It was strange to Emily how often in the day her feet took her to the sewing-room whenever there were a few odd moments to spare and it was not worth while settling down to anything. It was such a pleasant room, sparsely but brightly furnished and it had a big window overlooking the bay of Craitn which usually stood wide open.

As a rule a smiling face greeted Emily, but today the smile was faint, Kitty looked pale and worried.

"Is anything the matter, Kitty?" said her young mistress very kindly.

Kitty shook her head.

"You are sure, Kitty dear? You are not too—too unhappy here?"

"Happier than I thought possible," was the low answer.

"You are so good to me—if I could only help you a little as you have helped me—"

"You do help, my dear little Kitty," said Emily gently.

There was a little silence while each longed to confide her secret trouble to sympathetic ears—but failed to find the words.

Charles and Alice returned from Craitn in time for a late lunch. They were full of all they had seen and done and as Mr. Dennistoun had gone to Glasgow for the day there was no restraining influence on their talk, and their youthful and inconsequent chatter made Emily feel very old. She succeeded in rousing herself to take an interest in their doings in spite of the misery which darkly enfolded her. The tides of unhappiness are hard to understand, they ebb and flow without any perceptible cause and today was one of Emily's worst days, when the thought of Francis recurred again and again with almost unbearable poignancy. She tried hard to understand why this should be, why today should be so hopelessly dark and dreary. Was it the mere sight of Charles, his friend, which brought him before her eyes? Or was it the almost indecent happiness of the lovers which threw her own misery into bolder relief?

In the sweetness of her disposition Emily hoped and prayed that it was not the latter, for she did not like to think that Charles' gladness could bring her sorrow.

"I *do* think Laura is perfectly sweet," Alice was saying, her large blue eyes fixed on Emily with a dreamy expression. "So *different*, isn't she?"

"We are to bathe with them tomorrow," Charles added. "Laura says you are to come too, Emily—she was awfully disappointed you didn't come over with us today."

"They are going to have a fancy dress dance in the studio," Alice chimed in. "Won't it be too heavenly? I simply adore dancing. Just a few couples and the gramophone—it is the most delightful idea. I *do* think it was perfectly divine of Mr. Murdoch to suggest it."

"I could see he was thinking all the time what a lucky fellow I am," said Charles ardently. "He asked me if he could paint you—"

"Oh Charles, did he really! Oh how deliciously exciting."

"—but I said no, you can't paint the lily," finished the young man with a chuckle.

"Oh, but Charles—how silly," Alice protested. "It would be frightfully exciting, and we could give it to mother—she would adore it."

"Oh nonsense, Alice, think of the time he would take and we've only got a fortnight—at least I have before I go to France to mug up French. You know I promised father I would do that before going up for next term. Why, Goldie dear, it would spoil all our fun if you had to go and sit to him every day."

Alice made a little moue of disgust which was very attractive. "Silly boy," she said.

"Goldie!"

"You must not be selfish. It would be such a kindness to Mr. Murdoch—you told me he was poor, and mother would love to have a portrait of me. We must think of others, not always of ourselves and our own happiness."

This was said with such an angelic smile that Charles was at a loss to contradict her, and Emily who had listened to the discussion with a dawning horror was quite deceived. After all, it was but natural that Alice should wish to give pleasure to her mother and if she could at the same time give a much needed commission to a struggling young artist, it was all to the good. Perhaps it was good for Charles too, not to get his own way about everything, but the expression of disappointment on his young face went straight to his sister's heart.

The weather continued bright and warm and the bathing party was such a success that it was followed by others no less enjoyable. Harry and Alice absented themselves from these revels, on the score of the picture which had been started and which bade fair to be one of Harry's most successful portraits. He worked at it untiringly and Alice was always ready to oblige him with a sitting whenever he wanted it.

One afternoon when the others had gone off to bathe Harry and his sitter were left alone in the studio.

"Am I really as pretty as all that?" Alice asked him. She had dropped her pose for the time being and had come round behind the easel.

"Alice!" cried the artist. "You are a million times more beautiful. Sometimes I feel utterly disgusted with this wretched daub. How could any mortal man hope to paint *you!*"

She laid a cool hand on his and looked up into his face

with her big blue eyes. He was very good to look upon with his Grecian features and his fair skin.

"Harry—don't you know it is very naughty of you to say these things to me?"

"How can I help it!"

"You must be a good boy if we are to be friends," she told him with subtle innocence.

"You adorable little creature! You know, Alice, I think you are very like Dora with your fair curls and your sweetness—I always liked Dora better than Agnes."

"Dora who?" asked Alice, her eyes clouding a little at the mention of another woman's name—it was rather stupid of Harry to think that she was like anybody else.

Harry laughed teasingly—ignorance in a pretty girl could be very attractive. "Do you put your hair in curlers every night?" he wondered.

"No, of course not."

"Well you are not like Dora then."

"What *are* you talking about," she asked him peevishly. "Do you mean Dora Clarke? She is the only Dora I know—I used to go to school with her. She married one of the Humes—fearfully stuck-up people—her husband is the next heir to Eaglefold."

Harry shook his head—he was tired of the subject. The only subject which interested him for long was a pretty woman.

"Dear Alic,e there is nobody in the world like you—I wish I could paint you as you deserve to be painted. I should want to dip my brush in sunshine to paint your hair, and in the deep blue sea for your beautiful eyes."

"Have you ever felt the greyness of life, Harry?" she asked, looking up at him with an expression of trusting innocence. The sentence was culled from a favourite novel and Alice had found it effective on more than one occasion.

"My dear!" he cried. "How well you understand! Life is all grey with just sometimes a burst of sunshine. This poverty, this eternal struggle to make ends meet! Everyday the continual grinding at subjects which don't interest one but which *sell well*—Oh, how it all cramps one! And then you came here, Alice, and the whole world has blossomed."

"How wonderful!"

"Wonderful you," he breathed, his lips close to her little ear where the soft tendrils of gold hair curled so irresistibly.

Alice's heart fluttered. It was rather thrilling to be made love to in this fashion (Charles' inexperienced efforts fell far short of this). He was so good-looking too—

"My Fairy Queen," he continued, holding her so that the gold of her hair was against his cheek. "My beautiful Fairy Queen, how everything changes at your touch—how you could inspire me if only you were mine!"

She drew away from him at that.

"What would Charles say?"

"Charles!" cried Harry. "How can a mere boy like Charles appreciate you! Look into my eyes and tell what you see there."

Alice struggled like a bird in his clasp—he was going too fast for her. Flattered and attracted by his passionate admiration she yet retained a few grains of caution.

"Give yourself to me," he whispered, "and we will fly away together to the Ionian Isles, where the sun always shines on lovers and the sea is calm and warm and blue like your eyes—"

"There is somebody coming," Alice cried.

They sprang apart, and a moment later the bathing party trooped in, brown and sandy, with the usual accompaniment of soaking brown bath-towels. With them came Mr. and Mrs. Wick, a young couple who had taken a bungalow near the Murdochs for the summer months. They were a cheerful pair and fell in comfortably with the Bohemian atmosphere of *La Boiselle*.

"My hat, I am hungry!" Charles cried, throwing his bathing towel on the floor and stretching himself like a cat.

Alice looked at him with sudden distaste. His brown hair was in dark streaks upon his forehead and his grey flannel suit was creased and covered with sand, but Charles was quite oblivious of the fact that he did not look his best—he felt happy and comfortable.

The men of the party gathered round the easel while Laura and Ivette Jacquot laid the tea.

Charles had not seen the portrait before and he was agreeably surprised. It was very like Alice for it had caught her elf-like quality.

"You're a clever devil," said Wick suddenly.

"One does not often get such a subject," Harry replied, smiling enigmatically. "It brings out one's best work."

"It should," Wick said laughing. "I should think you must be quite sorry it is finished—"

"It is not finished," Harry replied. "The hair and the mouth are merely sketched in. It will take another week at least."

"Then it must remain unfinished," Charles said quietly, "because Alice and I go south on Tuesday morning."

"My dear chap, you can't take away my sitter before the portrait is complete," said Harry reasonably. "Can't you stay a few days longer?"

"No I can't," replied Charles. "I have to join the others at Dover on Wednesday and we all go on to Paris that day. I can't possibly back out at the last moment after promising to go—besides the picture is practically finished."

"You must allow me to be the best judge of that, Charles," Harry said with a smile.

"Oh, you lucky boy to go to my Paris!" cried Mademoiselle Jacquot. "But look you, why doesn't Mademoiselle Brunton stay on here for a leetle? She goes not to Paris—*hein?*"

"Why of course," cried Harry. "That's an excellent idea."

Emily looked at Charles and saw that in his opinion the idea was anything but excellent. His frank face was index to his annoyance but he did not speak, and before any more could be said on the subject Laura changed the conversation by saying in her quiet voice,

"We must have our little dance on Monday night then, so that Charles and Alice will be there."

"Oh yes!" Alice cried, clapping her hands in excitement. "I was hoping you had not forgotten. Oh, *what* shall I wear? We've only got three days to get our dresses—what will you wear Emily?"

"I don't think I shall come," Emily said quietly but this announcement was greeted with such horror by Charles and Laura that she was obliged to change her mind, merely for the sake of peace.

The rest of the afternoon was taken up discussing the dance and the preparations for it. Emily was quite determined that the Murdochs should not incur any expense over it as she knew that their existence was an exceedingly hand to mouth affair. Fortunately, Charles saw her idea and backed her up nobly, promising to bring the supper (which was to be prepared at Borriston) over to *La Boiselle* in his car.

"I thought this was going to be *our* dance," Laura whispered to Emily as they were coming away.

"So it is," replied her friend, wilfully misunderstanding the issue.

Laura shook her head. "You are a dear!" she told Emily with a smile and the situation was made plain to both of them.

On the way home Emily contrived to lose her two companions—not a difficult matter for they were too interested in each other to care whether she was there or not. She let them go on in front and followed in a leisurely manner, full of troubled thoughts. It was difficult to see just where and when her opinion of Alice had changed but in the last week Emily had come to the conclusion that Charles' future wife was by no means the young and innocent maiden that she seemed. Underneath that babyish exterior there was a woman of the world, subtle as the snake which beguiled her ancestress to destruction. Just how she knew this was hard to say. Other people took Alice at her face value and spoke of her as a "butterfly" or as a "delightful child" but Emily was very sure that she was neither the one nor the other. She was so lost in thought that when Charles appeared just in front of her she was startled as if he had risen out of the ground.

"Where is Alice?" she asked, looking round vaguely like someone awakened out of a deep sleep.

"Gone on," he waved his hand towards Port Andrew. "We've—we've quarrelled," he added hoarsely. "Oh, Emily, why do you stand there looking like that? Why don't you say something?"

Charles would have been astonished if he had known that the first thought which filled his sister's breast was one of thankfulness. It was with difficulty she repressed a cry of joy, but the next moment her natural sympathy reasserted itself on the reflection that Charles was not finding it a subject for congratulation. He would some day —of that she was sure—but just at present it was a bitter pill.

"Charles dear!" she said, taking his arm. "It was about that wretched portrait of course. I think you are right to stick to your plans."

"*She* doesn't," said Charles bitterly. "Of course it isn't her fault, it's that ass Murdoch. I wish he were at the bottom of the sea."

It was hard to know what to say, for she sympathised deeply with Charles and although she was sure that it was all for the best she was far too wise to tell him so. They walked on for a little in silence and then Charles burst out,

"He's turned her head of course. I don't blame *her,* poor little thing. He's frightened her—"

"Oh come, my dear!" Emily interrupted, she was seized with a hysterical desire to laugh at the idea of Alice being terrorized by Harry Murdoch.

"He has, I tell you. He was awfully angry, she told me, threatened to destroy the whole thing if he wasn't allowed to finish it."

"He wouldn't do that," Emily reasoned. "For one thing Laura wouldn't let him."

"A man must put his foot down somewhere," Charles said with dignity that was somehow rather pathetic. They reached the door of Borriston Hall.

"You're quite in the right," said Emily firmly. "If you give in now you're done," she added to herself as she watched him run upstairs two stairs at a time.

Alice did not come down to dinner, she sent a message to Emily saying that she had a bad headache and asking for "a little soup" to be sent up to her room.

Emily smiled as she gave directions for her guest's dinner. "A little soup and nothing more, Stephens," she told the tablemaid, and felt savagely glad that Alice would miss an ice pudding which she particularly liked. It was a queer feeling for so gentle a person as Emily to indulge in.

All the evening Charles wandered about the drawing-room like an unquiet spirit.

"The awful effects of love on a weak brain," said Mr. Dennistoun at last. "You and I score there, eh Emily? You would think the young woman was having a child at least instead of merely the megrims or the tantrums or whatever the modern generation likes to call it."

"You don't understand, sir," cried Charles, driven to desperation by his father's ill-timed humour.

Mr. Dennistoun rose heavily from his chair. "Don't be too sure of that, Charles," he said, as he left the room. "Women have always been the same and always will be—she'll make it up with you tomorrow."

They heard him laughing as he crossed the hall with his heavy tread to seek peace from the manifestations of love in the solitude of his study.

No sooner had he gone than Charles rushed to the writing table and sweeping aside the usual litter of ornaments and frames began to pour out his soul in a long impassioned letter to his beloved Alice. He took a fierce pleasure in humbling himself to the dust. She was right as always, and he wrong, this was the gist of his letter, and Emily, watching his face needed no further guide to its contents. It was more than she could bear, and with a little sigh of hopelessness she gathered up her sewing and went to bed.

CHAPTER 9
The Dance at the Bungalow

THE NEXT few days were full of excitement and bustle. Alice decided to go to the dance as a sea nymph and bought yards of green gauze at the little haberdasher's shop in the village. She commandeered Kitty to "run it up" for her, and spent hours in the sewing-room trying it on and picking it to pieces until even the patient little Kitty was exasperated.

"I'm afraid I can't waste any more time over it, Miss Brunton," she said at last. "You see I've got this Toreador dress to alter for Mr. Charles—perhaps you could finish it off yourself."

Alice's eyes flashed dangerously. She seized the mass of filmy material out of Kitty's hands and flounced out of the room, pausing at the door for a Parthian shot—

"You had better take care, impudent creature, I'm not so blind as your beloved mistress—"

"What do you mean?" Kitty cried, the red blood flushing her pale cheeks to deepest rose.

"I mean *I know your secret*," was the cryptic reply.

Charles was almost as excited as Alice and very nearly as fussy over his dress. Since the quarrel his relations with his betrothed had been even more of the devout lover than before and Alice who was the soul of good-nature when everything went right, forgave him handsomely—and decided to stay on till the picture was finished. Meanwhile the dance lay between them and the parting and beyond the dance neither of them could look.

But no joyous anticipation filled Emily's horizon, she would much rather have gone to bed than spend half the night looking at the other people dancing. Nobody would want her as a partner, of that she was assured. Charles and Harry would probably think it their duty to ask her to dance but the rest of the company were to be friends of the Murdochs, strangers to her. She would either be a wallflower or else a duty to be tooled round with heavy courtesy and left with thankfulness the moment that good manners permitted.

She tried to explain her feelings to Laura with the earnestness of a condemned criminal asking for a reprieve but Laura only laughed at her friend's fears and held her to her promise to come to the dance.

"Dear Emily, we'll be wallflowers together," she said lightly—and then she added more seriously, "don't fail me, my friend."

A hasty glance at Laura's face did not elucidate the mystery of her serious words, for she was smiling in the old inscrutable manner; but the words had had their effect and there was no more talk of Emily's not being present at the dance.

She had been so determined not to go that she had not contemplated the important matter of a fancy dress but now that it was settled irrevocably something would have to be done. There was no time to *make* anything, for the great affair was fixed for the following night so Emily took some keys and ascended to the garret where there was an old iron-bound chest full of discarded finery. Here she found a flowered silk gown which had belonged to her grandmother and with Kitty's eager help it was let out sufficiently for Emily's modern figure to squeeze into it. The little yellow shoes which went with the dress were hopelessly small for a modern girl's healthy foot, but she managed to find a pair of black satin shoes with red heels which had belonged to her mother and with these she had to be content.

A more conceited woman than Emily would have been content with the image which confronted her when she looked into her long mirror and saw the dainty old-fashioned figure looking back at her appraisingly. There was a softness combined with dignity in the drapery of the golden silk which suited Emily as few other dresses would have done. Kitty who had helped her young mistress to dress and to pile her dark brown hair in curls on the crown of her shapely head was well satisfied with the results of her labours.

"There won't be anybody there so pretty as you," she said, with a shake of her serious little head.

Emily laughed gently at the naïve prophecy; she wondered whether any other guest was dressing for the ball with such absence of excitement and anticipation as she was. Her one longing was to escape the ordeal and go peacefully to bed, but for Laura's sake she must see it through. There was something troubling Laura, for she was by no means her usual placid self, the calm of her nature was ruffled and although Emily had no idea what had caused the disturbance she was none the less ready to help in any way she could.

The day had been spent by herself and Charles in helping the Murdochs to prepare the studio for the entertainment. Harry's paintings in various stages of completion had been stacked in an outhouse, together with practically all the furniture the little bungalow contained. The larger of the two bedrooms had been converted into a supper room, the smaller into a cloakroom for the repairing of damaged garments—most necessary to a fancy dress dance.

"Where are you going to sleep?" Emily asked when she saw Charles and Harry emptying the room of furniture.

"Sleep!" cried Harry gaily. "We're not going to *sleep*, we're going to 'dance till the sun breaks through'—and then some. Begone Morpheus, thou over-rated god and make way for Bacchus and Terpsichore."

They all laughed at that, but Laura's eyes were tired already, darkly shadowed with insomnia, and Emily wondered if there were something desperately the matter or if it were merely the effort of living up to the youthful enthusiasm of her husband. He was so much her junior not only in years but in mind and character as well. She tried to persuade Laura to come back to Borriston for the short night which would follow the dance but without success.

The gramophone had already begun to blare forth the melancholy tidings that it had "no bananas today" when Charles drove up the rutty track leading to *La Boiselle.*

"*Do* hurry Charles, I *knew* we would be late," Alice said fretfully.

"We're not late," Charles replied shortly, "and I can't possibly race the car over this blinking road."

Alice flung herself back into the corner of the car with an air of resignation. She had been more than difficult all day and Emily had wondered several times how the none-too-patient Charles had kept his temper with her. It was a relief to all three when the car drew up outside the bungalow from whose open door a shaft of light shone out welcomingly into the darkness.

The new arrivals were hurried into the cloakroom to remove their wraps and Emily noticed with amazement that her companion's small hands were trembling with excitement. It seemed strange that a girl who had been out so much, and had attended balls in London should be thrilled with this small amateur affair. Alice's behaviour savoured more of a débutante at her first party than that of a London belle. Such thoughts were quickly swamped in consternation caused by her first glimpse of Alice's frock—what *had* she done to it?

She was standing before a cheval glass with a wrapt expression on her small fair face, admiring her rounded arms and the graceful turn of her neck. Twisting her lithe body this way and that to get the effect of its contours and its sinuous beauty. For none of Alice's admirers was more conscious of her loveliness than that young woman herself.

To the horrified Emily it seemed that what there was of the dress only served to reveal every line and curve of Alice's figure. A few thicknesses of green gauze with fluttering ends reached to the girl's knees, her arms and neck were bare and white with powder, and her short fluffy hair was curled loosely about her face and neck. How *could* she have come like that? How *could* she have so mutilated the pretty frock which Kitty had made for her? It was too late now to do anything, too late to speak to her. Emily knew that nothing she could say would be taken in good part, it would merely alienate the self-satisfied Alice to criticise her appearance. It is my fault, thought Emily desperately, I should have taken more interest in her frock, I was angry because she was rude to Kitty and this is my punishment. Oh my poor Charles, what have I done to let you in for this.

Fortunately Alice was not at all interested in her future sister-in-law's opinion so Emily was spared the choice between offending Alice's delicate sensibilities and telling a falsehood.

She followed the sea nymph into the studio which was lighted by a dozen Chinese lanterns and decorated with paper ribbons and flowers from Borriston gardens. Dancing had begun, and the room was filling rapidly with gaily decked figures of apaches, pierrots and pierrettes, brigands, gypsies, flower-girls and more dignified impersonations of historical characters. Harry was already fox-trotting energetically with a dark girl who wore the scarlet petticoat and short black jacket of Carmen. He was dressed as a French artist from the *Quartier Latin* in a velvet coat and an exaggerated silk tie, whose deep blue colour showed up the fairness of his skin.

Laura, attired in a Dutch Costume, was still busy receiving guests. The white cap with its wings of muslin suited her well, she was flushed to prettiness with the excitement of the moment. Two long plaits the colour of ripe corn hung down below her waist. Just at present she was too busy to be disturbed, and Emily let her eyes wander round the transformed studio with interest and pleasure. Her trained mind was taking in its store of impressions which might lie dormant for years before germinating in the soil of her imagination.

Then, suddenly, it was all gone, and with a sick flutter of her heart she realised that Francis Hood was standing beside her.

He was dressed as an eighteenth century Highwayman with a dun coloured riding-coat, and leather boots which reached to his thighs. A pistol was stuck jauntily in his belt and in his hand was a three-cornered hat trimmed with gold braid. He looked more immense than ever and more dominating. Emily held her breath and tried to still the beating of her heart, which surely must be audible above the din and clatter of the latest fox-trot. Fool, she said to herself, you might have been prepared for this, you might have schooled yourself better. It seemed to her that everyone in the room must realise the significance of their meeting, must be able to read her shameful love for him and his indifference to her.

Francis could see that his sudden appearance had agitated Emily and he began to wonder—madly, with an up-springing of hope which would not be stilled—whether it had been wrong to go away from her as he had done, without a word of farewell. Whether, after all, Laura had been right and he wrong. Whether, in short,

Emily loved him. If that were so, if Emily cared, he had made her suffer. Instead of sparing her he had made her suffer, he had behaved more like a cad than the fine gentleman he had imagined. Pride had been at the root of it, pride and cowardice. He had made her suffer because he was not brave enough to tell her the whole truth, because he was too proud to humble himself before her. He had been so sure that she did not care, so certain that her attitude towards him had been, all along, one of friendly tolerance for her brother's friend. If he had suspected a deeper interest he would not have dared to come back like this, he would have felt it unfair to Emily, but sure of her safety he had dared the encounter. Laura had been so persuasive, and the need to see Emily once more (only once, said the tempting voice) was so great.

Something of this flashed through the mind of Francis as he stood looking down at the dainty figure in the old-fashioned gown. It was as perfect as she was—manlike he could describe it no further—he could only see that her throat, the ivory pillar so well remembered, was encircled by a narrow band of black velvet. Below the band was a little creamy hollow, and it was there that Francis Hood wanted to kiss Emily.

"Come," he said at last, and before she could protest he had swept her into the circle of dancers with a strong arm about her waist. Tonight was his, he would take the pleasure of it, drink the cup to the dregs and tomorrow she should hear the whole story of his life and make her choice.

When the dance was finished Francis guided his partner to the open door and they went out together into the cool darkness of the starry night.

Somehow all the anger that Emily had cherished against this man, and all the shame that he had caused her, was melted away and forgotten at the first touch of his arm about her waist. There was something in his firm touch which set her throbbing heart at peace, and, while he held her no differently from another partner, her woman's instinct told her that he loved her.

They walked up the little path which led towards the sea, and for several minutes there was silence between them, for after the glare and the noise of the dance-room the quiet of the outside world was awe-inspiring. Behind them was laughter and the chatter of merry voices, before them the sea lay gently heaving in the warm dark, so quiet that a sprinkling of stars was reflected on its indigo surface.

"Emily," said Francis at last, "will you forgive me, if you can? I thought I was doing right to go away and leave you, but now—now I begin to think that I was wrong."

"I thought we were friends," Emily said, a trifle unsteadily. It was so hard to resist him when he spoke in that deep slow voice of his, so hard to keep one's pride from toppling in the dust.

"We can't be—friends," Francis replied, and in spite of himself his voice trembled. Emily was so near to him in the starry darkness of the night, her shoulder touched his arm as they stood on the little path together. The darkness was sufficient to wrap them round so that they stood together in a curtained place. Below them the dancing had begun again and the monotonous wail of a one-step came faintly to their ears but this merely served to isolate them more completely from their kind.

A little shiver of doubt shook Emily when she realised the significance of her companion's words. He was going too fast for her, she had the sensation of being swept along by an impetuous torrent. What, after all, did she know of this man, beyond the fact that he was Charles' friend—and Laura's—beyond the fact that in spite of all her efforts she loved him? That might have been enough if Emily had been eighteen, but at thirty-one the reckless courage of youth has gone, it is replaced by a fear of change difficult to overcome.

Francis realised what Emily's hesitation meant, she was frightened, she did not quite trust him—why should she trust him after his behaviour to her?—and the last remnants of his pride vanished, leaving only an infinite tenderness.

"Emily," he said, and his voice was very deep and gentle. "I don't want you to say anything—I don't want you to promise anything in the dark. I want to tell you everything about myself—everything. But I can't tell you now, we are not ourselves tonight tricked up in these strange clothes. I don't feel as if I were real—or as if you were real. This isn't the time or the place for serious talk." His strong hand closed over her small trembling fingers tenderly, protectingly, and looking down she was struck afresh by the beauty of his hand—the fine long sensitive fingers and firmly knit muscles. "Meet me somewhere tomorrow—that ruined hut on the sandhills will do—and I will tell you everything—"

A dormant fear which had lain all these long months at the bottom of Emily's subconscious mind impelled her to say, "Francis, tell me one thing—is it a woman?"

"You are the only woman in my life," he replied quietly.

Emily looked up and met his clear gaze, and read his love for her in the soft brightness of his eyes.

"Francis!" she whispered.

He knew then that she was his for the taking, but he steeled himself against her weakness and against her sweetness which went to his head like wine. She was his for the taking, he might hold her in his arms, might press his mouth upon hers and upon the soft hollow below the velvet band where the pulse beat unevenly in her throat—but he had said that she should choose knowing all, not blindly and inadvisedly, not moved to emotion by the unexpected meeting and the seductive beauty of the night, and cost what it might he would keep his word, he would not take her till knowing all she came to him of her own volition.

Emily did not question him further, it was characteristic of her that she was content to wait for his explanation until he was ready to give it. Besides it was obvious to her as it was to him that this was no fit spot for a serious conversation. Even where they stood at some distance from the bungalow, couples frequently strolled past them with careless talk and easy laughter, and already their absence from the dance-room would be noted and commented upon.

"Come," Francis said suddenly. "You have been out here long enough in that thin pretty frock—it was foolish of me to have forgotten a wrap for you."

Once more in the whirl of a fox-trot with Francis' strong supporting arm guiding her, the memory of those few yet vital words seemed unreal as a dream. After all the months of doubt and humiliation it was hard to believe in the happiness which had come to her so suddenly. For the time being the happiness was enough; enough to know that her love, so far from being an unwanted, shameful thing was returned in full measure. Beside that sure knowledge the disclosure which had been promised to her seemed unessential. Francis' love for her was all that mattered, and so with a light heart she gave herself up to the enjoyment of the moment.

Glimpses came to her of the other dancers, of Alice flitting round like a sea-green fairy in the young painter's arms, of Charles and Laura bending over the gramophone, feeding it indefatigably with tunes. Of Ivette Jacquot, a gypsy to life, talking, in her animated mixture of French and English to a bewildered looking sailor boy. But none of this was vital to Emily, and it seemed to her as if the music, the floor, even the other revellers were merely there as a background for herself and Francis. A background which faded more and more into unreality as the hours sped on.

Laura watched her two friends with a very real joy in their evident happiness, a joy which partly eased the pain and anxiety which she was suffering on her own behalf. It seemed strange to her that anyone could enjoy the long hours which she found so tedious. The monotonous screech of the gramophone set every jangling nerve on edge, the whirl of the couples made her sick and giddy. It was not the first time since their marriage that Harry's affections had wandered away from her, caught by a passing fancy, stirred by the breeze of romance, and Laura knew that it would not be the last. In a way she was sure of him, for their affection was based on fundamentals—principally on his need for her in his times of weakness and temptation. But she loved him so deeply that each time he strayed away it seemed as if the very fabric of her being was torn in pieces—as if her naked soul must be visible in its agony to the densest observer.

The almost elfin beauty of the girl and her flaunting youth made it even harder to bear, and each time that the perfectly matched couple swung into view a spasm of sheer physical pain caught at her heart. Charles was suffering too but his pride forbade the words which trembled upon his lips. Laura's heart bled for him as she saw his eyes follow the flimsy green drapery round the crowded room, and she longed to comfort him but was powerless to find the words.

Even when he was not dancing with Alice, Harry avoided Laura, not because he feared her recriminations for he knew as well as she did herself that she would not take him to task for his flirtations—that had never been her way. It was his own feeling of guilt which kept him from her side. It will all come right, Laura told herself firmly, for the dance could not last for ever, and the picture must soon be finished and then Alice would go away and Harry come back as he had always come back, full of self-reproach and remorse for his errant fancy.

The dance was nearly over before Emily had a chance of a few words with Laura, and even then it was with difficulty that she escaped from her exigent partner.

"Go and have a drink with Charles," she said, with a mischievous twinkle in her eyes. "I'm tired of you, Francis. I want to talk to Laura."

The two young men went off together laughing at her autocratic tone and Emily sank into a vacant chair beside her friend with a little sigh.

Laura turned to her with very real affection shining on her face. "Emily, you are lovely, really lovely my dear. Are you enjoying yourself?"

Emily nodded, her eyes sparkling with excitement. It was so like Laura to be glad of her happiness, so like her to add to it by loving words of admiration. But for Laura's persuasions Emily would not have been here at all, she would have missed Francis and all that he stood for. It was difficult to find words, but somehow she made Laura understand her gratitude.

"I'm glad," said her friend simply. "More glad than I can say. Francis is good. I know a lot about men and I know Francis well. Trust him, Emily."

"I do, I do," was the reply.

Just at that moment Alice was whirled past them, her green gauzy draperies fluttering in the dance-stirred air, her small elfish face turned upwards to the man who was her partner. For the moment it happened not to be Harry.

"What do you think of her dress?" Emily whispered. She felt a sudden need for Laura's verdict, perhaps in this Bohemian atmosphere it was not so out of place as she had feared.

It was obvious that Emily had not noticed the more serious breach of convention of which her future sister-in-law had been guilty, and to Laura this seemed fortunate if rather incredible. She had been so certain that everyone in the room must be aware of Harry's infatuation for the green sea nymph and of her own shame.

"Harry is delighted with her dress," she said, trying to speak naturally. "He told me when he first saw her that it was the most artistic dress here."

"I wish there were more of it," Emily replied with a little laugh.

"Don't worry!" Laura added comfortingly. "She's so very young and—and pretty. It suits her somehow—"

"I wonder what Charles thinks of it," Emily mused, but to this even Laura's ingenuity could find no answer.

The dance, which had seemed a short interval of bliss to Emily, and an eternity of torture to Laura was now beginning to lag. Dawn was breaking over the sea and the grey light of coming day put the Chinese lamps to shame and showed up the tinsel frocks and haggard faces of the dancers with merciless accuracy.

"Just one more dance, Emily," cried Francis, striding up to her.

"Just one more," echoed a dozen voices. And once more the indefatigable voice of the gramophone blared forth the monotonous soul-destroying music of the latest fox-trot.

Then for a space all was bustle and confusion, as the tired guests fought irritably for their wraps in the tiny cloakroom, and packed themselves into the motors and cabs which had come to take them home.

"Come with us," Emily whispered to her friend. "Come with us, Laura. There's a room ready for you, my dear, you are so tired and there's no place here for you to rest. I can't bear to leave you here like this—"

But Laura shook her head resolutely, she could not forsake her post. She watched the Borriston car—the last to leave—bump slowly down the uneven road and turned back into her devastated house with tear-filled eyes.

CHAPTER 10
Retrospective

DAY was fully come, the sea was flooded with gold, gold touched the roofs of the houses in the village and changed their squalor to fairyland. A golden window in the coastguard station shone like a morning star and winked a pale defiance at its parent sun. Dew sparkled on the trees and flowers in the garden like handfuls of brightest jewels. It was the most beautiful hour of the twenty-four, this hour of sunrise, and to Emily it was symbolic of her life—the night of darkness and doubt had gone and the sun of love was rising in her sky. For long she leaned from her window watching the sun mount in the heavens and gain in heat and power. She was too happy to go to bed—these moments were too precious to be lost in sleep. She looked back along the grey level of her life and marvelled how she had borne it. Thankfulness filled her heart, making her very humble and yet hopeful. It was true there were still obstacles to be surmounted before the course of love could run smoothly for her and Francis, but with Francis at her side she could laugh at obstacles. "With Francis"—how wonderful those words sounded to Emily's heart! She knew then, for the first time the utter *comfort* of love and clasped the warmth of it about her like a cloak. The comfort of being essential to the well-being of another, of being cared for and considered above everything—of being perfect in a loved one's eyes.

Emily was all this to her lover and in that hour of sunrise when the innocent new day was issuing from the womb of night, her thoughts were clear and bright. She seemed to see the different issues grouped in her brain like a well-planned novel. They were waiting, ready to march into place at the sound of the trumpet—waiting as she was waiting, not impatiently, for Francis to make the first move.

There was no impatience in this period of waiting for Emily—that must be understood—she was too happy in the present. She would have lived happily in the consciousness of Francis' love for long before demanding a further step in their intimacy.

The future frightened her a little. She shrank from it, not because she distrusted Francis, more because she distrusted herself. This life, this grey level of usefulness and dreams she knew so well, she was adequate to its demands. Deep in a groove, was that it? Perhaps. Emily's days of rebellion were few now, the grey level had claimed her for its own. Only now and then when the wind whined in the wide chimneys and the sea roared its challenge to the solid earth did her wild heart break its bonds and fly forth to join the tumult. For the rest it had dwelt in dreams, in the thickly-peopled mist of its own imaginings and the real world was strange, unknown, rather terrifying. Francis had awakened her from her world of dreams, had awakened her to reality. And for a while the newly born butterfly which was Emily's world-conscious self hovered on a twig, stretching its wings to the warm sunshine, spreading them tentatively, a little frightened of trusting itself to their untried strength, a little loath to leave the shelter of its twig for the unknown yet tempting beauties of the flower-garden.

Emily gave a little sigh of sheer happiness—so this was love! She was filled with peacefulness and content. She did not long for Francis now she knew that he was hers—that mad shameful longing was over as the night was over. The steady flowing of Emily's thoughts seemed to her like a river which bore her on round bends and past strange places, and well-known places on its winding course. She thought of Laura now, and the trouble in that still face, the strained expression of her eyes. Had she been lacking in friendship not to find out what was the matter with her friend? She tried to recall the conversation they had had and found in it no cause for disquiet. Perhaps Harry was the cause of those finely etched lines on his wife's face. Emily went over her impressions of the dance but found that she had none of any importance beyond that one figure which was complete in every detail. The rest was a mere background, a whirl of gay figures, multi-coloured as a kaleidoscope, a monotonous hum of dance-music, a swish of dresses and a mingling of perfumes in the heavy air. But, clear and distinct, the moments stood out when she and Francis had escaped from the crowd and stood alone beneath the wide still canopy of stars. "We can't be friends," he had said. They were men's words, men's feelings. Emily felt she could be friends with Francis very easily—for the present she wanted no more. She was grateful to him for his generosity in not taking advantage of that moment of weakness when she would have given him her lips. Grateful, yet with a very vague idea of what it had cost him to refrain.

Tomorrow—nay, it was today—she would see him. She must escape by herself immediately after tea so that she would be at the little hut soon after five o'clock. He would be there first, waiting for her as he had promised, ready to tell her everything. Surely the tale that she was going to hear could not be so very serious when all was said and done. Some boyish escapade perhaps, nothing more. She would laugh at it, very gently of course, would smooth the anxious wrinkles from his eyes till he was forced to laugh with her.

What then? Her father—well that would be difficult and unpleasant, no doubt. He would mock her, his cruel humour would not spare her feelings. She could hear in her imagination the dry chuckle, the sarcastic tone. "Dear, dear, so you're in love are you, Emily—what does love feel like at your age? You're sure it's not your liver that's wrong?"

Oh he was bitter, but what mattered it? She and Francis together could weather worse storms than that. From their sure haven of love and trust and happiness they could pity the warped soul though they could not understand. Now, with the prospect of escape before her, Emily could look at the figure of Mr. Dennistoun dispassionately. She had said to Charles that he was like a cruel little boy, tearing the wings off flies and delighting in their agony. And it seemed still that she could find no better metaphor. He was cruel for the sake of being cruel, for the sheer delight that his cruelty gave him—the soul was warped.

A soft little wind began to blow from the sea, ruffling Emily's hair and cooling the fevers of her brain. She shivered a little and rose from her knees by the window to complete her preparations for bed. She had no more than a few hours for sleep; Kitty would call her early, in time for her to give Charles his breakfast before he left for the south. There was little hope of Alice being down to say "Goodbye" to him. Mr. Dennistoun was going to Glasgow by car, and she must remember to tell Duff to come back for her father after taking Charles to the station. Poor Charles, his love affair did not appear too rosy at present, and if he persisted in his determination to marry Alice he was in for a lifetime of misery.

These thoughts filled Emily's mind until she climbed into bed, but once lying there with her two dark plaits of hair upon her gently heaving bosom they faded, and once more the figure of her lover filled her imagination. She whispered drowsily,

"Goodnight—Francis—dear."

And was asleep.

The day after the dance was a busy one for Francis Hood. He awoke to find Laura and Ivette already hard at work scrubbing the floor of the studio which had recently been such a scene of revelry. He was lying on a mattress on the floor of the kitchen for he had given up his bed on the divan to Laura. The sound of work and talk came to him very clearly through the thin partition, and rising hastily he threw himself into the fray, carrying in the furniture and helping to remove the withered flowers and paper decorations. Harry was very silent and Francis noticed that he avoided Laura as much as possible. It was obvious that all was far from well between these two. Their trouble was no mystery to him, but he was too sensitive to butt in where he could do no good. Laura was capable of managing her affairs without his bungling aid; she had weathered such difficulties before. He had a profound regard for her wisdom.

By afternoon the bungalow was looking more like its usual self, only cleaner, and the four workers were all pretty tired and very dirty. Francis, glancing at his watch found that he would just have time for a bathe before setting forth to meet Emily, and calling out his intention to Laura who had gone to lie down till supper-time he seized his towel and made for the beach. Harry was nowhere to be seen and Ivette had an ingrained horror of the cold sea so his bathe would be a solitary one—solitary except for the thought of Emily which went with him over the sandhills like a warm and living presence.

He made for a little cove amongst the red sandstone rocks which was his favourite place. The rocks were warm and sheltered him from the wind, the water was deep and green, the surface warmed with the July sun, the depths cool and refreshing. He plunged in, a lithe and beautiful figure, white as an alabaster statue and came up spluttering and gasping as the chill of the water caught his breath. Then, as his circulation reasserted itself and the water felt less cold, he struck out nobly for the sea and felt the power of his fine limbs as the water raced and eddied under the swift strong strokes of arms and legs. Gad! It was good to be alive!

Returning more slowly from his swim he lay in the warm sunny cove and gazed up at the blue sky with its scattered clouds, his limbs moving gently like those of some giant white octopus in the clear water. And now he began to think of the disclosure which he had promised Emily, and to wonder what she would make of it all. Would she be brave enough to take the risk—a man without a name, a man who did not know what vile blood coursed in his veins, what heritage of evil was his to pass on—

Oh that was it, that was where it caught you out, this namelessness which was his. Emily must weigh that factor of it before she gave herself to him, must count the cost which she might have to pay. Dear Emily, he visioned her face, pale and beautiful in the light of the stars, softly flushed beneath the swinging lanterns of the dance-room, a perfect oval beneath the dark softness of her hair. He was glad now that he had been able to resist the temptation of her weakness, glad that he had been given the strength to behave decently. She must know all before committing herself—that was the right way to build their house which must last till death, on firm foundation in the clear sunlight of truth and honesty.

And if she said yes, if knowing all she did not shrink from his love, he was now in a position to offer her some kind of surety for the future. He had matriculated well, and had a fine chance before him which he was determined to make a rung on the ladder of success. It was a chance that many of his fellow graduates would give their ears to have, while yet realising that he had more right to it than they. Sir Addison Field the great brain specialist had offered him an assistantship. It carried little pay and meant much hard work but Francis was not afraid of work. Under this man he would have the opportunity of studying at first hand that marvellous brain-surgery which had become a household word during the war, that brilliant progressive science of the greatest brain surgeon in the kingdom. The man who had revolutionized textbooks, who was a law unto himself in the most subtle science of all. It was lucky for Francis Hood that Sir Addison was slightly eccentric; he would not have experienced men as his assistants. "Give them to me young," he was wont to say. "They've not so much to unlearn." It was thus that Francis had stepped from the university into a position which many men infinitely more experienced than himself might have envied. He took no credit to himself for the zeal and the tireless industry which had brought him to the front and had caused his professor—a friend of Sir Addison—to write of him as "the most brilliant surgical student we've had since F—d."

The promise of advancement was sweet to Francis Hood for many reasons, but chiefly because it gave him something to offer Emily—a hope at the least. He could wait for her if need be, wait years if he had her promise. Without Emily this brilliant opening would be but dust and ashes. Not that he intended to lie down and moulder whichever way she decided, that was not his idea of playing the game. He would work like the devil in either case, but whereas on the one hand Success would be a joyful stepping-stone to Emily, on the other it would be an anodyne for his pain and at best the reward for a duty performed to suffering humanity.

The latter may sound a fine aim, but to a young man demanding love it looks a poor second best.

As Francis rubbed himself into a fine healthy glow and raced back to the bungalow across the prickly grass the buoyant spirits of youth reasserted themselves and in his optimism Emily was close to him, his for the taking—his, as she had seemed last night when he had held her graceful body in his arms, and walked with her beneath the starry heavens.

CHAPTER 11
What Took Place at Pennybrigg Station

THE LITTLE house seemed strangely quiet when Francis got back to it after his bathe. He supposed that Harry was out. He often went out the whole day and generally returned with a sketch or sketches of the sea—small but eminently saleable. There was a big market nowadays for small pictures and Harry had a flair for them; he was gradually becoming known by these little seascapes of his which he referred to slightingly as bread-and-butter-scapes. The undoubted talent which Harry possessed was never so apparent as when he was painting the sea. He seemed to get the actual movement of it—you could almost hear the waves.

Francis peered round the studio for a small sketch which was a favourite of his and which he intended to buy from Harry when he had ten guineas to spare. It would look well in the consulting room, he decided with a little humorous twist of the lips at the thought. The sketch had got lost in the upheaval occasioned by the dance and could not be found. Francis seized his brushes and tried to brush his unruly mop of hair into some semblance of order, he found himself whistling gaily.

He had scarcely whistled more than a few bars when he heard the door of Laura's room open, and looking round he saw her standing there.

"Laura!" he cried. "Why do you look like that? What is the matter?"

She made a tired helpless gesture with one hand.

"Harry's gone."

"Gone!"

"With Alice."

Francis strode across the room and put his hands on her shoulders, his doctor's brain registered the impression that her face had aged incredibly, yet she was perfectly calm. Another woman might have been hysterical, tearful, angry. Laura was none of these, she was merely *aged* by the tragedy which had befallen her.

"Tell me about it," he commanded her, impatient for once of her innate dumbness.

Laura tried to tell him—

"I saw it coming," she said, passing her hand across her brow in a bewildered manner. "At least I knew Harry had fallen in love with her. He often does, you know, Francis, but usually it just passes—and I hoped when she went away it would—just pass, and he would come back."

"Where is he now? How long has he been gone?"

"I think he must have gone to Pennybrigg, there is a train from there about five o'clock. He can't have been gone long."

"Perhaps he has just gone out for a walk—"

She shook her head.

"No, he has taken a suitcase with his best clothes."

Francis opened the door of the bedroom and saw that the room was littered with clothes. Harry had obviously packed in a hurry and discarded all but the actual

131

necessities of life. He looked at his watch and made up his mind quickly.

"Listen," he said, "I am going after them to stop them, I can just do it if I run. The thing is madness. Don't say anything about it to Ivette, it will be better for you both if she knows nothing. Don't worry, my dear," he added gently. "I shall bring him back with me."

"Francis!" she whispered, and for the first time since Harry's flight her eyes were sparkling with tears. "Be kind to him, he's such a child—he doesn't mean to hurt me."

Francis seized his Burberry and drew it on to cover the deficiencies of his toilet after bathing—

"My God, women are saints!" he said, and with that he vaulted out of the open window and sped across the fields towards the station.

Pennybrigg was four miles off, perhaps less by the field path, and it was twenty to five when he left the house. He planned as he ran. Cold reason must be tried first but if that failed he must have recourse to strategy or even brute force. He was absolutely determined to take Harry back to Laura if he had to carry him the whole way. He smiled grimly at that thought. Alice could never hold the weak Harry, it would mean shipwreck all round. Pray God he would be in time to save Harry. He cared less about saving Alice, she was none of his business, let Charles look after his own belongings—he was well rid of the baggage in any case. But it was different with Laura, she was defenceless inasmuch as she loved Harry too dearly. Knowing his utter worthlessness she still loved him. Francis could not understand this, he merely knew it as an indubitable fact and put it down to the wonderfulness of women in general and of Laura in particular. It was this love which had raised Harry from the mud in which he wallowed, saved him from utter degradation. No man was worthy of such love, Harry least of all, and the foolish boy was giving the gold in exchange for tinsel—Laura for Alice—mad, crazy, boy!

How long would this tinsel satisfy him? How long would it hold him from the clutches of his vice? Only Laura knew the fight which day by day she fought for the soul of her husband, only Laura could have told of the nights when she sat up with him, watching by his bedside, struggling against the craving to which, alone, he would have succumbed. The ups and downs of his illness were more of a strain on her than on the patient himself for he leaned on her with his whole weight, and in his weakness spared her nothing. The stony path lacerated Laura's feet as she bore her unwilling burden by the weary hills of life.

If need be Francis was prepared to betray his friend's weakness to the girl—that was the last weapon in his armoury, but one which he would not scruple to use if others failed.

It was fortunate that Francis was in good training for his run. As it was his limbs were trembling when he reached Pennybrigg and his breathing was laboured and difficult. A hasty glance round the small station assured him that he was in time; the train was not yet signalled. He had few enough minutes to do what he had to do but he was confident of success. They should not escape him now, whatever happened.

Harry had crossed the narrow iron bridge and was to be seen upon the other platform waiting for the ticket office to open. This was all to the good, for if he could get Alice alone it would be easier to convince her of the folly of her elopement. He guessed that she would be in the waiting room, and strode along the platform oblivious of the interest which he was exciting by his heated appearance. There might be other passengers in the waiting-room, it was usually full of farmers' wives with babies or bundles, but Francis did not care for them. He would say what he had to say supposing the place was stiff with people. Alice must take her chance of that. He did not intend to spare her, nor, having come so far, to let the couple slip through his fingers for any scruples of that kind.

Alice was standing near the door of the frowsy little waiting room, she drew back when she saw Francis Hood and tried to escape his notice, but he followed her into the place, which was fortunately empty, and shut the door.

"Now," he said peremptorily, "just what are you doing?"

There was no reply to that—perhaps he did not expect one. He continued, "You are going away with Harry—I discovered his absence rather too soon for his convenience. I am here to prevent this mad thing from happening."

"You can't," she gasped.

"I can and I will," was the confident reply. "Both for your sake and his. You are not big enough to hold him, not strong enough. And he—my God, he's not fit to black

Charles' boots, you must be crazy!"

"It's no business of yours."

"My friends' affairs are my business," he said in a gentler tone. "Go home before you've messed up your life and his—and Laura's."

The last word was a mistake, and he knew it as it left his lips, it raised suspicion in her mind and she laughed scornfully.

"Of course, I might have guessed that Laura sent you. You're *her* friend, I know all about that."

"You know wrong then," he replied. "This is my show entirely."

"Once and for all your interference is useless," said Alice proudly. "Harry and I are everything to each other, we understand one another perfectly."

"Are you so sure that you understand him?" the pitiless voice questioned. "Has he told you that he is a confirmed drunkard—"

"It's not true."

"—that Laura married him when he was without hope in the world. Nursed him back to life, remade him, kept him straight? Has he told you that he still has lapses when the old craving seizes him with renewed force and even Laura's hold on him is not sufficient to keep him straight? Are you ready to give up your whole life to this man, to—"

"I thought you were his friend," she cried trying to shut out the terrible truth which shone in this man's eyes by holding her hands before her face.

"I *am* his friend," said Francis gravely. "Do you think I

would interfere with your despicable affairs if I were not? Do you think it would be the act of a friend to stand aside and see him wrecked?"

"Wrecked!" she echoed indignantly.

"Why yes," was the reply. "There are not many women who would stick to Harry Murdoch when they found out the truth about him. Isn't it better to know the truth now than to find it out too late?" He saw now that she was weakening in her resolve and added with the guile of a diplomat, "I want to save you both—from a terrible awakening."

Alice knew suddenly that it was all true, and a vision of the future rose before her and turned her faint with horror.

"Oh I didn't know," she wailed. "How could I know? There was nobody to tell me. He said he loved me—" She was utterly broken, the naked truth which shone in the strange man's strange grey eyes had torn the wrappings from her fine romance and shown it in all its ugliness. "Oh what shall I do," she cried in a strangled voice.

"There's still time," Francis said with a tingle of compassion in his voice. He could afford to be compassionate now, for he had won hands down, won even before the other actor in the little drama had appeared upon the scene. He knew that come what might Alice would not go with Harry. She was as helpless as a child in his hands—crushed, broken, terrified. The thing had been almost too easy.

It was at that moment that the door of the waiting-room was thrust open and Harry's voice said, "My God, *there* you are, Alice, I've been searching everywhere for you, the train is ten minutes late already—it's not signalled yet—too damnable to happen today—"

The high nervous voice died away into silence as its owner suddenly perceived the broad back of Francis Hood.

"Francis!" he cried. "What on earth are you doing here? How did you get here?"

Francis turned and confronted his friend. He was suddenly terribly sorry for the boy whom he had betrayed for his own good. It had been the only way to save him from his folly but it was a rotten way. If he had had the thing to do again he would have done the same—and yet—

"Harry," he said quite gently, "the lady has changed her mind—it's a privilege of the sex, you know. Off you go home, I'll see Miss Brunton into the Port Andrew train and catch you up in a few minutes."

"Alice!" cried Harry, "It's not true what he says—he can't prevent us—Alice, darling!" He moved forward to take her hand but she evaded him.

"I think I was mad," she whispered desperately.

"Alice, it's not true that you've changed your mind," he cried again, but this time she did not answer him, only stood with downcast eyes and twisted her handkerchief between her damp fingers. It never occurred to her to doubt the word of this big red-haired stranger—perhaps he carried TRUTH too legibly stamped upon his earnest face—neither did it cross her mind for a moment that anyone could expect her to carry out her original plan in the face of the revelation which had just been made. She had imagined herself in love with Harry but she loved herself more—too much to face a future full of hideous risks and sordid possibilities.

All she wanted was to get back to Borriston as quickly as she could, it had become a place of safety and she was frightened now, frightened of Harry and of the awful mistake which she had so nearly made. Curiously enough in spite of his hard words to her she was not frightened of Francis Hood. If she could only get back to Borriston Hall before Mr. Dennistoun returned from Glasgow and found that she had gone, all might yet be well. Why had she been such a fool as to burn her boats like that? Oh *why* had she? thought the shallow little worldling. But if only she could get back before Mr. Dennistoun's return nobody would ever know what had happened, or nearly happened. Neither Harry or his red-haired friend would give her away for it was to their interest, and Laura's, to keep the whole thing dark. She could thus carry out her original plan to marry Charles which had been overset by the superior attractions of the handsome young artist.

Her love—or what she termed her love—for Harry had vanished completely in a moment, there was nothing left of it. His tall slim body had suddenly ceased to attract her, she felt no more interest in him than if he had been the veriest stranger. What madness had possessed her she wondered, had she really been in love with him or was it an illusion based on falsehood and now slain by truth? As if in a dream she saw Francis take the weakly protesting Harry by the arm and start him off in the direction of Craitn with a gentle push. "Go home to Laura and ask her forgiveness on your knees," he was saying, and Harry, overborne by his friend's strength of character and the queer compelling power of his commands went in a dazed manner, the two first class tickets for Glasgow still clasped tightly in his nerveless fingers.

Alice wondered for a moment what Francis Hood had said, that had sent her ex-lover home so meekly. She did not realise the weakness of Harry's character, undermined by his indulgence in his vice, neither did she appreciate to the full the strength of Francis Hood.

He was a man who took Fate and moulded her with firm hands, who took men and bent them to his will. During the war this gift for command and the genius for leadership had been of supreme usefulness. It had brought him to the front and placed him in more than one dangerous corner. His superior officers had early marked him down as a born leader of men and if any arduous task was to be done there was always somebody who knew, somebody who said, "Better send Hood's company, they'll do it if it can be done." That was the impression that Francis Hood gave you, the impression that if anybody could do the difficult thing, the dangerous thing, *he* could. It had raised him from the ranks by leaps and bounds and his scathelessness in the midst of death had only increased the respect which he claimed by his courage. He was a mascot to his men; they would have followed him to Berlin and then some.

Thus, in a company of brave men and born leaders of men whose fathers and grandfathers before them had led their men to battle, Francis Hood, the nameless waif, had taken an honoured place. It is a strange world.

"Sit down, Miss Brunton," said Francis when he returned to the waiting room and found the trembling girl standing in the same place. "Sit down, there is a train for Port Andrew in twelve minutes. I will wait and see you into it safely." The words were kind enough but the tone of them showed plainly the speaker's contempt for Alice. The whole affair had been so futile and childish, so impossible to understand in the light of his own firm purposes. That two people could be such fools as to risk everything for a moment's infatuation was hard to credit, and yet there was one thing still harder and that was their being so easily dissuaded from their purpose. They were bits of thistledown blown by the passing breeze yet capable of wrecking the lives of others by their mad caprice.

Alice sat down on one of the black horsehair sofas in the ugly little waiting room, and after a glance at his watch Francis sat down too. Emily would be waiting for him on the sandhills, waiting (with that quiet patience which was all hers) for him to come. It was no use regretting it. He could not have behaved otherwise under the circumstances, could not have gone selfishly to his own joy with the three lives in jeopardy. That was not the way to build. He must see her tomorrow and give her a full explanation of everything. She would understand that he could not keep his appointment—he was not afraid of that, she was not unreasonable as were so many of her sex. No indeed, he could trust Emily to understand everything. In comparison with Alice's shallowness and fickleness the constancy of Emily shone like a steady flame lightening his darkness.

Francis was so lost to the world in thoughts of his beloved lady that he did not hear a hastily driven car arrive at the station entrance and he was literally dumb with surprise when Dennistoun's bulky form filled the doorway of the waiting room.

"So there you are, my fine lady!" he jeered. "Surprised to see me, eh? I got home from town a bit earlier than usual and the servants told me that you had gone. I thought it sounded a bit suspicious so I came after you to make sure. Quite a little romance isn't it, heavy father and all," he chuckled dryly and then added with sudden sternness. "Come along with me, young woman and no nonsense. I'll stand no fuss from either of ye—there's to be no romantic elopements taking place from my house, kindly understand that. You'll go home to your mother tomorrow, I'm through with you, I'll have no promiscuous hussy for my son's wife." He turned to Francis and added, "Ye can take her and welcome for all I care, but not while she's under my roof."

"But sir!" cried Francis who now perceived the mistake into which Mr. Dennistoun had fallen.

"Oh, it's you, is it?" said Mr. Dennistoun, peering up at the tall figure in the shabby Burberry coat. "The budding doctor! Well I'm blowed—thought you'd a' had more sense."

"But it's not me," Francis cried with more force than grammar. "I mean I don't—I hardly know her."

"Tired of her already, eh?" laughed the old man delightedly. "Pretty quick work that, isn't it?"

Alice shivered as she followed Mr. Dennistoun to the waiting car. Everything had been discovered, there was no hope of concealment now. She was too cowed to attempt any explanation of her abortive elopement—besides what did it matter if the old man thought Francis was her lover? It was better perhaps, seeing that Harry was married and Francis not.

Francis, however, was not of the same opinion, he pursued Mr. Dennistoun to the door of his car, protesting more and more wildly that it was not his intention to elope with Miss Brunton, that he barely knew her, and imploring Mr. Dennistoun to listen for a moment while he explained everything.

But Mr. Dennistoun, perhaps not unnaturally, was quite unimpressed by the frenzy of the young doctor and handing the subdued Alice into the car he instructed his chauffeur to "Drive home like hell" and lay back rather wearily amongst the soft cushions.

"You explain to him, Miss Brunton," cried the unhappy Francis as the car leapt forward and disappeared down the road in a cloud of dust.

Alice Brunton had no intention of trying to explain anything to the irate old gentleman at her side. She had suddenly remembered that the red-haired man was the same highwayman who had shown such marked attention to Emily on the previous night; *that* accounted for his intense anxiety to make Mr. Dennistoun understand how matters really stood. It was rather a joke, thought Alice, and it would do her ex-future sister-in-law a lot of good to hear Mr. Dennistoun's version of today's affairs. Ridiculous for a woman of *her* age to behave in such an outrageous manner with a man; it had been the talk of the whole ballroom. Yes, it would really serve her right—and with these agreeable reflections Alice was able to banish the thoughts of her own foolish behaviour into a convenient corner of her mind.

She hated Emily with the vindictive hatred of a small nature for one immeasurably nobler and bigger than itself. Emily had disapproved of her almost from the first, had taken Charles' part in that absurd quarrel. Emily had even dared to see through her pretences of altruism and was too simple and straightforward to hide the fact that she had done so. Why, it almost made up for the humiliations of the afternoon to feel that at last she could get a bit of her own back on Emily.

CHAPTER 12
Troubles and Perplexities

EMILY waited for Francis until all hopes of his coming drained away, and a sick dread took place of the eager expectancy in her heart. It was like the draining of her very life-blood and the simile struck her as she sat there with her watch before her and watched the long minutes pass. It was thus that people bled to death.

Walking home across the Machers, her eyes bent upon the ground, she revolved in her mind every possible cause for his non-appearance, yet none of them satisfied that inner craving for the truth which stayed itself trustingly upon the honesty of Francis and upon his love.

"He has done this before," she told herself, "and now he has cheated you again. He has funked the explanation which he promised you—that is the obvious reason for his non-appearance. It must be worse than you thought, this bar to your happiness, it must be some terrible thing that he can't tell you. He is faithless, make up your mind to that." But at this her heart cried, "No, no, he will write or come to see me, it will all be explained—he will explain everything, he must, he must!"

Emily had just arrived home when the car drove up to the front door and her father descended followed by Alice in her travelling hat and cloak. Emily did not know that Alice had gone out; she had imagined her resting after the fatigues of the previous night so the sight surprised her.

She was still more surprised when Mr. Dennistoun beckoned her into his library and closed the door.

"Alice will go home tomorrow," he said heavily. "I have no more use for her," and then the whole incredible story of the afternoon was hurled at her head.

Emily's heart was so trusting, her belief in her lover's honour was so strong that at first her father's story sounded in her ears like a fairytale which had no foundation in fact. It was absurd to think that any man could be so needlessly brutal as to let one woman wait for him at a solemnly arranged tryst while he calmly eloped with another—it was utterly beyond credence. There must be—there was—some quite sensible reason for this apparently inexplicable behaviour—Francis would tell her everything and make it all clear.

During the recital of her misdoings Alice preserved a downcast mien, she contradicted nothing and made no excuses for herself. By this course of action—or inaction—she made it impossible for Emily to ask the hundred and one questions which were trembling on her lips—when had she met Francis and where? How had the elopement been arranged? Why was it necessary to carry out their marriage in this underhand manner as they were both free to marry each other when and where they pleased? And then again, why had they pretended to be strangers on the previous night and gone through the elaborate ceremony of introduction? Emily remembered with a shiver of horror that Francis had asked to be introduced to "Charles' best girl", and that he had grumbled because he supposed he must dance with her.

Was all this elaborate tissue of lies necessary? Emily could not see why it should be. She had arrived at a further step in her deductions before the full agony of it dawned upon her—Francis' attention to herself. Was that all part of the "blind"? Was his appointment with her at the ruined hut merely a decoy to get her away from the house at the hour of Alice's departure?

It all fitted in so damnably if you took the thing at its face value, fitted in like the pieces in a puzzle, edge to edge, and the picture of Francis' betrayal of her grew with each piece. How he must have smiled at her gullibility, how he must have laughed behind her back when she fell so neatly into the trap, when she leaned to him in the starry darkness and offered him her lips. Oh Francis! What awful monster is this that has suddenly assumed your face and your form—is it possible that you could be so base?

Emily never knew how she got through the remainder of that day. She had no recollection of sitting down to dinner with her father and Alice, no remembrance of what had been done and said. It was not until she was safely in her room, alone for the night that the numb paralysing horror lifted from her brain and she flung herself face downwards upon her bed and wept soundlessly until the dawn.

Francis soon caught up the reluctant Harry and the two walked back to *La Boiselle* together. Neither of them spoke a word. Francis stole a few sidelong glances at Harry's Greek profile and wondered what was going on in that queer unbalanced artist-brain of his. He had made up his mind to say nothing, leaving everything to Laura. She knew Harry much better than he did and could deal with the situation as she thought best.

Laura was watching for them out of the window and when she saw them approach she opened the door. There was something so calm and strong about her as she stood there with the sunshine on her corn-coloured hair that Francis felt a sudden wave of comfort. Laura stood for common-sense and everyday things, she looked as though nothing tragic or melodramatic could come near her.

"Come in, Harry," she said quietly. "You must want your tea, it is all ready."

Francis pushed Harry in to the doorway.

"I am going for a walk," he muttered.

"But you have had no tea either," Laura said solicitously. Destinies might hang in the balance, yet her men-folk must be fed with tea and scones at the proper hour.

"No, I'm not hungry—I'm going down to the sea for a little," Francis replied. It was obvious that she would manage Harry best left to herself and he felt that he had assisted in enough "scenes" for a long while to come.

"Wait then," she said, as he turned away. "There's a wire come for you—I'll give it to you if you wait a moment."

She went into the house and returned with an orange envelope in her hands.

"I hope it isn't bad news—I've always hated wires since the war," she said as she gave it to him.

"You forget I have no relations to die," he replied, a trifle bitterly.

Laura did not answer that, she went in to her husband who was waiting for her and closed the door.

Left to himself Francis wandered down towards the sea. His thoughts were full of Emily—his first impulse to go straight to her and explain everything. On second thoughts however, it seemed better to wait. He did not wish to compromise Emily in the slightest degree until she had heard his story and accepted him with open eyes. Alice would probably go home tomorrow and he would walk over to Borriston Hall in the morning and see Emily.

Francis suddenly found that he was very tired and half dazed by the swift passage of events; he sat down on the sands and clasped his hands round his knees.

If it had not been for Harry and Alice and their absurd behaviour he would have seen Emily by now and everything would have been cleared up between them —how maddening it was! A wave of sheer rage swept over him and for a moment he wished that he had let them go and reap the fruits of their folly.

How could Laura take life so calmly? Was her attitude right or wrong?

The sea lapped gently on the yellow sands and the gulls, emboldened by his stillness strutted about the beach within a stone's-throw of him.

Surely it was more than two hours since he had bathed in that sunlit sea, it felt like a lifetime.

After a little he remembered the telegram which Laura

had given him—what could it be?

He tore it open and remained for a moment gazing at it in surprise.

"Come at once to take up duties, chief assistant down with influenza. Addison Field."

When he had taken in the full import of the message Francis sprang to his feet and half unconsciously drew out his watch. It was too late now to catch the night express to London, he must leave early tomorrow morning. A wire to Edinburgh for his gear to be sent direct and another to Sir Addison would settle matters. Yes, tomorrow night was the earliest that he could be with Sir Addison.

But then what of Emily?

Almost before he knew what he was doing he had started off along the sands in the direction of Borriston Hall. Somehow or other he must see Emily tonight; he must see her, if only for a few moments, just to explain why he had not been able to keep his appointment with her.

Francis stopped at Port Andrew Post Office for a moment and sent off a wire to Sir Addison Field saying that the earliest he could be in London was tomorrow night and that he would come straight to Harley Street from Euston Station.

That done he walked quickly up the steep High Street to Borriston Hall. The last time he had entered the high iron gateway was the night that he had dined here—the night when Emily had told him of her writing and all that it meant to her. How wonderful she had seemed to him —how far above him in every way! And now he had learned that although she was an author, talented above the average, she was also a woman with a woman's heart. He had held her in his arms and—almost—he had kissed her.

These thoughts so filled his mind that he did not notice Mr. Dennistoun who was taking his usual walk up and down the terrace before dressing for dinner. Unfortunately Mr. Dennistoun was not so blind, he saw Francis approaching and watched him with rage and amazement.

Was it possible that the man had the effrontery to come *here?* To pursue Alice to the sacred precincts of Borriston Hall itself?

Mr. Dennistoun had not yet recovered from his adventure of the afternoon. In spite of his boasted strength the excitement had told upon him; he felt out of sorts and was therefore in a thoroughly bad temper. The sight of the very man whom he considered responsible for all the trouble calmly walking up the front drive was not calculated to soothe his feelings.

"What the devil are you doing here?" he cried, placing himself in Francis' path and glaring at him savagely.

Francis was so completely taken aback at the suddenness of the challenge that he had no reply ready.

"Get out of here at once," Mr. Dennistoun continued. "I'll have no philandering half-baked doctors coming about my house."

"But sir, you are making a mistake," Francis began,

raising his voice a little in the attempt to make himself heard.

"Don't shout at me—I'll not listen to a word."

By this time Mr. Dennistoun's face had become quite purple and Francis (with his medical knowledge) feared that he was going to have an apoplectic fit.

"I can explain—" he said, trying to speak soothingly.

"Away with you, away with you!" cried the old man brandishing his stick and making as if to attack the gigantic Francis single-handed (for, with all his faults Mr. Dennistoun was no coward). "Away with you, I say. Get out of my grounds this minute or I'll call the gardeners and have you kicked out of the gate like the cur you are. How dare you show yourself here! Get out I say."

Francis was obliged to retire or he would have had the stick about his ears. He had no wish to engage in combat with Emily's father nor to be forcibly ejected from the grounds of Borriston Hall by the gardeners.

As he walked back over the Machers he tried to review the whole situation with a calm mind and to weigh its perplexities.

Even if he delayed his departure until the midday train tomorrow there was no certainty of his being able to see Emily. She was like a princess in a fairy castle guarded by a dragon—near, but unattainable.

The risk of delay was great, for he had wired to his chief to say that he would come, and he knew well that the great surgeon was capricious and exigent. It would be madness to risk his whole career by failing to take up his duties at the earliest possible moment.

There was only one thing to be done, he must write to Emily; write her a full account of all that had happened and trust to her good sense to see things in the right light. Emily would never wish him to put his inclinations, or hers, before this clear call of duty. Emily could be trusted to understand—thank God for that!

When Francis got back to *La Boiselle* he knew by the demeanour of Harry and Laura that their reconciliation was complete. Laura looked her old calm self; the deep shadows beneath her eyes were the only traces of the suffering through which she had passed. She accepted Harry's attentions with the slow tender smile of a mother towards a repentant child.

Ivette Jacquot had been the witness of so many domestic upheavals that she did not attach much importance to them. She was feeling depressed at the imminence of Francis' departure, for she had looked forward to having the young doctor as a fellow guest for some time. He amused her, and Ivette liked being amused. Harry and Laura were dull, especially when all was well between them. When Harry was in his wife's bad books it was not quite so dreary, for then he fell back on Ivette and the two of them were naughty children together.

Francis noticed that Ivette was unusually silent but he was too modest to guess at the cause; the moods of his companions mattered very little to him tonight. What Harry had said to Laura in extenuation of his conduct was *his* affair, and if Laura were too easily forgiving that was hers. Francis had played his part in averting the tragedy and he was pleased that it had been successful, he was too busy revolving in his brain phrases for his letter to bother any more about other people.

He settled down to his labour of love when the others went to bed and dawn found him still hard at work upon it, covering sheet after sheet of Laura's notepaper with clear round handwriting.

This letter, besides being an exposition of facts, was also the first love-letter that Francis had ever written. It was therefore a bulky affair when it was finished, more like a young parcel than billet-doux. Francis sealed it with Harry's signet ring which was lying as usual on the writing table.

The letter was now ready, but containing, as it did the very life-blood of his heart Francis felt that it was too precious a thing to be entrusted to the tender mercies of His Majesty's Mail—why not deliver it himself and have done with it?

The idea was no sooner conceived than it was acted upon, and Francis was soon walking across the waste land towards Port Andrew with the letter in his pocket. It was still very early morning, and the dew lay thickly upon the long spiky grasses and covered the turf with white moisture. A lark rose from his feet and flung itself into the bright sky singing as if it would burst its little heart.

"By Jove, you're happy!" said Francis Hood, and he went on his way cheered by the spirit of joy. The sky and sea were of a bright deep blue, and in the clear air the little town of Port Andrew seemed very near, each roof and gable outlined against the morning sky.   Francis was no poet, he had lived too practical a life for poetry to appeal to him very much—he had always been too busy working at whatever there was to work at to have time for poetry—or women. But this morning there were both in his heart, poetry and a woman—they were curiously linked together. He tried to remember a poem he had read; how did it go—

'The year's at the Spring'—it wasn't but that was a detail, poetic licence—'The day's at the morn'—yes that was right. (How sweet the clover smelt from that field where the stream ran! It was like the essence of honey.) 'Morning's at seven'—well Summer Time had something to say to that—'The hillside's dew-pearled'—By Jove, so it was! These poetry Johnnies knew something, they could put it all into a picture for you. Dew-pearled, a lovely word that, and *true,* for the pearly dew clung to the hillside like a soft cloud of jewels. What else was there— 'The lark's on the wing'—there he was, singing his little heart out for very joy—'The snail's on the thorn; God's in his Heav'n—All's right with the world!'

Francis walked along in rather a humble mood after that. The world was all right—God's world—it was men's world which so often went wrong, and if Emily turned him down . . . But he must not think that, he would try to keep an open mind until the answer to his letter came. Three days should be ample for that, he had begged her not to delay if she could help it; in three days he would be in London hard at work with Sir Addison Field but her letter would follow him there—in three days he would know if all was right with his particular world.

154

The big house was astir when he reached it, windows had been flung open to the fresh morning air and a sleepy maid was washing the doorstep. She was too sleepy to be much surprised at the appearance of a young gentleman at the hour when most young gentlemen were fast asleep in bed, and she moved aside to let Francis go past her into the hall.

"This letter's for Miss Dennistoun," he said. "Will it be all right if I leave it here on the table?"

"She'll get it when she comes down to breakfast," was the reply.

Francis placed his precious packet upon the hall table where it would catch the eye of the young mistress the moment she came downstairs. That done he felt for the first time fatigue; he turned and walked back slowly to *La Boiselle* to prepare for his journey.

CHAPTER 13
The Sea nymph's Picture

WHEN Francis got back to *La Boiselle* he found Laura waiting for him.

"My dear, where have you been?" she said.

"I delivered my letter in person," replied Francis laughing shyly. "You see I've never written such a long letter before, Laura, and I wanted to be sure that it reached her safely."

"You did not see her at this hour?"

"No, but I left it for her—she will get it first thing."

"She is a lucky woman," said Laura with her rare smile, and then she added, "I have packed your things so you can have an hour's rest. Two sleepless nights is a bad start for a journey and you will be very busy when you arrive in London."

"You are a brick," Francis said, "but don't worry about me, I'm as strong as a horse and I shall sleep in the train."

He lay down on the divan but he did not shut his eyes; he watched Laura as she moved noiselessly about the room, setting out the white cloth and the blue cups and saucers for breakfast. What a dear woman she was!

He was glad that she and Emily were friends—Laura was a good friend to have. She never wrote letters unless it was absolutely necessary, and then they were colourless and dull, but she was always the same when you met her again, there was no need to make friends with her anew.

The portrait of Alice stood on an easel at the end of the studio and Francis compared the two women and marvelled once more at Harry's blindness. It was a good portrait but it flattered Alice, Francis thought. Her face was etherealised, it was fairylike. Here was an elf-child dreaming of midsummer nights, of dancing in fairy glades, of riding over the waves beneath the moon. Even her lover had been unable to give her a *soul*.

Laura saw the direction of his eyes and she came and stood near him for a moment in an undecided way.

"Francis," she said, "you've done so much for me that I feel ashamed to ask you anything more, but I wish you would take that away with you."

"Alice's portrait?"

"Yes."

"But, my dear girl, how can I? It's not mine."

"I know, but Charles won't want it now—and—and I can't bear it. If you don't take it I shall go mad."

Francis sat up and looked at her.

"What would Harry say?"

"Nothing—he doesn't want it. The affair is finished."

"It is worth money," he pointed out.

"Take it and sell it then," she replied, "or burn it—only for God's sake take it away."

"All right, I'll take it," he said soothingly. "We'll do it up in paper."

They were busy tying up the parcel when Ivette Jacquot came in to breakfast. She had on her hat and signified her intention of walking to the station with Francis. Harry was still in bed and his guest decided to depart without saying goodbye to him. There was still a certain amount of tension between the two. Harry would soon forget what had happened and be quite friendly again but in the meantime silence was best.

Ivette enlivened the breakfast table with her usual chatter, promising to meet Francis in town some time and let him take her to the theatre.

"I shall keep you to that," cried Francis, throwing himself into her mood. He was feeling anything but gay and the Frenchwoman's badinage helped him over the difficult moments. It is easier to be gay than merely cheerful when your heart is sore.

Ivette continued to chaff him when he had said goodbye to Laura and they were walking across the fields together to the station.

"Your wife will be a lucky woman, Monsieur Francis."

"How so?" he enquired, looking down at her *piquante* little figure with a smile. She looked so completely out of place in the country scene with her swinging cape and her high heeled shoes. Yet in spite of her Parisian attire she was a stout little walker and seemed to be able to keep up with his strides without any difficulty.

"She will have so many sisters," replied Ivette demurely.

Francis laughed. "You will be one of them, I trust, Mademoiselle Ivette."

"Ah bah! You English!" she cried. "What Frenchman would have made a so banal remark?"

"I'm sorry," Francis said meekly, he always felt rather

like an elephant attacked by a bumble bee in these passages of arms with the Parisienne, but he enjoyed them all the same.

"I will forgive you," she replied, "because you are born English and so you cannot help your stupidness but before I forgive you there must be a penalty."

"I hope it will not be a serious one."

"Do not fear, my friend," said Ivette archly. "I shall not ask for a kiss like the frog in the fairytale. Your penalty is just to tell why you are taking away this so pretty picture of a sea nymph."

Francis laughed with real amusement—what an inquisitive little creature she was! He saw now that she had been leading up to this question all along but instead of asking it straightforwardly like anybody else she had approached it from an angle all her own.

"Does Mademoiselle Ivette think it an incongruous subject to hang on the walls of a doctor's room," he said innocently. "Surely a doctor has a heart like other men and may therefore be captured in the meshes of a sea nymph's hair."

He was getting his own back now and enjoyed mystifying his tormentor.

"The picture is yours?" she asked, him, glancing at him with a sidelong sweep of her dark eyes.

"Most certainly, since it was given to me."

"It is then, another sister for your wife? Have I guessed right, Monsieur Francis?"

"No," he said, suddenly grave. "No, you have not guessed right. I don't think I want this sea nymph for my sister, Mademoiselle Ivette."

Their walk took longer than they expected and Francis had no time to buy a ticket, he jumped into the train when it had begun to move and slammed the door.

"Goodbye," he cried. "Remember you are to meet me in town."

"*Au revoir, mon ami*," replied Ivette waving the scrap of cambric which she called her handkerchief.

The train slid past her, gathering speed. Ivette watched it idly, and then suddenly she gave a little gasp of surprise. In the last carriage, which happened to be a half empty First Class she saw a fair head bent over a book—a fair head that she recognised at once—it was the sea nymph.

Francis lay back in the flying train with a little sigh of relief. The need for sleep was upon him, his brain felt like cotton wool and there was a weight upon his eyelids. In a few moments the rumble of the wheels died away and he was fast asleep, his breathing as even and regular as a child's.

It was strange that Francis' sleep was so peaceful, and that no evil dreams disturbed its depth. We are such insensitive beings that events may occur within a few miles of us, events which affect our whole lives vitally, and we slumber happily or lose ourselves in roseate daydreams unconscious that the hand of man or Fate is moving in our affairs.

This was so with Francis Hood, for while he slept so happily, his letter, far from finding its way into Emily's hands, was on its way to London in the very train in which he was travelling, in Alice Brunton's tortoiseshell fitted dressing case.

She took it out once or twice and looked at it indecisively. Her impulse, prompted by innate curiosity, was to open it, but the big seal with its quaint device guarded it in some strange way from her eager fingers. There is an air of importance and of inviolability about a seal, especially if it be large and red and stamped with design of doubtful meaning. Alice felt baulked. Should she open it? No. Should she burn it unread? Again no, it was too mysterious a packet to thrust into the flames without having glanced within. What then was to be done with the tantalizing thing? It was difficult to decide, and decision was therefore postponed in favour of the latest novel of Alice's favourite authoress which she had been fortunate enough to pick up on the bookstall.

Before settling down to read her novel she reflected idly that Fate had played into her hands that morning in more ways than one, perhaps to make up for the scurvy tricks she had enacted on the previous day. It was lucky that for once she had been downstairs before Emily; lucky that she had thought of questioning the maid as to how the bulky package had arrived upon the hall table; lucky that she had had time to slip it into her bag without being seen.

Alice was sure that the letter contained the true account of her abortive elopement with Harry and she had no wish for that to become the property of Emily and her father. It would suit her better for the affair to remain as it was—inexplicable, a mad escapade—and to die a natural death. She had also the usual distaste of being proved a liar, though she would not have put the case in those words for, mark you, she had told no lie but merely remained meekly silent under the torrent of abuse which Mr. Dennistoun had poured upon her.

There was nothing more to be done in the matter; she must just go home and trust that her next affair would have a more successful termination. After all, there were as good fish in the sea as ever came out of it. She had been fond of Charles in her own strange manner until the more attractive artist had appeared on the scene, but it was not in her to regret things for long. Charles was rather dull when all was said and done and his relations were simply hateful. She hoped that she would never see any of them again. And with that amiable thought in her fluffy head she opened her novel and was soon lost in its morbid depths.

CHAPTER 14
Ivette Makes Le Café

IVETTE Jacquot walked home across the fields deep in thought. She had been born and brought up in an atmosphere of secret intrigue and now once more she breathed her native element. Putting two and two together she made a convincing five!

These English with their coldness and their prudish mien—what hypocrites they were!

Every now and then she stood still and gave a little chuckle of wicked joy. Here was Francis Hood, by way of being so honourable, going off to London with his friend's fiancée. It was pretty low down, thought Mademoiselle Jacquot. A Frenchman would at least have waited until they were married.

When she reached the bungalow it was empty, her host and hostess having gone off together for the day in their Bohemian fashion. Harry's comings and goings depended on the whim of the moment and Laura was his bond-slave. Ivette was not worried at the prospect of a day spent in her own company. As long as she had a novel and unlimited cigarettes she was quite happy. She saved the kitchen fire from total extinction and put the kettle on to boil. A cup of coffee would be nice after her long walk.

As she flitted to and fro with a clatter of high-heeled shoes on the polished floor of the studio she sang in a thin sweet high-pitched voice,

*"Mon père avait cinq cent moutons
Mon père avait cinq cent moutons
Dont j'étais la bergère - Lan leré lan la
Dont j'étais la bergère.*

*Quand je pesais mes blanc moutons
Quand je pesais mes blanc moutons
Le loup—*

A knock at the front door interrupted the song in the middle of the second verse. Ivette ran to open it and found Emily Dennistoun standing upon the doorstep.

"Ah *mon amie!*" she cried. "This is indeed a pleasant surprise—*voilá* I am left all alone today. I was about to drink some *café* all by myself—you will join me, *chère mademoiselle, n'est ce pas?*"

Emily was rather taken aback at this rapturous greeting from Ivette, she had not had much to do with the Frenchwoman and neither understood her nor liked her. She had walked over to *La Boiselle* with the intention of seeing Francis and asking him for some explanation of his behaviour—anything would be better than the uncertainty she was enduring.

"Where are they all?" she asked as she followed Ivette into the studio.

"Who knows except *le bon dieu?*" replied Ivette. She perched herself on the edge of the table, and fitting a fat cigarette into a long green holder she began to smoke like a chimney. Secretly in her queer tortuous soul she hated Emily Dennistoun. She was jealous of her friendship with Laura, of her elegance and the air with which she wore her deplorable clothes, but it was never Ivette's policy to show her feelings—hence her enthusiastic greeting. Today Miss Dennistoun was tired. "She looks plain and forty," thought Ivette hugging herself with delight. Aloud she said, "Mademoiselle Dennistoun is looking tired."

"I *am* tired," replied Emily simply. She sat down in Harry's basket chair and looked at the Frenchwoman thoughtfully. What a queer little creature she was!

"Mademoiselle will wait here until Laura's return?" Ivette said at last.

"I really want to see Mr. Hood," Emily said frankly. "I suppose you don't know where he has gone."

Ivette laughed. "I have just seen him off in the train for London," she replied. "But with anyone so deep as Monsieur Francis that may mean anything—" She lifted her hands towards the ceiling and rolled her eyes knowingly. "He and his so lovely sea nymph, how does any mortal know where they have gone?"

"You mean they have gone together?"

"*Mais oui, Mademoiselle*, they have gone together—but do not despond, your brother Monsieur Charles is well rid of that sea nymph with her baby face and her—her —grown-up heart."

"It may have been—just coincidence."

"You mean because they travel together? Why then should he take her picture to hang on his wall? Why then did he say to me that his heart is caught in the meshes of the sea nymph's hair?"

"I see," said Emily slowly. "He said that to you?"

Ivette waved her cigarette holder gaily; she was

enjoying herself thoroughly for she was a born mischief-maker. It was amusing to watch Miss Dennistoun's face.

"He said that to me," she continued, "and when I say to him, 'Ho ho, Monsieur Francis, this is another sister I suppose!' (for you must know mademoiselle that it pleases me to tease *ce jeune homme* about his so many sisters) he reply to me, all grave of a sudden, 'No no, it is not for a *sister* that I want my sea nymph.' "

"I see," said Emily again. "He said that to you."

"He said that to me," repeated Ivette, "with his serious English face. *Ma foi*, he is earnest that young doctor—he make you do what he wants. I am sorry for his patients for he will not listen when they say, 'This medicine is too nasty, I will not take it.' He will just look at them with his eyes and they will have to drink it—every drop."

In spite of her aching heart Emily managed to smile at the picture of Francis standing over his patients while they drank their medicine.

"I think you are right, mademoiselle. He will cure his patients in spite of themselves. But now I must go, I haven't time to wait for Laura today." She rose as she spoke and drew on her gloves. "Thank you so much for the coffee, it was excellent—we don't seem to be able to make good coffee, and yet there is nothing so very difficult about it, is there?"

Ivette rose to the bait and accompanied her guest to the door explaining volubly how to make *le café*.

"Heat well the pot!" she cried, as Emily turned to go. "That is the great secret of it."

When Emily reached the deserted bathing hut upon the

Machers she sat down and let the full tide of her misery sweep over her.

Who would have thought that Francis Hood could do a dishonourable thing? And yet he had stolen his friend's fiancée, had deliberately eloped with her twice. Emily did not know much about men—she had really seen very little of life—but she had heard that they were sometimes swept off their feet by a beautiful face and she supposed that this is what had happened to Francis. "His heart had become tangled in the meshes of her hair—"

That was what he had said to Ivette Jacquot and he had added that he wanted the sea nymph but not for his sister.

Well, there was no need for all this secrecy for neither she nor Charles was likely to pursue them or interfere with their arrangements. There was such a thing as pride, Emily summoned all hers to her aid.

First of all she must take Francis out of her heart, she must fill her life with other things and think of him no more. It should not be so very difficult to do, for, after all, she had not seen him more than a dozen times or so. She looked back along her life and found it grey and even, with just this one love affair standing out in bold relief.

"Perhaps if I had travelled a lot—" she thought, taking up handfuls of sand and letting the yellow grains trickle between her fingers. "Perhaps if I had travelled about the world like other girls I might have grown used to this sort of thing. It would not hurt so. Perhaps my perspective is wrong because it seems such a big thing to me. Other girls have been kissed at dances and it has meant nothing—and I was not even kissed. To him it was just an interlude, he said more than he meant because he was excited and the moon was bright. He *said* he did not feel like himself in those strange clothes. "But oh Francis!" she cried, "I would not have minded if you had done it all openly, it is all this dreadful secrecy, this plotting and scheming that I can't bear."

After a little while she rose and walked home slowly, and it seemed to her that her life was over and that nothing would ever matter to her again.

However sad we are, however wrecked our lives, we must go on with our daily task, for there are others in the world besides ourselves and although their lives have crises also, they do not coincide with ours. Emily got through her day somehow, she counted linen and ordered her household as usual and was thankful to have some employment for her brain. Dinner, *tête à tête* with her father, was the worst ordeal. He had not recovered from his ill-humour and everything was wrong. Emily sat and listened while he cursed Alice and Charles and the "red-headed doctor" with a nice impartiality. If Charles were half a man he could have held his girl . . . if the girl were worth a farthing she would have stuck to Charles . . . if the doctor fellow . . . But here his feelings overcame him and he fairly choked with range.

"Damn him," he cried. "Damn him with his ugly carroty hair, how dare he philander with Charles' girl—a sneaking hound, that's all he is—why the man's been here to dinner, (you remember Emily, that night we opened the last bottle of '87 port?) He drank it too, damn him, drank my port—"

Emily bore it with a set face in which her lips showed in a thin red streak, and when she escaped she went upstairs slowly like an old woman, leaning upon the bannisters for support.

"It is not always going to be like this," she told herself. "It can't be, something must happen soon or I shall go mad—"

The need for human sympathy, human companionship was so strong in her that she went along the passage to Kitty's room and knocked at the door.

Kitty was lying on her bed in a tumbled heap and at first in the dim light Emily did not see her.

"Where are you, Kitty?" she cried and then added, "My dear, what is the matter—are you ill?"

She went over to the bed and found her hand seized in a hot damp clasp.

"Oh Miss Dennistoun, I can't go away from you—don't send me away—I don't want wages or anything if only I may stay with you."

"What do you mean? I am not going to send you away!"

"Mr. Dennistoun said I was to go. He sent for me this afternoon—he has given me a month's wages and I am to go tomorrow."

"But why? You have done nothing wrong."

"He has found out something about me."

"I am sure it can be nothing very bad," said Emily gently, she sat down on the bed and stroked the little hot hand which held hers so tightly.

"No—at least it is nothing that I can help—"

"How did Mr. Dennistoun find out about it?" Emily asked, trying to arrive at the mystery by a round-about way.

"Miss Brunton told him—at least I'm sure she did. You see I was the one who told Mr. Dennistoun that she had gone and taken her suitcase. The others were too frightened to tell him and you were out—and—and so Miss Brunton said she would be even with me. She guessed my—secret."

Emily listened to the rather mixed explanation with utter bewilderment.

"Kitty dear," she cried, "what is it all about? I want to help and I can't unless you tell me. You see that, don't you?"

There was a little silence and then a small muffled voice said, "I'm going to have a baby."

For about a minute Emily was so surprised as to be absolutely speechless. Kitty's married life had been so short and ephemeral and had left so little impression upon her that Emily scarcely remembered that it had happened. She looked upon Kitty as little more than a child.

"My dear," she said at last, "there is nothing to be ashamed of in that. I think I should be proud."

The figure on the bed moved a little.

"Would you?"

"Yes, and glad too. I think I should feel that it was a present from Joe. Something to comfort me—something to—to love."

Emily's voice was very tender as she said this, it was the great need of her own big heart—something to love.

Unconsciously she had been looking for it all her life, the great need had been only partly satisfied by those with whom she came in contact, temporarily stilled by the creations of her brain, but she was so made that she would never be completely at rest until she could feel the small clinging hands of her own babies about her neck.

"Yes," said Kitty softly. "I feel that sometimes, but oh Miss Dennistoun if I have to leave you I shall die—I know I shall. Mr. Dennistoun says I'm not fit for my work but really I can manage quite well, and I don't mind about my wages if I could just stay near you."

"I will take care of you," Emily said, soothing her like a child. "You must not worry any more because it is so bad for you. I will take care of you, but you must promise not to be ashamed any more. I am sorry you did not tell me about it before—I can't think why you got such a foolish idea into your little head. Perhaps it is just because you are not quite yourself." She went across to the window and pulled up the blind so that the little room was flooded with white moonlight. "Look Kitty, how pure and beautiful the moon is tonight. Your heart must be like that—calm and peaceful and pure—for your child's sake."

Kitty watched with her big brown eyes and understood—to a certain extent—what her dear lady meant.

"I will try," she said. "I feel much better already—and you will let me stay with you if I am good."

"I will keep you near me and take care of you," Emily promised, and then she shut the door softly and went away to her own room.

BOOK 2

CHAPTER 1
"The Time and the Place and the Loved One"

HELEN ROE stood at her garden-gate and gazed down the dusty road towards the station.

Behind her was the little house which she had beautified; it shone in the afternoon sunshine like a polished jewel, every window seemed a diamond, reflecting the glancing rays of sun, and the brasses upon the door gleamed like much fine gold. On either side of the paved walk which led from the gate to the door, pink hollyhocks grew to giant size, which phenomenon Miss Roe attributed to the richness of the soil, and the gardener to the indubitable fact that "a woman ruled the house". "They allus grows like that when a wumman rules," Marr told her with a shake of his shaggy head. "Now you should just see mine, not more 'an a foot high they aren't."

"H'm," Helen Roe had replied. "Try giving Mrs. Marr a bit of her own way sometimes. It would be cheaper than a cart of manure—"

She smiled a little now as she thought of the conversation and the man's puzzled face. It amused her to tease Marr about his superstitions but he was a good gardener and had worked well, grasping at vague ideas and carrying them out with a slow efficiency which had gained his employer's respect. The garden was really beginning to look well now; things had grown up and burgeoned in the soft air. It had taken longer than the house, for you cannot hurry a garden. But the result was good.

When Helen Roe first came to Longmeadows, eight years ago, she found a fusty old-fashioned house surrounded by a tangled garden. It was the chance of her lifetime and she allowed no sentimental scruples to mar her pleasure. She made a clean sweep of all the drab old furniture and carpets and furnished the house afresh, choosing every small detail with care. Dark oak and bright chintz were skilfully combined and the result more than repaid her for the trouble expended. It took her a long time and much hard work, for money was a consideration, but eventually it was all finished, even to the last pink cushion on the drawing-room sofa, and Miss Roe sat down quietly amongst her possessions and told herself that she was happy, her dream of life fulfilled.

But possessions—even if they be the fulfilment of dreams—do not make up for the loss of human companionship. Helen found herself a lonely creature; in spite of all her brave talk she missed Emily with a slow dull pain which was as difficult to bear as constant toothache.

The house was perfect—but she wanted Emily's confirmation of her opinion. The situation was delightful—but she wanted to show it to Emily.

It must not be supposed from this that Miss Roe was discontented with her lot; she loved every tile upon the red roof of her house, every bright flower that bloomed in her rejuvenated garden. She loved the green lawns sloping from the back of the house and merging into boggy meadows which fringed the brook; here cattle stood knee-deep in mire, contentedly chewing the residue of their last meal and ducks floated upon the slow-moving water like celluloid toys.

All these things pleased Helen Roe and flattered a secret and innocent vanity. She had lived all her life in other people's houses eating their bread and pandering to their unreason so it was wonderful to taste freedom and independence. She quaffed great draughts of it and was insatiable.

The very cattle, although not her own, added to her feeling of importance, were they not growing fat upon her grass?

For the first time in her life Helen's feet were upon her own soil and the thought thrilled her. The Roes had been landowners from time immemorial and the tradition lingered in the last of the line, lingered secretly but strongly. For the love of land and the greed for its possession is as strong a passion as the lure of drink and more insidious.

On the particular afternoon which we have in mind, Miss Roe's possessions were evidently far from her thoughts. Not once did she remove her eyes from gazing at the dusty road to rest them with pride and affection upon the flowers in her garden; not one glance did she spare for the shining windows or the lazily smoking chimneys of her house. Several times she removed the glasses from her straight little nose but only to polish them with a small piece of "shammy", which she always carried about with her for the purpose, to replace them and once more to peer down the road.

It was quite evident that something unusual was about to happen; Miss Roe was expecting somebody.

Presently she drew a crumpled telegram out of her pocket and gazed at it with shining eyes. It was quite unnecessary for she already knew it by heart though it had only arrived that morning.

> "Roe Longmeadows St. Mary's Brook
> Coming to you today and bringing Kitty
> expect us about 6 o'clock Emily."

It seemed too good to be true! In a few moments she would have Emily in her arms—Emily here in her own house, under her own roof—sitting down at the small round polished table with her and eating her food—Emily in the garden, walking through the meadows with her—

A lump rose in Helen's throat and a mist dimmed her eyes—too good to be true—

The very wording of the telegram seemed perfect to Helen Roe. It had given her a warm thrill of happiness to realise how implicitly Emily trusted her friendship. They had scarcely met for eight years. Mr. Dennistoun was so selfish that Emily was practically a prisoner—a few stolen hours in a London hotel when Emily was in town with her father was the sum total of their meetings for that period, yet in spite of this Miss Roe was overjoyed to find that her child could and did depend upon her love as surely as if they had only parted last week. Emily might have wired, "May I come," but she knew that was not necessary. There was no doubt in her mind as to her reception and to Helen it seemed that Emily's complete trust was an index of her own faithful heart.

Helen supposed that the reason for this sudden visit was a break with Mr. Dennistoun. At last, after all these years he had reached the limit of his daughter's patience. She had been expecting this same thing to happen ever since she had left Borriston Hall but now that it had come it found her surprised. Emily had endured for eight years. What new indignity, what further tyranny could have roused the longsuffering woman to flight?

Yet, in a way Helen was not surprised. Re-reading Emily's most recent letters she had found in them a flatness, a weariness of spirit. They did not flow with the same smooth rhythm which made all Emily's writing a thing of joy to the critical. There was a forced gaiety about them—

Only a very intimate friend could have discerned the change but to Miss Roe's keen mind and loving heart it was palpable. She knew Emily so well, had watched the gradual unfolding of wings as shown forth by her writing, had rejoiced when sketches and essays which fell so swiftly and easily from Emily's pen became more and more assured and graceful, and showed ever a deeper psychological knowledge and a more profound sympathy with the sorrows of the world. Helen had followed with palpitating interest the slow growth of the beautiful character whose first faltering steps she had guided with such care. She managed all the business part of Emily's authorship and as each new bundle of manuscript arrived she fell upon it as a starving man falls upon his food and found each meal more delectable than the last. It had been borne upon her more and more that the separation from her darling (which had seemed at the time to be an unmitigated evil) was really the lever raising Emily's talent to sublime heights and deepening and ennobling her character. For it was in the loneliness and the solitude following Helen Roe's departure from Borriston Hall that Emily had found her soul.

There was only one cloud in Helen Roe's horizon and that was occasioned by the thought of her second guest. Why had Emily thought fit to bring anyone with her? She was considerably puzzled as to Kitty's status for Emily's letters had been full of the girl and from these she had drawn the conclusion that Kitty had become almost like a friend to her lonely mistress. Should Kitty be relegated to the kitchen and have her meals there with apple-cheeked Margaret or would Emily want her in the dining-room? What a bore that would be! Helen swithered from one idea to the other and was still undecided when the station fly hove in sight and sent all her ideas to the four winds.

Emily's face framed in the dark square of the window showed that the incredible had really happened—incredible because blissful beyond all human deserts—and Emily had arrived at Longmeadows in the flesh.

Lucky Helen Roe, now in the very truth your dreams are fulfilled! For as you hold your child, the child of your heart, tightly in your arms you have at last "the time and the place and the loved one all together."

As regards poor Kitty, her hostess' doubts were very easily resolved. The long journey had tried her severely and she arrived at Longmeadows in a half-fainting condition. Bed was obviously the only place for her. Helen asked no questions and would listen to no explanations until her guests were fed and rested. A glance at Emily's face had shown her that something very serious had occurred. It was strained and white and it seemed to have aged in some subtle way. There were dark shadows round the eyes and faint lines about the sensitive mouth.

Nothing of this escaped Helen but she kept her thoughts to herself as she flitted through her house carrying hot water and towels and chattering inconsequently.

The two friends, the old woman and the young one, dined together at a round oak table which was drawn close up to the open window. It was still quite light and the view from the window was very beautiful—meadows and woods stretching up to the skyline where the sun was beginning to set, tinging the fleecy clouds with palest pink.

Although there was so much unexplained between Emily and Helen, neither of them felt any awkwardness, they knew and trusted each other too well. They talked of immaterial things, of the latest book and of flowers. Emily was rather amused at the interest taken by her hostess in her garden for this was new since the days of Borriston Hall.

"You need not laugh Emily, wait till you have a garden of your own," Helen said and then wished the words unsaid, for they evidently aroused painful thoughts in her guest's mind.

From the garden it was an easy step to the house. Emily expressed her admiration of its arrangement and colour with a quiet appreciation all her own. She could do so in all honesty for it appealed to her immensely after the ornate luxury of her home. She liked it all from the shining glass and china which took the place of silver on the polished table, to the coloured rugs upon the polished floors.

"It is very peaceful, Helen—very safe," she said, trying to find words for the inexplicable feeling of relief which was beginning to pervade her soul.

Apart from that one exclamation which came from her heart and showed her deep need of peace and safety, Emily said nothing to give her friend any idea of the turmoil and disorder within her. It was always her way to put her house in order before opening the gates even to her nearest and dearest, and Helen, knowing this well, was content to wait.

When dinner was over and dusk had fallen they went out together into the fragrant warmth of the garden. The scent of night-stock was in the air and the white flowers gleamed like a heap of snow. From far below came the soft low of cattle as they sought a comfortable resting place for the night.

"I suppose I am as blind as the proverbial bat," Emily said, when they had walked up and down the terrace once or twice in silence. "Until Wednesday I had not the smallest idea that Kitty was going to have a child. Her married life seemed such an episode—so terribly short and ephemeral—it seemed to have left so little impression upon her." Emily paused for a moment and then went on in a lower voice, "I blame myself for not seeing how it was with her. I have been very selfish—letting my own troubles blind me to hers."

"She hid it from you," Helen suggested.

"Yes. At first she did not understand—she is very young in some ways—and then she became frightened and ashamed and tried to hide it but people were beginning to notice. Poor child, she has suffered, and so unnecessarily. If anything happens I shall never forgive myself—"

This was the old Emily—so tender towards others, so passionately unforgiving of herself.

"You have not changed," Helen said softly.

Emily pressed the thin arm against her side but did not answer—in words. She went on to tell her old friend about the break with her father.

"The moment I realised the truth about Kitty I went to him and asked him if he would let me have her there at Borriston for her confinement. I won't say it was the first request I had ever made to him but it was certainly the first for eight years. He refused unconditionally—"

Helen felt the arm in hers tremble and guessed something of the struggle which had taken place.

"He said a great many unkind things," the soft voice continued, "and eventually ordered Kitty out of the house."

"I can see him," said Helen grimly.

"That settled it, because you see the child is fond of me and she had nowhere to go—nowhere except to her stepmother in the village. I was not going to let her go *there*. I explained that to Father, but he would not listen."

"So you told him that you would go too."

"Yes. He said then that I was a beggar and not a chooser and reminded me that I was dependant on him for my food and clothing."

"I hope you told him that you were no such thing," Helen said indignantly.

"Yes. I told him about my writing and that I had every reason to believe that I could make enough to keep myself and Kitty without his aid. He was very angry."

"He would be," Helen admitted, smiling a little in the darkness at the picture which Emily's words had painted.

"Since the Brunton affair he has been more trying than usual," added Emily.

"Emily, that was a most extraordinary affair—you never explained properly about it."

"I simply can't, Helen," replied her guest sinking on to a garden seat and pulling her cloak about her as though the air of the summer night had suddenly become chilly. "I don't understand it myself. There is something—something I don't understand. I can't tell you yet—perhaps some day—"

"You are not sorry that the engagement was broken

off?" said Helen Roe after a few minutes silence.

"Oh no, Charles is well out of it," came the swift reply, "only I fear it will leave him bitter and unsettled for the time being."

"You did not covet her for a sister-in-law?" asked Helen. She felt there was a mystery here and longed for a clue to it.

"She is—just—*worthless*," Emily replied thoughtfully. "And yet—Oh Helen, I can't understand it—there must be some good in her that I didn't discover."

"It must have been well hidden," thought Helen, but she did not say anything aloud. She was watching Emily's face and the agony which had suddenly clouded its sweetness at some secret thought.

"She was jealous of me," Emily continued rather incoherently. "I don't know why because she had all she wanted. She disliked me from the first—I couldn't find the road to her heart—yet she was so pretty—"

"Tell me why Charles broke it off."

"She eloped with another man," Emily said in a low voice. "Father caught them at Pennybrigg Station and brought her back. Charles was in France with some friends—undergraduates—and Father wrote him the whole thing. It was a terrible letter." She covered her face with her hands as if the shame of Alice's conduct and her father's frank exposition of it was in some way her shame.

In a sense it *was* her shame because despite all that had happened she still felt that Francis was hers. She had given him her heart and she could not take it from him. Yet her head told her that he was unworthy of her love, that he was a cheat and a liar, that he had deceived her who trusted him, had broken his promise and betrayed his friend.

"Emily, don't fret so over it my dear," Helen said, trying to find words of comfort for a grief she could not understand. "It was nothing to do with you—not your fault in any way."

"Oh no," was the whispered reply. "Yet Father seemed to blame me for it—seemed to feel that if I had taken pains to make her like me it would not have happened."

"Sweet reasonableness was never his strong point," said Miss Roe primly.

Emily laughed, a little hysterically, and drew her friend down beside her on the seat.

"Oh Helen, you are such a dear, so strong! You make me feel a child again and I've been feeling so dreadfully old lately."

"You won't go back to him," said her old friend comfortingly.

"I don't think so," Emily replied. "I have made no plans yet. I may go to Charles when he comes down from Oxford and help him to start his shop."

"You know you have a home here always," said Helen quickly. "By all means let Charles have his shop, but he can get a wife to help him with it—and I'll have you which is precisely what I have always wanted."

"Dear Helen," said Emily affectionately. "I know I can rely on you but—but you must let me pay for—for being here. You can't—Kitty and I will eat you out of house and home—until we find some place to go for Kitty to have her child."

"Hoots!" cried Miss Roe indignantly. "And what's wrong with this house, pray, that the girl can't stay here for her baby? As for eating me out of house and home, *you* won't cost much to feed and the little widow less, judging by her supper tonight which wouldn't have nourished a fly. Charles can come too if you want him. There's the attic room for him and enough food for the lot of you. And as we are on the subject, you may as well know that you're my heir so it will all come to you sooner or later and you may as well have it now, and benefit by it, as when I'm in my grave." And the little woman looked at her heir with such an expression of rage and fury that Emily laughed outright. So spontaneous and so infectious was the laughter that Helen was obliged to join in it, and did so after several ineffectual attempts to look hurt at the untimely mirth.

CHAPTER 2
Still Waters

ON SUNDAY morning Emily and Helen Roe went to church together. It was a grey day, calm and peaceful, the clouds hung low over the green meadows and the rolling tree-capped hills. Across the fields came the slow tinkle of the church bells as they tolled out a simple hymn.

"You are very happy here, Helen," said Emily as they climbed over a stile into a lane hedged with honeysuckle.

"I am now," Helen replied. "It was rather lonely before you came. You see I have not made many friends—not real friends. People are a little afraid of me, I think."

"How foolish of them!"

Helen laughed. "I'm not really very terrifying, am I? But I frighten them with my manner and I'm too old to change it."

"You like the rector or the vicar—I don't know what you call him in these parts."

"Yes, there is no nonsense about the man. He's not eloquent but his sermons are worth listening to."

The church was a beautiful old building, cool and dim with tall narrow windows and high-backed pews. Emily looked about her with a restful pleasure—the atmosphere evoked peace and reverence.

The whole service seemed beautiful. The fine words of the liturgy pleased her critical ear and thrilled her to the depths of her being, the voices of the boys in the choir enveloped her with their innocence and purity.

Presently she knelt and asked forgiveness for the sin of disobedience which she had committed in leaving her father's house. It had been a great wrench and she was feeling the effects of the strain but what else could she have done under the circumstances? She honestly believed that Kitty would die if she were sent away under a sort of cloud, and besides she had given her promise. How could she let the girl go away after that?

When Emily arose from her knees, her eyes lighted on a coloured window of the Virgin and Child. The Mother was sufficiently like Kitty to arrest her attention; she had the same big questioning brown eyes, the same dark hair. To Emily in her sensitive state it seemed a sign, comforting and reassuring, that she had chosen the right path and that all was well.

"Let us hurry," said Helen when they came out of church. "If we once stop and talk to anyone we shall never get away."

The sun had broken through the clouds and streamed down in a golden flood onto the little green churchyard full of old monuments and mossy stones.

They went through the old-fashioned lych-gate and turned into the narrow lane where the white dust lay deep like driven snow. Emily's troubles were lightened, she felt too happy for speech. With her arm through Helen's they walked on together in silent companionship. They had not gone far when a thud of hooves broke the absolute stillness which surrounded them, and looking up,

Emily saw a man riding towards them on the soft turf which bordered the lane.

"Here is Sir Joseph Leate," Helen said, her cheeks growing pink with suppressed excitement. "He is a great friend of mine—practically my only friend in St Mary's Brook and I do want you to like him—"

She had no time to say more for Sir Joseph swung himself out of the saddle and came towards them with the reins over his arm. Emily saw that for all his agility the man was not young. He had thick white wavy hair and a clean-shaven face covered with a network of small wrinkles. His keen blue eyes were like those of a sailor, they gave one an impression of long sightedness, his mouth was straight lipped and mobile.

"I hoped that I should meet you," he said to Helen as he took her hand. "I have not seen you for a day or two and I thought you might be at church."

Emily liked his voice, it was full and deep without being loud. She set great store by the voices of those she met and was ready to smile at him when he turned to her to be introduced.

"So it is really you," he said, returning her smile with a flash of white teeth. "Please do not think that I am forward; I have known you for a long time, not only through your books but also through your friend. It is impossible to be for long with Miss Roe without making the acquaintance of Miss Dennistoun."

"You put it very nicely, Sir Joseph," said Emily, laughing.

"How otherwise could such a nice thing be put?"

"Perhaps like it was put by an old fish-woman at home. I had helped her daughter a little when the times were hard and, when I went to see the old lady she said to me, 'Weel Miss Dennistoun, here y'are in the flesh,' and she added a trifle sadly, 'I've bin that deaved wi' the very name o' ye that I expeckit something bye-ordinar.'"

Sir Joseph laughed heartily at the story and turned to walk home with the ladies, his horse following contentedly behind.

"I know enough 'braid Scots' to be able to follow your story perfectly, Miss Dennistoun," he said. "But you have put me in an awkward position for I hardly know you well enough to say what is in my mind. Perhaps I may be allowed to say this much however: it has given an old man much pleasure to meet a lady whose work is of such high literary quality and henceforth her books will give him even more pleasure because he has had the honour of her acquaintance."

A little twinkle in Sir Joseph's blue eye took away from the pedantic strain of his speech without impairing the compliment, and Emily felt that he was both humorous and sincere. She had never liked a man more in the first few moments of her acquaintance with him.

"You seem to know all about me," Emily said with a little smile, "but I am not so fortunate."

"Ah!" he exclaimed. "My history is easily told— Winchester, Oxford, the bar and then Parliament. Not a very exciting story I'm afraid."

"I should have guessed that you were a sailor."

"How nice of you, Miss Dennistoun! It was a dream of

mine, for my ancestors were all seafaring men, with many a wild adventure to their credit and discredit. We Devon folk have the sea in our blood, you know—"

"Are you coming to lunch, Sir Joseph?" Helen asked, interrupting him suddenly in her usual abrupt manner. "There's roast chicken and apple tart."

Sir Joseph laughed outright and looked sideways at Emily.

"It was some time before I got used to our friend's downright speech," he said whimsically. "Some time before I discovered all that it cloaked."

"It cloaks nothing," put in Helen. "I merely say what is in my mind."

"I still maintain that it cloaks a great deal," he replied. "Your abruptness is as much a covering for your thoughts as the whole of a diplomat's outfit. You deceive of set purpose although you say you have no use for the finer arts of pretending. To return to your invitation I accept it with my humble thanks *for the pleasure of your company* and for no such material reasons as roast chicken and apple tart. You should know me well enough by now to realise that such mundane things never cross my mind."

"Hoots, man!" cried Helen laughing. "They will cross your lips soon enough. Away with you and your diplomacy—what's the use of it between friends?"

"That is true," said Sir Joseph with sudden gravity. "It is a fine thing to have friends who can be treated with absolute candour."

"I've no use for any other sort," Helen said.

By this time they had reached the little house, and Helen hurried in to tell Margaret to lay another plate for lunch, leaving her guests to follow more slowly. Sir Joseph tied his horse to a convenient tree.

"Do you ride, Miss Dennistoun?" he asked suddenly.

"I used to," she admitted, "but it is ages since I was on a horse."

"I wonder if you would ride with me sometimes," he said, looking at her hopefully. "This horse is an ideal mount for a lady and there are delightful rides about here."

"I should love to," Emily replied simply. "I want to get some writing done but my afternoons will be free."

"I do hope you are going to make a long stay with Miss Roe—she is rather lonely sometimes," he said, and then added in a quieter voice, "The people here do not understand what a splendid person she is."

"I know, it is a pity. I should like to stay but my plans are rather uncertain," Emily said, incoherently. "I feel like a prisoner released suddenly and unexpectedly—I may be recalled—I don't know what to do with my freedom. I don't even know whether it is right for me to have it."

Sir Joseph was puzzled, he was anxious to make the right answer to this woman who was beginning to interest him so profoundly.

"Isn't freedom always right?" he asked her, feeling his ground and watching the expressive face.

"I used to think it was so easy to tell right from wrong," she said thoughtfully, "just like telling white from black or cold from hot, but now—"

"It is easy to tell cold from hot when you are sitting under a shady tree looking on at the battle of life; it is when you descend into the arena yourself and take a hand in the fray that values become lost and feelings mixed."

"I am a looker-on," Emily said with a shade of sadness in her tone. "I have never done anything—I am a looker-on at life."

"Not you! Your writing shows that you have suffered, that you have joined in the battle. Lookers-on may see most of the game but they don't feel the bumps and the bruises. You must *feel* to write as you do."

She shook her head and smiled at his earnestness.

"I have always wanted to *do* things, not just to think and write about them. You who have travelled and seen foreign lands cannot imagine how narrow one gets always living in the same place."

Sir Joseph did not answer that directly. He said, "How I enjoyed that little sketch of yours in the *Wheatfield Magazine*—the old fisherman mending his nets while the sunset flames over the sea. He looks up and sees it—*really* sees it for the first time in his life, and realises the promise which it gives of dawn. I can't put it so beautifully as you did. He sees all that it promises *him.* Another DAY, more beautiful than the one which for him is so nearly at an end—'For mine eyes have seen the glory of the Coming of the Lord.' "

Emily was moved; she could not make a light reply.

"It is well worth writing for those who understand," she said softly.

They walked up to the house in silence.

The small household at Longmeadows settled down to quiet routine. Emily wrote every morning and in the afternoon she was free to walk with Helen or ride with Sir Joseph. The latter, true to his word, took her for some beautiful rides and Emily enjoyed them even more than she had expected.

She had never met a man of Sir Joseph's stamp before, so widely travelled and well-read, yet withal sensitive to her every mood. His brain challenged hers, while his personality charmed her. He drew her out and set her at her ease with his fine air of old world courtesy.

One day she and Helen walked over to tea with him at St. Mary's Place. The old house stood four square to the sea overlooking a bay which was full of fishing boats. It reminded Emily of her home though there was a softness about it—a misty softness which was not like the sharp clarity of the north. Their host showed them all over his domain. Parts of the house were old and of these he had the history at his fingers' ends. He had the gift of making the past live again and his blue eyes blazed as he told them the battles which had been fought in the neighbourhood and of hardly less exciting smugglers' escapes.

"Your ancestors must have been rather a bad lot," Emily told him, laughingly.

"No worse than the Scots reivers that your old Border families are so proud to own," replied Sir Joseph. "Look at Wat of Harden—the man was an absolute villain. I own it is a queer thing to take so much pride in the roguery of one's ancestors, but we all do it."

Sir Joseph walked home with his guests and dined at

Longmeadows. The house seemed strangely small after St Mary's Place—small but eminently cosy. They sat round the fire and talked until it was late and the moon had risen to light Sir Joseph home.

"Don't forget you are riding with me tomorrow," he said to Emily as he rose to go.

When he had gone the two friends went back to the drawing room and stood looking at the fire for a few moments in that strange silence which often follows the departure of a guest.

"Why did you never mention Sir Joseph in your letters to me," Emily said suddenly.

"I often *nearly* mentioned him," replied Helen, flushing a little. "But I was so afraid that you would be 'deaved with his name' like the fish-woman, and I always hoped that you would come here some day and meet him yourself: I wanted you to like him."

"I should be difficult to please if I did not like Sir Joseph!" Emily said, looking at her hostess in some surprise.

"I want you to like him *specially*," Helen continued, fixing her eyes on the fire which glowed redly on the broad hearth. "I can see how much he admires you. Oh Emily, how perfect it would be if you were settled here quite near me for all my life!"

"You matchmaker!"

"But it is not only for my own sake that I want it, not just an old woman's selfishness. It seems to me—it has always seemed to me—that you and Sir Joseph were made for each other. You like the same things and see life from the same standpoint. He is such a dear—almost good enough even for you, Emily. No man could be *quite* good enough in my opinion. Perhaps I am a fool to speak to you about it but I can see how much he is attracted to you and I do not want you to be taken by surprise."

"I shall never marry," Emily said.

"My dear, he would never interfere with your liberty or your work. He would only take what you could give him easily and freely. A woman gets lonely when she grows old—her friends die or scatter—oh my darling, I don't want you to have a lonely life like mine."

Emily saw the tears in her friend's eyes and she replied gently. "It is because of a dream that I can never marry. I dreamed once of a perfect lover. But it was only a dream. He went away and I shall never see him again. It hurt me dreadfully—it still hurts—but I am glad it happened because it was so beautiful."

"I didn't know——" Helen said.

"I didn't tell you because I simply could not speak of it."

"But Emily, if it is really over and he has gone for ever, couldn't you think of Sir Joseph? He is so kind and good and you could make him happy."

They said no more upon the subject, but long after Helen Roe had gone to bed Emily sat gazing at the dying embers of the fire.

She liked Sir Joseph so much, his quiet friendship and understanding healed her deep wounds and restored her self respect. Francis had gone from her forever, perhaps by now he was married—a little shiver went through her body at the thought and she hid her face in her hands. But thinking about Francis was a luxury which she had forbidden herself and she soon raised her head and looked the future in the face.

Why should she waste her life in pining after a man who had thrown her off like an old glove? Why not take her life in firm hands and make something beautiful of it? With Sir Joseph she would be safe and happy, already she knew him well and was fond of him. Helen was right, he was good and kind. He wanted her—so Helen said—and it seemed that nobody else did. She knew without any false modesty that she could enrich his life and make him happy.

At this time Emily felt cut off from all her family. Her father had not written a word to her since she left his house and Charles, who was always a bad correspondent, had become even more inarticulate than usual. He sent her a postcard to say that he was back at Oxford and then relapsed in silence.

Emily feared that Charles was very miserable and in this she was not far wrong. Alice's elopement had been a severe shock to him, for although he had seen that she was flighty and easily flattered, he had never believed her capable of infidelity to him. Mr. Dennistoun's letter had opened his eyes to the utter worthlessness of Alice and now, looking back, with the knowledge of what she had done clearly in his mind, Charles saw her for a frivolous selfish creature. When he went back to Oxford he did not see Alice and he imagined that she was married to Francis. That hurt more than anything—the fall of his idol, his beloved and admired Francis Hood.

Charles would rather have died than have believed Francis capable of such meanness and deceit, yet the facts were clear, too clear to be denied.

He was so embittered by his disillusionment that he could speak of it to nobody. He flung himself into all the "rags" and gaieties of the term in the effort to forget his troubles.

CHAPTER 3
Stormy Skies

IT WAS a glorious autumn, the trees of the forest flamed red and gold in the pale sunlight, and the red berries formed thick upon the holly.

Kitty was very happy at Longmeadows. She had come through dark shadows into the sunlight of kindness and sympathy, and she was near Miss Dennistoun—this was all she asked of life. She busied herself about the house, trying to show by deeds the gratitude and love which filled her heart. At first Helen Roe felt a little jealous of the place that this girl had taken in Emily's heart but Kitty was so humble and unassuming and had such a naturally sweet disposition that Miss Roe very soon came to love her and spoil her as much as Emily did. She followed her round the house with glasses of milk which she believed would fatten Kitty and bring back the roses in her cheeks.

Kitty's baby was born in the second week of November. The night was cold and stormy with a promise of snow in the air. The wind howled dismally in the chimneys and sent the smoke bellying into the rooms in grey gusts.

Emily was reminded of the great storm at Port Andrew when the life-boat had gone out to save three men and had returned with two. Joe's child was to be born on just such a night as that on which he met his death. There was the same grim energy in the shrieking wind, the same malignant force.

Perhaps it was the turmoil of Emily's own feelings which made the storm seem so ferocious; she was frightened and miserable. Kitty was very dear to her—how dear she was only now realising.

Banished from Kitty's room she wandered about the house like a lost soul and finally found refuge in the drawing-room where Helen was seated pretending to read the *Times.*

A small frock, still unfinished with the needle sticking in it, lay on the table where Kitty had left it. There was something pathetic about the unfinished garment. Emily felt the tears sting her eyes.

She could bear it no longer, the helplessness, the inactivity was crushing her, she ran upstairs for her cloak and dipped out at the front door into the rushing fury of the night.

The wind caught at her dress, she fled before it, a leaf borne upon its breath. The leaves went with her, whirling round her head as she crossed the meadow and climbed the wide rolling hill crested with trees. It was a favourite walk of hers and had grown familiar to her but tonight it was strange and wild as her own heart.

The tattered clouds sailed by like the remnants of a defeated army, hiding the bright moon for a moment and gone the next. The pattern of their grotesque shape passed swiftly over the land and vanished like a dream.

Emily's soul was in tune with the storm, she suffered with it, suffered as only those can whose art lives upon their nerves like a hungry animal. Suffered all the more because she was gentle and sweet in every-day life. She was like the quiet pastoral English country that smiled in the sun. The storm came to her heart and roused its slumbering rage, changing the familiar scene to a nightmare of madness. What did it all mean—where did it come from? Whither was it going?

She reached the hilltop, blown there by the wind's rough force, and stood there upon the crest of the hill amongst the tortured trees which bent and groaned and shed their leaves like rain. She leaned against the wind and the leaves flew past her into space, catching in her loosened hair and rustling in her ears.

For a long time Emily stood there while the wind plucked at her dress like a live thing and gradually the burden of depression lifted from her soul. A new strength came to her from some unknown source, a realisation of her own power, her own importance.

In the dark immensity of the night she was a small thing but not helpless. She was no leaf to be seized and blown whither the wind listed. The storm was strong but she was stronger, she could fight the wind if need be.

Presently she turned and looked back at the little house which lay far below her in the valley. The lights in the windows beckoned to her, speaking of human ties and human needs. She gathered her cloak round her and went home down the hill, fighting against the wind and glorying in her strength.

Helen met her at the door, relief struggling with amazement in her small white face.

"My dear girl, where *have* you been?" she asked. "I have been hunting everywhere for you."

"I can never resist the wind," Emily answered rather shamefacedly. "I expect I look mad, don't I?"

She did look dishevelled for her hair was tangled with leaves and twigs and her cloak was torn with brambles but Helen was too thankful to see her alive to be critical of her appearance.

"Go and tidy your hair," she said gently. "Kitty has been asking for you—it's all over—quite all right, Nurse says."

The baby was a little girl and from the first they called her Josephine after the father whom she would never know. She was a pretty creature with blue eyes and fair hair and cheeks as pink as Helen's roses. She was good and happy as all babies should be and gave very little trouble to her adoring nurses. In fact it was Helen's complaint that the baby was always asleep when she wanted to play with her. In spite of this drawback however, Miss Roe became an efficient nurse and her queer matter of fact way of treating Josephine seemed to suit that infant extraordinarily well. She always spoke to Josephine as if she were a grown up person.

"Go to sleep now, Josephine," she would say as she put the baby in her cot. "I am going down to have my tea but I will come back soon—go to sleep at once, dear." And Josephine invariably did.

CHAPTER 4
The Fairy Godmother

IT WAS a fine afternoon in December, the air was crisp and bright, the ground hard as iron with white frost. The station fly, a big clumsy brougham which had seen better days, came lumbering down the road and stopped at the gate of Longmeadows with a creak of brakes. The driver climbed down from his perch and opened the door.

"This is Longmeadows, sir. Miss Roe's 'ouse. But it looks ter me as if it was shut up. Was they expecting you today, sir?"

The young man stepped out of the gloomy interior of the cab with a sigh of relief. He had not enjoyed the uncomfortable journey.

"Thank you," he said as he paid the extortionate fare demanded by the cabman. "Thank you so much, *please* don't wait, I'm not a millionaire yet. When I make my fortune I shall hire you for a whole day."

He turned then, and pushed open the gate, leaving the cabman to growl and drive off slowly down the road.

The house did seem deserted, the blinds on the ground floor had been drawn down and the doors were locked but the young man took comfort in the plume of smoke which curled lazily from one of the chimneys. He tried ringing the bell and knocking on the doors but neither had any effect.

He was about to give up the problem in disgust when he saw a small cavalcade approaching across the fields. It was a long way off but the young man had sharp eyes and distinguished the members of it easily. He sat down and waited for them somewhat impatiently for he was not in the best of tempers and the small check annoyed him.

The whole household had turned out in honour of Josephine's christening which had taken place that afternoon. They had walked to church across the fields to take part in the short service. Josephine was now a member of the church and had also the inestimable boon of two adoring god-mothers bestowed upon her. She had slept soundly through it all, only waking for a moment when the water touched her forehead to grunt with displeasure.

Josephine's god-mothers took their duties seriously—all the more so because the child was fatherless. They discussed her future eagerly as they walked home. In fact they were so engrossed in Josephine's future that they did not see the young man until they had almost reached the spot where he had sat down to await them.

"Look, Miss," cried Margaret who was carrying the baby. "There's a gentleman in the garden."

For a moment Emily's heart fluttered—could it be Francis? And then she saw that it was Charles and hurried forward to meet him.

The first glance at his face told her that something was wrong, he was very pale and dark shadows lay beneath his eyes.

"Is Father—all right?" she asked anxiously.

"Good Lord, yes! In full bloom," Charles replied bitterly. "I've been sent down, that's all. Thought you'd like to hear the good tidings from my own lips."

Emily took his arm and they walked away from the others who were approaching slowly. She felt sick with apprehension—what had he done? What new horror was there in store for her?

She realised the necessity for a quiet talk with her brother before they could face the keen eyes of Helen Roe. Helen was hard in some ways, she could not make allowances for Charles, and Emily saw that he had suffered. She felt that it would be a calamity for them to meet while Charles was in this mood.

Helen watched them disappear with some surprise.

"Who was that?" she said, turning to Kitty.

"It's Mr. Charles. Something must be wrong for him to come unexpectedly like this. Oh dear, what can it be! I wonder if Mr. Dennistoun—"

"What nonsense, Kitty," interrupted Miss Roe, brusquely. "Surely the young man can come and see his sister when he likes. What should be wrong? If you had a grain of sense you would come in and help me to make the tea instead of standing and staring after an innocent young man as if he were a banshee."

Kitty smiled to herself as she followed the irate lady into the house. Miss Roe's sharp tongue, always most in evidence when she was frightened or upset, had ceased to terrify Kitty. She knew her hostess too well and loved her too much to mind it any more. Besides, she had discovered the tenderness and womanliness of the heart which was hidden beneath the rather forbidding manner.

Emily did not return to Longmeadows until late in the evening; she had dined with Charles in the little inn at St. Mary's Brook. She looked tired and worn but her eyes had the serene expression of one who has accomplished a task to her satisfaction.

Helen looked up from her sewing with a characteristic turn of her small head.

"I suppose Charles has done something foolish," she said, going straight to the heart of the matter with her usual directness.

Emily nodded, she never minded blunt speech and she was used to Helen.

"He has been sent down from Oxford," she said simply.

"My dear!"

"Yes, it is unfortunate—and yet I don't know, he was doing no good there, just wasting time and getting into slack ways. Charles is no scholar."

"I know that," said Helen grimly.

"Don't be too hard on Charles," Emily pleaded. "He was in a wild miserable state after his affair with Alice. This escapade was simply a boy's prank—he has told me all the circumstances. It was utterly foolish of course but there was nothing vicious about it. Several others were mixed up in the escapade and Charles with his usual luck has been made the scape-goat."

"Silly boy!" Miss Roe said.

"Yes, he sees that now, he is sobered by the disgrace."

"Your father will not like it."

"Of course Father is furious. Charles went up to Port Andrew and they had a stormy interview. I wish I could have been there."

"My dear, you have carried Charles on your back for long enough—let the boy stand on his own feet."

Emily smiled. "That's what I want to do," she admitted. "Charles will be the better for some responsibility—he is to have his shop."

"How?" enquired Helen Roe brusquely.

"Very easily, dear Helen," Emily said. "You forget that I am a woman of property and therefore in a position to play fairy godmother—"

"You are going to sell out those shares in the S-P-" Helen cried aghast.

"Why not? The money may as well be used as remain idle."

"Idle?" Helen cried, throwing up her small hands in despair at Emily's unpractical nature.

"Well, not idle then," Emily said, trying not to smile at her old friend's horrified expression. "Idle isn't quite the word. I know I am getting good interest but you see I don't really need it. I have plenty of money to go on with and then there are those sketches coming out. Helen, I *do* want Charles to have that shop, and if I can only help him to this, the dream of his life, and settle him in a business which he is capable of managing—"

"You will be happy, and a pauper—isn't that it Emily? How can you be so foolish? You have broken with your father, and now you calmly tell me that you are going to give away all your capital, every penny of which you have earned yourself by your writing—"

"If he makes it pay—" Emily began.

"If!" cried her friend. "Is there the remotest chance of his making it pay in these days of slack trade and high taxes? Charles has not the moral fibre to stick in through times of adversity."

"I think you wrong him," said his sister.

"Don't blame me if you lose every penny," Miss Roe added grimly.

"I promise not to blame anybody," Emily replied gently, but firmly. "Not even myself, for I shall have done what I think is right."

"Well my dear, of course you must do what you think best," said Helen Roe, melted by Emily's gentleness. "You know you can always come to me for anything you want—"

"I know," Emily said. "Am I likely to forget that?"

Helen rose from the low chair where she had been sitting and gathered her dressing-gown round her. It was late and she did not like late hours but she lingered for a moment hoping for Emily's confidence.

"I wish you were happy, child," she said softly.

"If I am not, it is ungrateful of me," Emily replied.

No more was said, but the two women parted for the night with unusual tenderness.

Charles spent the night at St. Mary's Brook and turned up at Longmeadows the next morning. There were still some details of his new venture to discuss with Emily before he could return to London and start work. He was so frightened of Miss Roe that he entered by the back door and found Kitty baking a cake in the kitchen. She was wearing a blue dress and a white apron and her hands were covered with flour right up to her elbows.

"Oh, Mr. Charles, what a fright you gave me."

"I want to see Emily," he said. "Go and find her like a good girl. Don't tell Miss Roe that I'm here."

Kitty gave a little gurgle of merriment, it seemed so funny for a grown up man to be afraid of Miss Roe. However she was a good-natured little creature so she squeezed the dough off her hands and ran to do his bidding.

Charles sat down on the table and lit a cigarette; he began to whistle, for he was very happy. At last his ambition was to be realised, at last he was to have his beloved shop.

"Charles!" said a voice behind him.

He jumped up as if he had been shot and turned to face Miss Roe.

"What on earth are you doing in my kitchen?" said Miss Roe in amazement. *"Smoking!"*

"Just a whiff or two, Roey," he said, calling her by the name he had always used as a child.

The name took Helen back about twenty years. She smiled and was lost.

"Come into the morning room, I want to speak to you," she said.

He followed meekly, and sat down in the saddleback chair opposite to her with a sinking heart—now he was for it.

"Now Charles, what is all this about a shop?" said Miss Roe sternly.

Charles was agreeably surprised at her question, he had expected a long lecture on the shamefulness of his behaviour in getting sent down from Oxford. The shop was a congenial subject—he launched into his pet scheme, rather diffidently at first but with increasing ardour. He could talk about his shop for hours on end without getting tired or repeating himself. Miss Roe began to get dazed, she was not used to such eloquence. The objections which she had prepared to damp the scheme were swept aside like straws, or merely served as goads stimulating Charles to further flights of rhetoric.

When Charles had first arrived from London he had been full of defiance, and angry with the whole world. Cast off by his father in a fit of rage and disappointment his one hope had been Emily. If *she* could not help him then indeed he was done for. He hoped for sympathy from her, and help towards getting a job, but never in his most optimistic moments had he thought that she could give him his heart's desire. Charles had not been able to believe his ears when she asked him if he "still wanted his shop" and had offered quite simply and naturally to "back his venture."

With this one gracious gesture Emily had thrown open the door of Paradise to Charles; he was immediately raised from the lowest depths of despair to the pinnacle of bliss. It was characteristic of Charles that there was no gradual transition. To him the shop was already in being, filled with choice furniture and clamouring customers. Emily had waved her wand and magic was accomplished.

All that he now needed was an outlet for his feelings

and this Miss Roe had unconsciously provided. He talked and talked until at last she was fain to cover up her ears and cry for mercy. They both laughed then and all constraint vanished—Miss Roe's lecture on his deplorable conduct was lost to posterity.

"Where's Emily?" he said at last.

Helen motioned him to come to the window and they stood there together looking out. It was a glorious view, field upon field stretched away to the horizon but Charles did not look at the view. His eyes were fixed on two riders coming up through the meadows together.

"Hullo!" he said, looking at Helen in surprise.

"It is Emily and Sir Joseph Leate," said Miss Roe significantly. "Emily has been riding with him a lot, it is good for her and she enjoys it!"

"Who's the fellow?"

"Sir Joseph Leate, he has a big place about three miles from here. He is not young, but very nice and—and sporting. I do hope you will like him, Charles."

"Why?"

"Oh well, he's a great admirer of Emily's."

"So that's way the wind blows!" Charles exclaimed in a surprised voice. Like many brothers he could not understand how other men could find anything attractive in his sister, and Emily had always seemed old to him and "on the shelf" so to speak.

"She never said a word about him to me," he added in a hurt tone.

"Is it likely she would?" Helen asked grimly. "You don't give anyone much chance of speaking about anything—

you are full to the brim of your own affairs. Besides, I don't think she has quite made up her mind yet."

The riders now cantered up towards the house and presently they dismounted and came in together talking and laughing.

The wind had blown a faint colour into Emily's cheeks and the exercise of riding had brought a sparkle to her eyes. She looked years younger and full of vitality. It was obvious that Sir Joseph admired her for he could hardly take his eyes off her face.

Emily had been telling him about the new scheme and had aroused his interest; perhaps anything that concerned Emily would have interested Sir Joseph.

"I have been hearing all about you," he said to Charles as they shook hands. "You must come over to St Mary's Place sometime and give me your opinion about my furniture. I've got some rather nice old things stowed away in an attic. They want renovating—carefully."

"I'm your man, sir," said Charles, laughing excitedly at the prospect of his first customer.

After that all was plain sailing. Charles was easily persuaded to talk about his shop, he told Sir Joseph exactly how he proposed to run it.

"I know of a splendid man who will do all the manual part of the work," he said. "He was badly crocked in the war but he is an excellent carpenter and knows a lot about antiques. Of course I can't pay him much at first, but he has a small pension so he won't mind that and I thought of giving him a commission on what I make."

"That sounds a good plan," replied Sir Joseph.

"He has a wife who will cook for me," Charles continued, warming up to his theme, "so that makes everything easy. I've had my eye on the couple ever since I began to think about the scheme. Pring is an awfully enthusiastic fellow. I wired to him this morning and he is going to meet me in town to discuss everything. The only thing now is to find rooms—fairly central and yet not too expensive."

"That sounds rather difficult," Helen said. She was the only person who was not completely in accord with Charles.

"It's up to me to find them," he replied confidently. "Emily has made it all possible and I feel that the right place is waiting for me."

Luncheon was a very cheerful affair, for Charles was in excellent spirits and his gaiety was contagious. Nobody could be dull for long in his company. He forgot his old fear of Miss Roe and sparred with her in a ridiculous fashion. Sir Joseph liked the boy and showed that he did so by drawing him out on his pet subject and deferring to his opinion. It was obvious that the two men each had more than the usual amateur's knowledge of old furniture.

After the meal was over Charles and Emily were left to settle their business arrangements, and Helen accompanied her old friend round the garden. She found Sir Joseph a little distrait and guessed that his thoughts were elsewhere.

A few Christmas roses bloomed feebly upon a sheltered paling. Miss Roe drew her guest's attention to them with pride.

"Wonderful, wonderful," he said absentmindedly.

"What about pruning them?" Miss Roe asked him. "I never think Marr is severe enough with the pruning knife."

But even this subject, usually so absorbing, failed to draw much response from the baronet.

"What do you think of Charles?" she said at last, almost in despair.

Sir Joseph came down from the skies at that question. Charles was not the subject of his dreams but he was near enough to it.

"I like the young man, he is so enthusiastic and energetic—what a comfort it is to find enthusiasm in the young. Nowadays it is the fashion to be blasé and lazy."

"Do you think he knows anything about this old furniture business or will he lose every penny of Emily's money with his nonsense?" asked Miss Roe with her usual straightforward abruptness.

"I think he knows a good deal about it, but whether there is an opening for a shop of that kind in London, I cannot say. I know very little about London—it is too noisy for me."

Charles returned to London by the night train. He was anxious to get everything fixed, not to lose a single moment. Pring met him at the station and the two put their heads together over a suitable position for the shop. They pored over a map of London, marking out the possible streets with a red pencil. Charles was very serious and thorough over it.

What he wanted was difficult to find and might have taken months had not Fate played into his hands. It seemed as if some good fairy had taken a hand in the game—perhaps to make up for the delinquencies of the sea-nymph.

One fine morning, when Charles was in a hurry, he took a turning off Piccadilly to avoid the crowd and presently found himself in Trump Street in a quiet backwater with old-fashioned houses on each side. These houses had been turned into large flats and half way down he espied one with a card "To Let" in the window.

It was a large double flat with two large rooms on the ground floor which would make ideal show rooms for they were well lighted and capacious. Upstairs there was a small kitchen and living room for Pring and his wife and three other rooms for Charles to make use of. The flat belonged to a portrait painter who was starting on a leisurely tour round the world and was therefore quite willing to let the place for two years at a moderate figure.

Charles fell in love with the place at first sight. It fulfilled all the conditions that he considered necessary for the success of his venture, combining a central position with ample accommodation. He wrote screeds to Emily lauding its amenities and she replied by return telling him to settle with its owner at once.

CHAPTER 5
The Curiosity Shop

THE OLD CURIOSITY shop was full of gloomy shadows which deepened rapidly as the sun sank. It was very quiet there except for the distant roar of London which never ceases. Pring was seated on a carpenter's bench beneath a skylight through which the last few gleams of daylight fell directly upon the delicate work he had in hand. His fingers were the deft and supple servants of his brain and beneath their capable touch the small Chippendale table upon which he was engaged took on a most elegant polish.

He bent over it lovingly, his face, its thin features ennobled by the sufferings which he had undergone, was both happy and intent. His grizzled hair, wavy from the root stood out in a kind of halo from his brow from the habit he had of running his fingers through it when he was pleased or puzzled.

Pring was so intent upon his work that he did not hear the door open and was considerably startled to hear his wife's voice close to his elbow.

" 'Aven't yer done yet, Alf? Tea's ready an' gettin' cold—I'm shore you can't see now ter french-polish that table."

She stood there in the gloomy work room like a whiff of country air, a fresh comfortable looking woman with round cheeks and greying hair, in a clean print dress and white apron.

"Yer right, Liza—this bloomin' fog 'as snuffed out every bit o' light there is. I'm jes' comin'. Is the young master in yet?"

"Not 'im," Liza replied. "But a young gent 'as come to see him—seems a noice young feller. I showed 'im into the sitting room an' 'e was that pleased that you'd 'ave thort it was Buckingham Pallis. 'An' so you're Missis Pring,' 'e says, friendly as yer loike. 'Mister Dennistoun's told me all about you,' 'e ses. Big tall feller 'e is. My, 'e *is* noice! But Alf," she continued in a lower voice, " 'oo is 'e? I'm shore I seen 'im before, 'is faice seems familiar like—"

"Look at that now," Pring said, interrupting his wife's garrulous tongue without ceremony. "Ain't that a little beauty, that taible? An' Mr. Dennistoun picked it up for an old song at that sale on Sat'day. Covered in muck it was an' not fit ter be seen—didn't escape *'im* though. My, 'e's a wonder."

"Is 'e maikin' it p'y?" whispered Liza, to whom this was the anxiety of her life. For she realised with native shrewdness that with the fortunes of the newly started furniture shop her own fortune and that of her beloved Alf were closely allied. To the bighearted woman her Alf took the place of all the children that she had never had and it was bliss to see him at work once more, happy in his chosen employment. His lame leg which had been severely wounded in the War and would never be fit for hard usage again was hardly any handicap to him in this new job. Liza would have lain down and let Mr. Dennistoun walk over her so grateful was she for Alf's sake.

"You bet 'e'll maike it p'y," Pring replied reassuringly. "It'ull taike time of course, for Rome wasn't built in a d'y, but the young master's got grit and 'e'll stick in till Doomsd'y. An' for old stuff, 'e's got a eye like a 'awk—a eye like a 'awk," repeated Pring, pleased with the descriptive phrase.

Just at that moment the outer door of the shop opened and Charles Dennistoun walked into his domain.

"Pring," he called excitedly, "Pring, Pring, Liza, Pring!"

"Coming, Sir," Pring cried, leaning over and picking up the crutch without which he could not walk a yard. There was a light in his eyes at the sound of Charles' voice which was good to see.

When he reached the front show-room he was in time to see two men stagger in carrying an oblong packing case while Charles danced round them beseeching them to be careful and showering contradictory instructions at them.

"Careful now—slowly does it—hurry up can't you—a couple of undertakers is all you are! Mind that table. Put it down here—no there."

" 'Adn't they better carry it through to the workroom?" Pring suggested.

"Yes of course—carry it through to the workroom—idiots, mind the door now—look out—LOOK OUT—clumsy fools! That will do—that will do splendidly—thank you. Thank you very much. Here you are—Good afternoon to you."

When the bewildered men had disappeared, amazed at the munificence of their tip, Charles did a solemn cakewalk round the packing case while Pring fetched a chisel and proceeded to open it with great care.

Soon the workroom was littered with straw and laths of wood and amongst the debris stood a small chest of richly carved oak. The front of the chest consisted of three panels and the heavy lid was made to match. In the centre of each panel was a diamond-shaped ornament. The whole chest was black with age and smoke and at first Pring looked at it doubtfully. Charles smiled at his puzzled face and seizing an oily rag began to rub the wood of one of the panels and soon the grime began to melt and some dark letters came to view.

They were both deep in the merits and demerits of their new acquisition when Liza returned to say supper was ready.

"Wot a dirty old thing!" she cried, guilefully.

"Dirty old thing indeed," Charles cried, catching her round the waist. "That, my good Liza, is a valuable Jacobean chest. Observe the diamond ornaments on the panels. When Pring has cleaned it he will find that they are of three colours—black, brown and light yellow. In the centre panel in black is some writing which is the initials of the owner. Round each panel is the peculiar ornamentation which for want of a better description is called the 'split balustrade ornament.' If you think I am going to give it to you to keep your Sunday clothes in you are much mistaken."

"I wouldn't put my Sunday clo'es in that old box for a good deal," Liza replied teasingly.

All this time Pring was scraping away at the chest with

great energy.

"I b'lieve you're right," he said eagerly. "I do b'lieve you've 'it on a genuine old Jacobean chest. You wait till I've cleaned it up a bit an' then we'll talk—my word, what a find!"

They were all so thrilled over the discovery that they had forgotten the "young gent" who had arrived earlier and had been waiting ever since to see Charles. He looked round the room for a little, interested in the photographs and Oxford trophies, until at last he began to realise that they had forgotten all about him. Certain feelings seemed to indicate that the hour for supper was approaching so he set out on a voyage of discovery and soon, drawn by the sound of excited voices, found himself in the workshop.

Charles was the first to perceive the newcomer.

"Francis!" he cried joyfully and then he drew back and his face paled.

"Hullo Charles—why, what's the matter, old chap?" he added in amazement. Charles was standing with his hands behind his back.

"Do you expect me to congratulate you?" he asked with elaborate sarcasm.

The Prings had vanished tactfully and the two men, once such friends, were alone in the big dim work-room.

"Expect you to congratulate me?" Francis repeated. "What the dickens are you playing at, Charles? Why, you don't imagine that I had anything to do with Alice Brunton's escapade, do you?" he continued, a sudden light breaking on him. "Good Lord, man, you *couldn't* think I was such a swine."

"I know all about it," Charles said angrily. "Father wrote and told me the whole thing, so you need not tell any more lies about it."

Francis was aghast, he had never imagined for a moment that Alice would leave the matter unexplained. It seemed dreadful to think that Charles had been harbouring resentment against him all these months and he unconscious of the fact. And Emily, what had she thought? Was this why his letter had remained unanswered?

"Charles," he said at last, "do listen to me like a reasonable man. Even a criminal is not condemned unheard. I swear to you the whole thing is a mistake."

"But Father saw you with her at Pennybrigg."

"I know, I know—but I was there on Laura's account. Surely you saw that Alice and Harry were—were fond of each other. I rushed to Pennybrigg the moment that Laura told me they had gone, and got there in time to stop them. I had just sent Harry home to his wife when your Father appeared on the scene and, quite naturally in the circumstances, he got the impression that I was going off with her myself. Nothing was further from my mind, I scarcely knew Miss Brunton to start with. Of course I thought that she would explain matters to your Father and—and I wrote to Emily and explained everything to her."

Charles listened, and could not help believing. The facts fitted in with all he knew and were much more easily credited than the first story of the elopement.

"How did you persuade Harry to go home?" he asked, more quietly. He was not quite ready yet to restore his friendship to Francis, he found it difficult to change his views so suddenly.

"Oh well, I persuaded Miss Brunton to change her mind—it was not difficult."

"You told her Harry's history?"

"A little of it. I had to stop the thing at all costs, Charles. It was so absolutely mad and disastrous."

"It was indeed mad and disastrous," Charles echoed. And then all of a sudden he laughed. "Good Lord, what a fool I've been. I see it all now of course—what an utter ass I was to doubt you for a moment!"

Francis gripped his hand and wrung it; he could not laugh very heartily for the affair had given him such a shock. He had gone to see Charles—his friend—so lightheartedly and had found a strange man, tight-lipped and pale.

What of Emily? As yet he could not speak of her. That would come later when he and Charles were sitting over the fire with their pipes going.

"Of course you'll stay to supper, old man," Charles said when he had laughed away all the constraint that was between them. "I want to hear about everything and get it quite clear in my mind."

"I want that too," was the quick reply. They went upstairs together to Charles' sitting room where Liza Pring was busy laying the supper table.

The room was furnished with the stuff which Charles had collected at Oxford—shabby leather chairs and

223

battered tables. They had weathered many a "rag" but were still comfortable and homely. When the curtains were drawn and the fire lighted Charles could easily have fancied himself back at the varsity.

"You are mighty comfortable here," Francis said.

His host nodded,

"It *is* a nice room but I'm hardly ever in it except in the evening. Come in and use it whenever you like—it will be awfully nice to have you here, old boy."

"Very nice for me," Francis countered. "You don't know what I have endured in lodging-houses and boarding-establishments since I came to London."

"I live very frugally," Charles warned him. "You won't get four course dinners with me—or ortolans in aspic. You see it is really all Emily's money so I don't feel justified in spending a penny more than I can help on myself."

"Your sister's money?" Francis repeated in surprise. "I thought your Father had relented and set you up in business."

"Good Lord, no," cried Charles and began to tell his friend all that had happened since they last met.

Francis listened in silence until the recital was finished and then he rose from the table and groped on the mantelpiece for his pipe.

"So your sister is at Longmeadows now," he said in a detached voice. "I hope she is quite well."

"I never saw her look better," Charles replied with a laugh. "She has taken on a new lease of life since she got away from Borriston. The truth is I'm expecting to hear interesting news about Emily one of these fine days."

"What do you mean?" Francis asked sharply.

"There's a fellow down there who is obviously gone on her," returned Charles in his modern jargon. "Quite potty about her in fact. He's Sir Joseph Leate, used to be in Parliament before he got his baronetcy. I looked him up in Debrett and found out all about him—very good old family and plenty of dibs—most suitable in every way. Why, what's the matter Francis?"

"Burnt my finger with your damned matches," was the ungracious reply.

Francis left soon after supper, he felt that he must be alone to fight the demons raging in his soul. Emily lost to him was bad enough, Emily in the arms of another man was sheer purgatory.

All these months he had waited on, hoping for an answer to his letter, swung between hope and despair. Gradually there had come to him the conviction that she had answered the letter by her silence. Perhaps she thought it the kindest way, perhaps it was too difficult for her to write a negative reply.

He tried to banish her from his thoughts. But in spite of all his care there were times when the thought of her came to him, obtruding upon his studies with gentle persistence until—despite his strength of will—he seemed to see her as she was that night of the ball, with her pale golden gown and high piled hair. And he seemed to hear the soft low voice asking him if there were "another woman" in his life and to catch the glow of love-light in her eyes when she offered him her lips. Sometimes, in his bitter moments Francis wished that he had taken her then and there when she was his for the taking; that he had swept her off her feet first and made his explanation afterwards. She would not have backed out of her bargain once made and sealed with the solemn kiss of betrothal whatever she might have felt. But at other times pride came to his aid and he told himself that no marriage could be a success unless both parties entered into it with their minds as well as their hearts as one.

Emily had made her choice and he was too proud and too humble to approach her again. And yet—and yet *could* there be any mistake about it, *could* she have misread his letter—

Cold reason answered that she could not but still one small hope lingered on and would not be smothered.

It was this small hope that had driven him to seek Charles at his shop and to try and learn from him the truth about his sister. Unconsciously Charles had given him a terrible blow—Emily was to marry another man, a man of good family, very suitable and rich with a large property, a man in fact with everything which he, Francis, so lamentably lacked. Here, then, was the answer to his letter.

Francis went through a bad time in the days that followed, his only solace was his work. He flung himself into it with a sort of cold fury, forcing his mind to think and dream of nothing else. All the morning he worked in the hospitals, and in the afternoons he attended any operations or important consultations with Sir Addison and took notes for him. He went to bed late, and rose early to study the books and diagrams recommended to him by his chief.

Sir Addison soon found that his new assistant was the most zealous and indefatigable that he had ever had, and took him more and more into his confidence. He began to depend upon Francis Hood, and finding him responsible and efficient he allowed him to perform several minor operations. These and other favours brought Francis the jealousy of his contemporaries. His lust for work made them seem idle, his single-mindedness made them seem gay and flighty. But for Charles, Francis soon had no friends.

Occasionally, therefore, when his work permitted, Francis found his way to the shop in Trump Street and foregathered with Charles. He found a kindred spirit in Pring, and the two would talk of their war experiences, an endless subject of conversation.

It seemed to Charles as he sat and listened to them, watching first one and then the other through a cloud of smoke, that there was something odd about Pring's manner when he talked to Francis Hood. Pring was always respectful, but towards Francis he was more deferential than usual. Sometimes he would break off in the midst of a story and sit looking at Francis with his head a little on one side and a strange bewildered expression on his delicate face.

Francis still had the picture of Alice in his possession; he could not think what to do with it. The picture was still tied up in the brown paper wrappings in which he and Laura had swathed it. One evening when Charles dropped in for a smoke, Francis broached the subject to him.

"Good Lord!" said the young shopkeeper. "I wonder if Harry wants to be paid for it."

Francis laughed.

"Hardly, under the circumstances," he said. "But take the thing if you want it."

"*I* don't want it," Charles replied quickly.

"Well, what am I to do with it then?"

The two young men looked at each other with puzzled faces, and then quite suddenly they both laughed.

"Here is a valuable portrait of a beautiful sea nymph and apparently nobody wants it. Shall we advertise that we are giving it away with a pound of tea?" Francis asked.

"You might send it to Alice herself," suggested Charles. "I can give you her Oxford address."

This seemed a splendid idea to Francis; he was anxious to get rid of the portrait for it only took up room in his none too spacious apartment.

He despatched it to Alice the next morning and we may be sure that it was hung in a place of honour in the little house at Oxford. Alice was her own most faithful admirer. Other lovers might come and go, but her own pleasure in her skin-deep beauty never faltered nor grew dim.

Alice Brunton does not come into the story again. We do not know whether she is still at Oxford, turning the heads of the susceptible undergraduates or whether she has succeeded in marrying into circles where a shop is merely a place for buying things—never for selling. We do not know whether the letter, which she removed from the table at Borriston Hall, has been opened and read, or whether it still lies in a deep drawer guarded by its large red seal.

The Alice Bruntons of this world are birds of passage, they flutter through the lives of others and disappear into the unknown. Their best friends are people whom they only met last week, people who have not had time to sound the shallow layer of beauty and gaiety and to find the emptiness beneath. We need not pity the Alice Bruntons while they are young for there is always a fresh selection of friends awaiting their turn—plenty of fish in the sea of life to fill the nets of a young pretty woman. It is when the Alice Bruntons grow old that they need our pity, when they are relegated to a loveless old age with no old friends to share their troubles and no new ones to be made. When their beauty and their gaiety are dead and they have no abiding interests within themselves to make their lives worth living.

CHAPTER 6
An Old Friend

CHARLES was very happy. He was full of plans for advertising his business and he worked early and late attending sales and supervising the renovation of the old pieces which he acquired. At first the money flowed out without any return and the two large rooms became stocked with furniture of all the best periods and makes, then gradually a few customers found their way to the shop and the tide began to turn. It was a great day for Charles and Pring when they sold half a dozen dining-room chairs of Dutch pattern to a newly-rich gentleman at St. Albans. The chairs were certainly genuinely old, and might, or might not, have been the work of Sheraton. At any rate Charles took what he considered a fair profit on them and the customer believed that he had made a good bargain. After this opening the little bell tinkled quite often. Things began to look up.

One morning Charles was busily at work drawing some designs for a corner cupboard. He had determined to strike out an original line in new furniture for flats. Furniture that would combine utility with beauty, and would be designed specially to fit into any odd corner that might be available. This he hoped would bring in more money as there would be a larger turnover in the cheaper lines. It would also be a good advertisement for him and would bring possible customers for his antique furniture to his shop.

His head was full of his plans when Mrs. Pring came to tell him that a lady had called to see him.

"A very pretty lady," said Liza nodding excitedly.

Charles put aside his work and went into the front show-room which presented quite an imposing appearance. He found the lady examining a very beautiful old Dutch lacquer cabinet which he had bought quite recently at a sale and for which he had paid a good sum.

"That is a very fine Dutch cabinet—seventeenth century," he said in his best professional manner.

"So I see," replied the lady and she turned and held out her hand.

"Laura!" he said incredulously.

"Dear Charles!" said Laura Murdoch. "I had to come and see you when I heard about your shop. You have really got it at last. Harry and I are in London for a time; he has got some illustrating work and is rather enjoying it."

"Laura!" cried Charles again. He took her hands and held them in a friendly grasp. "How jolly it is to see you!" he said in his boyish way. "It was good of you to come."

"You don't bear us any grudge?" Laura said in a low tone, voicing the fear which had nearly prevented her from coming. Charles smiled and shook his head.

"You mean about Alice—no I don't. To start with, it wasn't your fault, you suffered too. That night at the dance—" he stopped, realising that he had not seen her since, then as she did not speak he went on, "I realise now what a fool I was."

"You don't regret—anything?"

"Not for my own sake," he said vehemently.

"Then you will be friends with Harry?"

"Of course," Charles said. "You did not doubt it, did you?" Laura had doubted it and it seemed to her even now that Charles was extraordinarily magnanimous. He saw the puzzled expression on her face and answered the unspoken question.

"I am very happy here—she would not have let me have the shop, you know."

Laura could not help smiling; Charles was so naïve, so intensely boyish in his absorption in the one subject. He had been ready to throw up all idea of the shop for Alice's sake and now was equally delighted to wipe Alice out of his heart for the sake of his new toy. That it was an attractive toy Laura was ready to admit, she looked round the various fine pieces which Charles had collected and realised in a few moments that he must certainly have a real gift in this direction. The pieces were all good and beautiful in their own way and each possessed some special attribute to recommend it to notice.

Charles saw that Laura was interested and he immediately offered to show her round.

"I'm afraid I shall be wasting your time," she said diffidently. "You see I'm not a buyer."

He laughed at that and assured her that he only wanted an excuse to go round the showrooms himself.

"I know every piece and love it," he said. "They all remind me of some little incident. You see I go all over the country buying up furniture. Very often you can pick up bargains in country places if there are no dealers about, and by Jove I get a lot of fun over it. Look at this four-post bed, Laura. I picked it up in a Sussex farm-house. Jolly lucky it was because Sussex has been simply over-run with collectors. The old lady would have sold it to me for a song, she wanted a brass bedstead, but—well, I couldn't cheat the old body, she was such an old dear, so I sent her a first-class bedstead and gave her something into the bargain and we were both pleased. I wish you could have seen her face."

The four-post bed was certainly a beauty, and now that it was cleaned and polished it would have graced any collection, but Laura did not feel that it was the sort of bed for a sound night's sleep. She said something of this to Charles.

"Give you bad dreams, would it?" he chuckled. "Well, I'm not sure that you aren't right, but it is a pretty bit of oak and I'm very fond of it." He ran his fingers down the slip pillars with their gently swelling curves as he spoke.

Laura watched him, irresistibly reminded of a groom of her father's who used to feel the slim legs of her father's charger in much the same tender manner. She was half amused at Charles and his shop but the other half of her feeling was made up of a very real respect for his knowledge and enthusiasm. Emily had done well for her beloved brother by giving him his heart's desire. There was no doubt that the boy was now in his right element, he had gained poise and had, in fact, become a responsible and useful member of society.

Laura remembered that Francis had predicted

something of the sort, he had always up-held Charles even when his infatuation for the foolish Alice had called forth their derision. "He only wants something to stabilise him," Francis had said. "Something that will give him a feeling of responsibility. Mark my words, Charles will be a man one of these days."

Laura could now see that Francis was right—he rarely made a mistake in psychology. The only mistake he had made—as far as Laura knew—was in his relations with Emily. There had been a sad muddle there, the affair was mystifying in the extreme.

Laura was not by nature a meddler in other people's affairs, she held the creed that people knew their own business best, that each soul must work out its own salvation in its own way. Her life was by no means an easy one and her troubles had taught her the virtue of tolerance for the foibles of her fellow creatures. Added to this was a natural diffidence; she had not the gift of ready speech and she knew this well.

But in spite of this Laura felt that she wanted to do something to help those two friends of hers. She was sure that they were misunderstanding one another, she longed to see Francis and Emily happily married because she was so fond of them both, and because, knowing them as she did, she knew that they were well suited.

Shortly after Francis had left *La Boiselle* Laura had gone over to Borriston Hall and was amazed to learn that her friend had gone from home leaving no address. Francis was busy in London and answered her letters only with unsatisfactory post cards. The whole thing was puzzling in the extreme.

When she arrived in London and went to see Francis at his rooms she found him immersed in his work, and a tentative reference to Emily met with no response. Laura was too shy to probe further into his attitude and went home more bewildered than ever.

She was sure that they cared for each other, and she was also sure that Emily would not refuse Francis on account of his unknown parentage.

What then was the bar to their happiness?

Laura was still worrying over the problem when an advertisement of Charles' shop caught her attention and after some hesitation she sought him out, braving the possibility of a cold reception in the hope that he would throw some light on the mystery.

While Laura was in the shop two prospective customers appeared on the scene. Charles took charge of them in a business-like way and helped them to crystallize their vague requirements. One lady bought a Sheraton book-case on the spot and seemed pleased with her bargain, the other drifted off, promising to look in another day.

"It is awfully interesting, Laura," said Charles when they had both gone and the shop was once more empty save for themselves. "I love selling things to people."

"That woman would have paid more for the book-case," Laura said slowly.

"I know, but I made a fair profit on it, and by letting her have it for less than she expected, I have made a customer of her. She thinks she has got a bargain and she will come back for more."

Yes, Charles knew what he was doing, there was no doubt of it.

"Where is Mademoiselle Jacquot," said Charles suddenly. "Is she here with you—in town I mean."

"She went back to her beloved Paris," was the reply. "I sometimes think that Parisians are like fish out of water. When they leave Paris they gasp for their native element."

"What quaint ideas you have, Laura," laughed Charles. "Jacquot amused me, but I never thought she was like a fish—I saw no signs of gasping. I must tell old Francis about it next time he comes in."

"Does he come here often?" Laura asked, opening her eyes wide with surprise.

"Yes, he often comes in at night, isn't it jolly!" said Charles. "We often spend the evenings in my sitting-room; Francis mugging up bones while I do accounts or read books about furniture. There's always lots to learn you know, Laura—it's a vast subject and it teaches you history too. I never could bear history at school—dates are so dull—but now I wish I had stuck into it."

"Where is Emily?" Laura interrupted. Like many shy people she sometimes brought out the question with startling suddenness, like an explosion. Ever since she had entered the shop she had been trying to bring herself to ask for Emily's address but had failed to lead the conversation gently in that direction.

"Emily? Oh she's staying with Miss Roe at Longmeadows, having a high old time."

"I thought that she and Francis—I mean they—rather

liked each other," Laura said, stumbling over the words. "At the dance—and before that too—I always thought—"

Charles gave a ringing laugh. "Good Lord, you've missed it this time," he said. "Good old Laura, did you really think that? Why, Francis thinks of nothing but his bally work, and as for Emily, she's practically engaged to a chap who lives near Miss Roe. I met him when I was down there, an awfully nice fellow and simply crazy about Emily."

Laura said nothing, she always thought slowly and it was difficult for her to assimilate this totally unlooked for piece of news.

As she walked home through the crowded streets she tried to visualise Emily engaged to a total stranger but she did not succeed.

CHAPTER 7
A Neglected Opportunity

ONE SATURDAY afternoon Pring and Francis were sitting in the workshop together, talking as usual about the war. It was a thoroughly wet day, too wet for even Francis Hood to enjoy a walk. Charles had gone to Chislehurst to hunt up an old chair which he had heard about from a friend. It was unlikely that any customer would come and Pring was taking advantage of the slack time to get through some arrears of work; he could always work better when he had somebody to talk to.

The two were at it hammer and tongs when the shop-bell tinkled.

"Bother!" said Francis.

"You didn't learn that expression from Colonel D——, sir", said Pring chuckling. He reached for his crutch and hobbled to the front shop with his usual surprising agility.

Francis smiled. Pring was a man after his own heart; the fellow could be amusing without presuming in the slightest degree. He rose and stretched himself and extinguished the remains of his cigarette before following Pring into the show-room.

Who the dickens could it be, on such a vile afternoon, he wondered idly.

The unwelcome customer proved to be a tall woman in a long chinchilla wrap. She had a dignified face, covered with a network of wrinkles. Although she was old—very old indeed—she carried herself well and moved with grace and assurance. Coming out of the sunshine, the shop seemed dark, and full of shadows.

"I was told that Mr. Dennistoun had an oak cupboard—" she began, addressing herself to Pring and then suddenly her eyes fell on Francis Hood and the words died on her lips. He thought that she was going to faint and sent old Pring for a glass of water while he found a chair for her.

"It is hot in here," he said gently. "I think you should loosen your coat."

She loosened it with trembling fingers upon one of which there gleamed an old Marquise ring of exquisite beauty.

"Who are you?" she asked him. "For God's sake tell me who you are."

There was such real trouble and urgency in her voice that Francis could not be offended at the strangeness of her request, but before he could reply Pring returned with a glass of water. The old lady waved it aside and rose to her feet.

"You can show me this wonderful cupboard, I suppose," she said, placing her hand on Francis' arm and waving her stick towards the inner recesses of the showroom.

Pring looked at them doubtfully as they vanished through the door, his head full of wild fancies which were beginning to take shape. He knew that Mr. Hood was quite incapable of showing off the Jacobean Cupboard to a prospective purchaser—the peculiar beauties of its rich colour and dark lettering were a closed book to him—but Pring was too well-trained a servant to follow them when, very obviously, they did not want him. Then another point puzzled Pring—had the lady really come to the shop to buy that cupboard or was her visit for some quite different purpose? Or again, coming to see the cupboard, had she still an interest in it, or was that mild interest supplanted by a more vital one? And, last but by no means least, what was the reason of that sudden faintness which had assailed her at the sight of Mr. Hood? All these questions Pring found himself incapable of answering, and feeling too excited to do any more work until he had solved them to his own satisfaction, he hobbled off to find Liza and discuss the matter with her.

Once in the back show-room the old lady seemed to lose all interest in old oak. She sank on to a Jacobean settle, more notable for its beauty than its comfort, and surveyed Francis through a pair of tortoise-shell lorgnettes.

"You seem interested in me," Francis ventured.

"An old woman has privileges," she replied quite gently. "And since I am old enough to be your—to be your grandmother, you must make allowances for my years."

"May I ask why you are so kind as to interest yourself in me?" Francis asked.

She fenced. "Might I not be merely taken with your good looks?"

"I would have credited you with better taste," he replied, half laughing in spite of the excitement which was rising like a tide within him.

The lady laughed too. "There's nothing the matter with your looks," she told him. "Women admire your type. I've borne two sons as like you as peas, so I should know."

"Why do you tell me that?" he asked her, brushing aside all pretence and going straight to the heart of the matter.

Their eyes met frankly. She was seated very stiff and straight in the oak settle with one hand in a grey suède glove upon the wooden arm. Francis could see the tension of her thin fingers through the glove and guessed what she was suffering despite her calmness.

"Have you come to man's estate without learning the futility of asking a woman *why* she has said or done a thing?" she added. "Give me the privilege of my sex and let me ask your name."

"I call myself Francis Hood," he replied carefully.

She noted the form his answer had taken and meditated upon it for a few moments. The show-room was very quiet and shadowy, the golden light of late afternoon fell softly through the curtained windows on to the polished floor.

"Shall we be honest with each other?" she asked him.

Something within him rose eagerly in answer to her courage but he replied cautiously,

"Words cannot be unsaid. Be very certain first if you want to go further into this. You can leave it now without any trouble—I don't know who you are and if I did it would make no difference—"

"You are generous," she said softly.

He glowed at the tribute but continued urgently—

"Do nothing which may cause you regret. Think it over first and then come back. You will find me here if you—if you want me."

The old eyes filled with tears.

"Where have you come from?" she said, rising and doing up her fur as she spoke. "I did not know there was a gentleman left in this post-war world. It's either a gentleman or a fool you are, and I'm not sure which. But you are right, I will sleep on this and come back tomorrow. I've always been an impetuous woman and now I am an impetuous old woman which is a deal worse. You'll not run away before tomorrow," she added, looking up at him with sharp grey eyes not unlike his own.

"I shall be here," Francis replied gently.

He went out with her to her taxi which was waiting for her at the kerb and helped her into it for she was a trifle shaky after the stirring of long slumbering emotions. Neither of them remembered anything more about the Jacobean cupboard. It had served its turn and passed from their minds like the remembrance of a dream.

Francis turned back and re-entered the shop wondering why he had been such a fool as to throw away this chance of learning something of the mystery surrounding his birth and parentage. He did not doubt that he had held the key in his hands and had thrown it away. She would never return, for second thoughts would bring wisdom. The fears and doubts to which age is prone would counsel her to let sleeping dogs lie. He would never see her again, and the mystery would remain unsolved.

It was not that Francis wanted patronage or money or even recognition from his relations, he was independent now and with his foot firmly upon the first rung of the ladder which leads to success. All he wanted was to know what blood this was that ran in his veins, what attributes he had inherited from his unknown father. This body of his, so strong and perfect in its carefully cherished fitness, from whence had it come and what heritage of good or ill lay dormant in its cells.

Just to know that, just to be assured that some decent member of society and not a vicious rogue had fathered him, and Francis felt that he could face the world and his own future with a bolder heart and an easier mind. The very fact of his profession and the consequent realisation of the dangers and the freaks of heredity made him more anxious to get to the root of the matter and establish his identity for good or ill.

It may be thought that Francis laid too much stress on the physical body—to him it seemed that a clean and beautiful body was a valuable possession, something to be sanctified in order that it might be a fitting instrument of the spiritual intelligence therein embodied.

Pring's voice roused Francis from his thoughts.

"Well sir, did Lady Hume buy the cupboard?"

"Lady Hume?" echoed Francis in astonishment.

"Lady Hume of Eaglefold," affirmed Pring.

"Pring, are you sure?"

"Yes Sir, quite sure, though I 'aven't seen 'er for a metter o' thirty years. I was at Portman Square as third footman when I was young an' we always went up to

Eaglefold for the shooting. 'Er Ladyship 'asn't changed much really. She must be over eighty now and straight as a pine—wonderful lady she is."

Francis was so sure that the master joiner was mistaken that he did not trouble to check the flow of reminiscences. He lit a cigarette and flung himself into a chair, his thoughts a whirlpool of emotion too chaotic for expression.

"Fancy it being thirty years ago since I was at Eaglefold," Pring said, sitting down at his bench and beginning to work. (He was sand-papering the marks of hot dishes from a seventeenth century serving table which Charles had picked up at a country sale.) "Thirty years ago an' I remember Eaglefold like as if it was yesterday—the 'eather on the moors where the young gentlemen shot an' the pine-woods—what a smell they 'ad. I'd never bin out of London before an' it was like a bit out of a book ter me. The second footman thought it was dull, but not me, I liked it an' was sorry when we came back again to Portman Square. An' it's thirty years since we 'eard that Mr. Edward 'ad bin killed out 'unting. There was two young gentlemen an' Mr. Edward was the youngest. 'E was Madame's favourite son an' as nice a young gentleman as ever stepped. Like you, 'e was sir, if you'll pardon me, with hauburn air. I remember it as if it was larst week, such a shock it was ter me. We'd 'ad a bet on the Lincolnshire—'e was that kind of free an' easy gentleman but without standing nonsense you know—an' the 'orse romped 'ome, an' there was Mr. Edward dead. It broke Sir Hubert's 'eart that it did, for all he was such a

Sparting (be way of). 'E was never the same after Mr. Edward's death, an' when the eldest son—'e was Mr. 'Erbert of course—when 'e got killed in the Boer War Sir Hubert went melancholy and petered out. Never 'ad the spirit of Lady Hume 'e 'adn't. I believe Mr. 'Erbert was married an' left a son so 'e inherited Eaglefold. I'd left service by then, of course, but being sweet on one of the 'ousemaids—that was Liza, second of five she was an' pretty as a peach—I 'eard all about it, she kep' me informed so to speak, 'ow things was going in the family."

Francis suddenly realised that he had no business to be listening to Pring's revelations. He had refused the facts from the one person who had a right to enlighten him and he had demeaned himself by listening to gossip from the servant's hall. Pring was an old dear but he was terribly garrulous.

"See you later Pring, I must do some work now," Francis said, and he ran upstairs to his own room. But even in this sanctuary the demons of unrest pursued him demanding—

Who are you? Isn't it your right to know?

The next day was Sunday, Francis hung about the shop all day in spite of his inner conviction that Lady Hume would not return. The day wore away slowly, he could do no work nor settle down to any kind of reading. His hopes, such as they were, faded with the light; she did not come.

On Monday morning Charles returned from Chislehurst, bringing with him his usual atmosphere of blythe energy. Francis, who had taken a holiday from his work, appeared once more at the shop. He listened to all that Charles had to say and when at last he paused for breath, confessed that he had frightened away a possible customer.

"You're a nice friend to have," cried Charles with mock anger. "Come now, make a clean breast of the whole affair or I won't answer for the consequences."

Francis immediately plunged into the tale of Lady Hume's visit and of her subsequent departure while his friend listened wide-eyed.

"Good Heavens, man, never say die," he cried when the story was over. "The old thing may still come back—"

"No such luck," replied Francis, smiling in spite of himself at Charles' designation of the lady.

"Well if she doesn't come, we know who she is, we can find out about her quite easily—"

"No, I promised to do nothing in the matter and I intend keeping my word."

"Bah!" cried his friend in disgust. "You are the most unpractical creature that ever breathed. You ought to have lived in the days of the Round Table."

CHAPTER 8
"Old Unhappy Far-Off Things"

AS IF TO REFUTE all the psychological theories and deductions of Doctor Francis, Lady Hume returned that afternoon.

It was not her fault that her coming was delayed; she had spent the greater part of Sunday in bed worn out by the emotions of the previous day and unrested by a sleepless night. Her spirit was as courageous as ever but her body had served her faithfully for over eighty years and it was only mortal after all.

She came in a taxi as before but dismissed it before she entered the shop. She made no pretence of interest in the furniture, merely asking if she might see "Francis Hood".

Francis found her seated on the same high-backed oak settle. She looked very frail and tired and he guessed that she had not slept much since the last time he saw her.

"I suppose you thought I was not coming back," she said grimly.

"I—wondered," Francis admitted with a smile.

"And you regretted your quixotry in letting me away without hearing what I had to tell you. Oh, I'm not a witch, Francis Hood, merely an old woman who has seen a good deal of human nature during her long life." She took a little case from her leather bag and placed it in his hands. "Open that, and tell me if it recalls anything to your mind."

He opened the little case without a word and saw, as if in a dream, the picture of a face which had been dear and familiar to him in his childhood's days.

"My mother!" he said amazedly.

Lady Hume gave a little sigh; the tension had been so great.

"I thought as much," she said. "I was perfectly certain from the first moment that you were Edward's son. Do you think a woman does not know the fruit of her own body when she sees it?" Her voice faltered for a moment but she called on her reserve of power and continued steadily. "Edward was killed in the hunting field. The groom who was with him when he died said that his last words were 'Take care of Fanny.' This picture was in his pocket." She took a flimsy cambric handkerchief from her bag and wiped her eyes with it. Francis made a little movement of sympathy but she motioned him to be silent. "We searched everywhere for Fanny, but there was nothing to give us any clue to her identity, no letters—none of his friends knew of her existence, even Moresby, his great friend in the regiment had never heard her name. He was amazed when he saw the miniature, could hardly believe his eyes. The regiment was at Aldershot at the time and Edward had many friends there but none of them knew anything of 'Fanny'. If it had not been for the picture we should have thought that the groom had imagined it all or that Edward was delirious. My husband was inclined to take the latter view—he feared a scandal and was anxious to hush it up. It was scarcely mentioned in the papers—it was easier in those days, thirty years ago, to keep things out of the papers. You could do much with money and influence and the Humes had both. If she had come forward he would have done what he could for her but she did not come. I longed for her, I felt that she was a sacred legacy from my son. I would have welcomed her as a dear daughter because *he* loved her. It was a bitterness to me that he had not trusted me with his secret, yet I could not be jealous. Sometimes when women spoke to me of their sons' wives I felt jealous of them, but never of her, never of her, she was a part of Edward. I set half a dozen detectives to search for her but it was useless, there was nothing to go on, you see, but the groom's evidence and that picture which you hold in your hands. I tried to discover the artist who had painted it but it was hopeless. I never heard an echo of the affair until I saw you."

Francis did not speak at once, he was trying to piece things together, trying to solidify the vague images which arose out of the past. His mother had died so long ago that the memory of her was hazy to him.

"She did not mean you to find her," he told Lady Hume, groping for his thoughts and expressing them with difficulty. "She was terribly broken by my father's death. She thought that you would be angry when you heard of his marriage, she thought you would take me away from her. She used to frighten me about it when I was very little. Her people were Methodists you see—"

"And we are Catholics—poor girl, did she think we

would have taken her child from her!"

"I think so. I can't remember my father, and she never spoke about him to me for she was afraid that I would not be able to keep her secret. I don't know when I first began to suspect that Hood was not my name, to realise that I was nameless—not until after her death. She kept all that away from me, shielded me from the rough world. She did it for love of me but it was worse afterwards."

"How old were you when she died?" asked Lady Hume.

"I was about seven years old."

"And then what happened to you?"

"I was sent to Devonshire to an old Uncle of my mother's. He brought me up as well as he was able, and he was very good to me in his own way. He was a funny old muddle-headed bachelor, almost a recluse, but he allowed me to have my own friends."

"A queer up-bringing!" she mused.

"I suppose it was, but it did not seem so to me at the time. I had the run of the country and the sea-shore, I had my lessons and my dreams—"

"What were they?"

"To be a surgeon," Francis answered, for he felt that he could tell this woman everything that mattered and be understood. "From my earliest childhood I can remember doctoring sick animals and birds. Perhaps it was a queer ambition in a child—it was more than an ambition really, it was almost an obsession. I took out an Insurance Policy and borrowed money on it to pay for my college fees and my training. I shall pay it all back."

"You are very sure," she said, admiring the courage of

him.

"Very sure," he replied smiling.

"Have you any papers—the certificate of your parents' marriage or your birth?"

Francis shook his head.

"None."

"How are we to prove the marriage?" asked Lady Hume.

"How do we know there was a marriage?" Francis said grimly.

She drew herself up proudly. "My son was not a blackguard. He behaved foolishly but I will not believe worse of him. We *must* prove the marriage."

"You cannot search every registrar's office in the Kingdom. It would take a lifetime and hundreds in money."

"I have not much time," said Lady Hume, "for I am a very old woman. Time was when I had money enough and to spare but the war changed that. The Eaglefold properties are shrinking, they are being sold piece by piece to pay the taxes—we are paying for the War. I'm not complaining, for we land-owners are all hit the same. Sometimes I wonder if it is good policy—but never mind that. There are still the family jewels, they can be sold if necessary."

"Is it worth the trouble?" Francis said, perhaps a trifle bitterly. "I have done well enough as I am for over thirty years. I have told you my ambition—it is to be a surgeon."

"And I want you to be my grandson," she answered in a low voice.

The bitterness which Francis felt was only on the

surface and he could not resist such an appeal. He sat down beside her on the oak settle and took her small hand in his.

"Forgive me," he said gently, "but you see I know so little about you. Why do you want me so much? Are there not others belonging to your family who would resent my —my intrusion?"

"There is only Ernest," said Lady Hume. "He is Herbert's boy and has lived with me since his father was killed in South Africa. His mother died soon after his birth, she was a weak creature and she bequeathed her delicacy to Ernest. He is not like you," she added a trifle naïvely.

Francis smiled. "There is certainly nothing delicate about me—but what will Ernest say about the matter, have you spoken to him?"

Lady Hume shook her head. "Ernest never comes to London, he is at Eaglefold—he cares for nothing but old books and monuments. I do all the business of the estate and it is getting too much for me now—too much responsibility. This selling off the property—when is it going to end? What on earth is going to happen to us all?"

Charles would have been less than human if he had been indifferent to what was happening in his back showroom amongst the Jacobean oak. He was too keenly interested in his friend and too aware of what an important interview this was to be able to settle down to any kind of work. He lounged about, talking to Pring and pretending to study sales catalogues, only to throw them down in disgust when he realised that not a word of what he read was penetrating into his brain.

The interview was so prolonged that at last Charles made up his mind that it must have terminated without his knowledge. He tiptoed to the door and peered in to see if she had gone.

In spite of his caution Francis saw him and called out to him to come in.

"Lady Hume would like to—to ask you about that er—er—oak cupboard. This is my friend, Charles Dennistoun," he added deferentially.

Her Ladyship acknowledged the introduction with a little bow, and then she put up her lorgnettes and surveyed the cupboard gravely.

"I have been admiring it very much," she said untruthfully, "but unfortunately it is too large to go into the corner for which I require it. Could you copy it for me in a smaller size?"

"Of course the colour would not be quite the same," Charles said, immediately all eagerness at the prospect of a commission. "You understand that it is impossible to get that same rich deep brown—only age can accomplish that, and two centuries of polishing. The date of this cupboard is 1725. I could make you a tolerable imitation of it however, if that is what you would like."

Lady Hume agreed to this and Pring was sent for to take the measurements of the projected cupboard. He came at once, hopping along on his crutch, all eagerness for a job which would tax his craftsmanship.

"I want it to fit in under the stairs," said Lady Hume. "It

must be some inches lower than the original."

"If you require it for the east corner of the 'all, madame, it must not be more than five feet 'igh," Pring said, his aitches flying all ways in his excitement.

"What do you know of the east corner of the hall at Eaglefold?" asked the lady in surprise.

Pring blushed. His chief recollection of it was that it was dark and that he had kissed Liza there for the first time but he could hardly explain this to Lady Hume.

"I think he was footman at Eaglefold for a time," Francis said, rescuing him from his embarrassment, which was evident though inexplicable.

"Were you?" she asked.

"Yes, madame, I was under-footman at Eaglefold when I was a lad."

She was interested at once. "Let me see if I can remember, your name is—"

"Pring, madame."

"Pring, yes, and you married one of the housemaids—though how I remember that I'm sure I don't know, for it is years ago—"

"Thirty years," Pring said.

"Ah, thirty years ago." She paused then, thinking no doubt of other things more vital to herself which had happened at Eaglefold thirty years ago. In spite of these old tragedies which filled her heart and mind (or perhaps because of them) she could remember the marriage of a footman and a housemaid. She looked up at Pring and smiled.

"I'm glad I remembered. Is your wife—"

"She's 'ere madame," Pring said eagerly. "If you would come upstairs an' see 'er for a minute—or I could fetch 'er down."

"Yes, of course I'll come," was the reply and for a second time the cupboard made way for a human interest.

Lady Hume rose and motioned Pring to lead the way and together the two disappeared up the stairs to visit Liza in her shining kitchen.

Charles wrung his hands in mock distress.

"You and Pring will ruin me between you," he said to Francis.

"Yes, it's a bit hard on you, I own," Francis replied with a smile.

CHAPTER 9
The Knight in Disguise

ENOUGH HAS BEEN said of Lady Hume to show that she was not one to let the grass grow under her feet. The morning after her visit to the shop she descended upon the family lawyers, Messrs. Dutton and Tod, and stirred that worthy and long-established firm into reluctant activity. She also paid a visit to a high official in the Police Force and received a promise from him that he would do what he could to elucidate the mystery of her son's marriage.

Having put in motion such forces as she possessed, Lady Hume decided to have lunch with Francis Hood. It would be rather a joke to take him to the Berkeley which was a favourite haunt of her sister-in-law, Mrs. Digby Hume. Of course Mrs. Digby might not be there, but then again she might and her face when she saw Francis Hood would be well worth seeing.

Full of her amiable designs, Lady Hume took a taxi to the hospital where Francis was spending the morning and sent in a message asking him to come out and speak to her for a moment.

In answer to Lady Hume's urgent message, Francis came out to speak to her. He was bare-headed and the spring sunshine found bronze lights in his hair. Nothing of this was lost on Lady Hume.

"Come and have lunch with me," she said in the tone of

one whose invitations are not often refused.

Francis hesitated a minute.

"Is it wise?" he said in a low voice.

"Wise!" cried Lady Hume. "I've never been wise in my life and it's too late to start now! If you are jealous of your reputation—"

"I am very jealous of it," he replied quickly.

The two determined people glared at each other for a few seconds and then the woman laughed.

"Dear God, you are like your father!" she said softly.

Francis frowned at that. It remained to be proved whether his father was a desirable person to resemble, but he stilled the quick retort that sprang to his lips and explained to Lady Hume the reason for his hesitation in accepting her invitation.

"If I am really so like—like your son," he said quite gently, "it may cause awkward questions to be asked. Supposing one of your friends sees you with me—how will you explain me?"

"I will introduce you as my grandson," she replied impulsively.

"You will do no such thing!" cried Francis. "I will not be made the laughing stock of London. It would be different if you had proofs—"

"I don't need proofs," she interrupted rather pitifully.

Francis saw her lips tremble and his heart failed him; it was a very tender heart where women were concerned. Lady Hume was so determined to have her way that she did not, or would not, see the difficulties which beset her path. It was essential to come to some sort of understanding with her, yet he could not do that here in the street with the taxi-driver standing a few yards away like a graven image. Francis had not been brought up in the belief that servants can neither see nor hear. Besides, it was time that Lady Hume had some lunch, for it was now nearly 2 o'clock.

"I will get my hat," he said briefly.

As they drove off together, Francis tried to explain to his companion that they would land themselves in endless trouble if they proceeded further in the matter without strong proofs.

"I see what you mean," she said at last, "and I daresay you are right for I am only a foolish old woman after all, but there is method in my madness. Ernest is very frail, he will never marry, and my nephew, the present heir, is a hateful creature. If anything were to happen to Ernest—" she paused for a moment and then continued. "You see I am being quite frank with you. Mr. Dutton advised me not to take you into my confidence, but then he hasn't seen you. I wish I could make you understand what it would mean to me to see the place go to William Hume, to see him installed at Eaglefold with his foolish chattering wife. Of course I may not survive Ernest—God grant that I may not do so—but even if I were dead and buried I think these old bones would turn in their grave if that were to happen. It is hard to have borne two sons and —and—"

Her voice quivered with the intensity of her feelings and she lay back in the corner of the car and closed her eyes.

"You are feeling faint," said Francis anxiously.

"Open the window and tell him to drive round the Park," she whispered.

Francis obeyed, and the car turned in at the big gates and proceeded smoothly round the Park. The trees were now in bud and the grass looked very green and fresh. Two men were engaged in painting the seats and the smell of paint came in a strong whiff as they passed. Francis noticed these things subconsciously for his conscious mind was busy with the problem which Lady Hume had set him. He envisaged the possibility, nay the probability, of his rights being proved. If Lady Hume intended to prosecute her search with all the energy and influence she possessed it was more than likely that she would succeed in proving the legitimacy of his birth. (Despite his cynicism he had never really doubted the fact of his parents' marriage.) Supposing that the search was successful, what then? Instead of going through life a nameless adventurer, a stranger within the gates, having neither kith nor kin to care for, Francis would wake up one morning to find himself heir to an old name and estate.

From what Lady Hume had said Francis realised that the Humes were in financial difficulties like so many old families with large estates to maintain but this did not seem vital to him. He had spoken truly when he had said that his ambition was to be a surgeon. What really mattered to Francis was the fact that his father, though not altogether above reproach, came of good stock. Lady Hume herself was brave and true—what more could one ask? Already he loved her almost as much as he might have done if he had been brought up beneath her care in the orthodox way. She was so sincere that it was easy to know her, and there was something more that drew him to her, it was perhaps the bond of kinship.

Francis leaned over and took one of her hands in a firm clasp. She clung to it suddenly, with amazing strength.

"Oh help me, Francis Hood," she whispered. "I am so old and tired, and so—lonely."

"I will help you," he said gently. "We will discuss what must be done, but first I am going to give you some lunch."

"Tell him to go to the Berkeley," said Lady Hume grimly.

The luncheon hour was nearly over and the beautiful room was emptying rapidly. Francis chose a quiet table and ordered lunch to be brought immediately. He had been a little anxious as to whether his companion would be strong enough to walk, she looked so utterly worn out and so white and ill, but he need not have feared. When the car stopped she gathered herself together and walked into the big room with the air of a duchess—nobody could have guessed what the effort cost her.

Francis ordered brandy and made her sip it and she did as she was told, taking a kind of pride in his masterfulness. Presently a little colour came into her cheeks and she began to talk to him about Eaglefold.

"It stands quite near the river," she told him, "so that when the spate comes I hear it thundering below my windows. There is a great beech tree on the lawn where we have tea when it is warm enough. Behind the house the hills rise one behind the other, clad with pines, and, above the pines, heather. The boys loved the shooting—there is nobody to enjoy it now so we let it every year to Americans. You are fond of shooting, Francis?"

"I have never shot anything," he confessed, and smiled at her amazement. "My up-bringing was strictly utilitarian."

"You could learn," she told him.

"I'm afraid it does not appeal to me," he replied. "I don't want you to think me a prig—it isn't that—but when you have been studying for years how to heal and mend, it goes against your instinct to maim and kill birds and animals. I know I am not logical because I eat them when other people kill them for me—"

"You are honest anyway," said Lady Hume smiling with amusement. "You would not be a Hume if you were not."

They had finished their lunch by this time and Francis asked permission to light a cigarette. The dining room was empty save for a party of three people—two women and a man—who seemed to be taking an inordinate interest in Lady Hume and her escort. The older woman was tall and of a commanding appearance, her features were well formed and her white hair contrasted pleasantly with her pink and white complexion, but in spite of these attributes there was something repulsive about her. Perhaps it was the immobility of her face which had as little expression as a carved image.

The medusa-like stare of this woman affected Francis

most unpleasantly and at last he leaned forward and told his companion that they were being observed.

The latter looked through her lorgnettes and then laughed with uncontrollable merriment.

"It is Ethel," she said when she could speak. "I hoped we might see her. She is wondering who the devil you are —only of course Ethel is much too ladylike to have anything to do with the devil. Ethel Hume," she explained, seeing her companion's puzzled face. "The mother of the delectable William. Why, there is William himself with his mother and, to complete the party, his wife Dora. We are in luck—"

"Don't do anything—"

"Foolish," put in Lady Hume smiling. "Wasn't that what you were going to say? Very well, I promise not to introduce you to Ethel as my grandson, if that is what you mean. We will make sure first."

She had no time to say more for the Humes were coming over to speak to her. Francis literally trembled, for he had had experience of his companion's wit and he had no confidence in her discretion.

"Dear Louisa," said Mrs. Digby Hume as she shook hands languidly with her sister-in-law. "It is so delightful to see you looking so well."

"Charming of you," replied the old lady grimly. "Allow me to introduce a young friend of mine, Ethel. Francis, this is Mrs. Digby Hume, Mr. William Hume, Mrs. William Hume."

She had deliberately left out her young friend's name for she had promised not to introduce him as her grandson and she could not bring herself to introduce him as Francis Hood. That the Humes were aware of this omission was evident from their puzzled expressions and from the half-hearted way in which they returned Francis' bow.

Francis looked with some interest at this hateful William whom he was perhaps going to dispossess of an inheritance and as he looked at him any scruples which he may have had vanished into thin air. The man was so obviously a cad. Who but a cad would wear his hair waved and his moustache waxed into long thin wires? Like all the Humes he was tall and broad-shouldered with flat hips and long legs but in his features he resembled his mother and his colouring was blonde. The young men took stock of each other silently while their elders maintained a limping conversation. If Francis had retained any doubts as to his resemblance to Lady Hume's sons they would have been resolved by Ethel Hume's demeanour. She could not take her eyes off him, they were fixed upon him with a ludicrously bewildered stare. Her face, usually so devoid of expression, seemed to have been re-carved by a master hand to represent the personification of Consternation. The poor lady could scarcely answer her sister-in-law's sly remarks, so upset was she at this nameless apparition which appeared before her.

"I'm afraid I did not hear your name," said William Hume after a short pause.

"Francis Hood," was the immediate reply.

"Ah, one of the Hoods of Barlington, I suppose."

"Not at all," put in Lady Hume quickly. "My young friend can claim affinity with the famous Robin Hood of Sherwood Forest. Dora, you were last at school, no doubt you will remember all about him."

Dora blushed, she was never very sure of William's aunt. Sometimes she had an uncomfortable feeling that the old lady was making fun of her.

"Oh yes, I remember," she said with a lisp. "How romantic! But I always thought that Robin Hood was an assumed name—"

"Why, how clever of you Dora!" Lady Hume cried.

"He was also known as Locksley and Diccon Split the Wand," continued Dora, anxious to display her knowledge and encouraged by Lady Hume's admiration of her erudition, "but really and truly he was a knight in disguise and the scion of a noble house. And, when King Richard returned from the Holy Land, he restored him to his rightful position and gave him back his lands."

"Dear me! That is most interesting, Dora. Let us hope, Francis, that some equally romantic fortune is in store for *you.*" And so saying, the old lady rose, and gathering up her furs she sailed out of the dining-room, followed by Francis who was half amused and half annoyed at what had occurred.

Mrs. Digby Hume sank into a chair with a gasp of dismay.

"William! Dora!" she cried. "Who is that man? Who can he be? Can the dead rise to steal the inheritance of the living? Can Edward have had some secret entanglement and this man be the offspring? Edward never seemed to care for women—Oh, it is enough to make one weep to see the way this dreadful creature has foisted himself upon Louisa—"

"What makes you think that red-haired feller is a son of my cousin?" asked William, gathering the drift of his mother's lamentations with some difficulty.

"Can you ask that?" she cried. "But I was forgetting, you are too young to remember Louisa's sons as I do. Take my word for it, that is Edward's son—whether he is legitimate or not it is our business to discover."

"Don't let that worry you," said William sarcastically. "If he is a legitimate son of Edward's we shall soon hear *all* about it. Aunt Louisa is not likely to hush it up to spare our feelings. Today when she was makin' game of Dora her eye was as full of devilry as a vicious old mare's—"

"To be fore-warned is to be fore-armed," said Mrs. Hume sententiously. "I shall go and see my lawyer this afternoon."

"Much good that will do us, you old fool," mumbled her dutiful son as he followed her out of the hotel.

CHAPTER 10
"Porty"

THE NEXT FEW DAYS passed like a dream for Francis Hood. Lady Hume had put in motion all the forces that she possessed, and the result was amazing. Francis was interviewed by emissaries from Scotland Yard who plied him with questions until his brain reeled. No smallest recollection of his early days seemed too insignificant to be noted down in large black notebooks. Under this goad Francis was able dimly to remember an old nurse who had been with him when he was a child and who had been known to him by the name of "Porty". He had recollections of a stiffly starched white apron, cold and shiny to the touch and of a large gold brooch with a plait of black hair in it. All this and more went down in the notebooks to be referred to if necessary.

Charles was far more excited over the quest than Francis himself. He insisted that Francis should make the shop his headquarters for he thoroughly enjoyed the bustle of people coming and going and the incessant ringing of the telephone bell. He liked Lady Hume and had quite made up his mind that she was Francis' Grandmother. When the old lady was feeling dispirited she made a point of visiting the shop and having a talk with its owner. Charles was always ready to tell her what she wanted to hear and to sing the praises of his friend from morning to night.

One afternoon Francis came in to find the strange pair having tea together in Charles' sitting room. There was an air of suppressed excitement about them which communicated itself to Francis directly he entered the room.

"Come awa' in, Maister Hume and tak' yer tea," cried Charles gaily.

"What's this?" he wanted to know, looking from one to the other. "Has something been found?"

Lady Hume nodded, her voice trembled a little as she said, "They have found Mrs. Porter."

To understand the workings of Scotland Yard and their enormous resources would take a book to itself, and the finding of Mrs. Porter from the slight description which Francis was able to afford was always a mystery to the Humes and will ever remain so. Moles do their work underground and only the mounds thrown up from their tunnels disclose their activities to the farmer and so it is with the secret workings of Scotland Yard. Strange looking individuals in seedy tweeds with caps pulled well down on their foreheads had appeared at the shop from time to time and startled Pring and Liza by asking in mysterious accents for Francis Hood. These men belonged to the mole brigade of the Yard, though unlike moles they were by no means blind. How they worked nobody knew but themselves and their immediate chief. Suffice to say that they had strange sources from which they drew their information and their methods were not strictly official.

It was from this subterranean source that the solution of the mystery came. The old nurse "Porty" who had been with Francis when his mother died had been run to earth.

"Have you seen her?" Francis asked, looking at Lady Hume as he spoke.

"I sent Mr. Dutton," she replied. "I wanted to go but he said it would be better not. He is to come here—after."

"Of course she may not know—anything," Francis said.

They had not been waiting long when Mr. Dutton appeared. Francis, who had not seen the lawyer before, observed him with no little interest. He saw a short stout man with curly grey hair and a red face. Mr. Dutton looked more like a prosperous farmer than a lawyer.

It was obvious that the little man had important news to impart, he seemed absolutely bubbling with excitement, his small eyes twinkled with it, and he could scarcely wait until the introductions were over before plunging into his story.

"Mrs. Porter's information is most valuable," he said, addressing himself to Lady Hume. "It should go far to prove the validity of Mr. Hood's claim."

"I make no claim," said Francis firmly. "I must have this point clearly understood before we go any further. I have been nobody for so long that I am quite used to it. I won't say that I don't want to know who I am because that would be foolish and untrue but I make no claim to be anybody, and I would prefer to remain independent than for there to be any dubiety about my position."

"Need we go into that?" asked Lady Hume, who was anxious to hear what Dutton had to say.

"Yes we must," replied Francis.

Mr. Dutton was looking at him with a strange

expression on his round cheerful face.

"There is little dubiety about your position, young man," he said slowly. "Anyone who knew Edward Hume from the time he was a boy, as I did, would not need further proof of your paternity than your amazing likeness to him—"

"And he's every bit as pig-headed," added the old lady with a chuckle.

They all laughed at that.

"Come now," said Mr. Dutton. "You are all anxious to hear about Mrs. Porter. I took a bus out to Hampstead Heath where the good lady has a small house, very clean and comfortable. At first she was a little difficult but I was able to convince her that by telling me all she knew and answering my questions she might be able to right a wrong and make several people happy. Once this little difficulty was settled my troubles were over, she sat down and told me all she knew, glad in a way to get the secret told. Perhaps it would be too strong to say that it weighed on her mind—" He paused for a moment and then continued—"About thirty-four years ago Mrs. Porter was engaged as a sort of cook housekeeper by a young couple who lived at Hampstead Heath. They called themselves Hood, but Mrs. Porter soon discovered that it was an assumed name. She also saw through the thin pretence of Mr. Hood's business which kept him away from his pretty little wife for such long periods at a time. Before very long she used the privilege of an older woman—more of a friend than a servant to the lone young wife—and taxed her young mistress with being no better than she should be. Whereupon the irate lady produced marriage lines which proved that Edward Cameron Hume had married Frances Edwina Hood on a certain date at the Parish of Holborn, London. You will understand that Mrs. Porter gave me this information in a diffuse form, partly a narrative and partly in reply to my questions. I am condensing it for you in the desire to be as brief as possible and to allay your natural anxiety."

"Thank you," Lady Hume said.

"After this revelation, made in the heat of the moment," continued Mr. Dutton, "the young bride began to get frightened and she made Mrs. Porter promise not to reveal the information. Mrs. Edward Hume (as we must now call her) was afraid that her husband's people would be angry with her for marrying their son, and she also feared that her child, shortly to be born, would be taken from her and brought up in the Catholic faith. She herself was a Methodist—something of a fanatic on the subject as far as I can make out. In view of Mrs. Hume's excitable state and her interesting condition, Mrs. Porter was obliged to consent. She was evidently very fond of her young mistress who was a pretty creature—"

"She was," said Lady Hume, and added on seeing Mr. Dutton's surprise, "I have a miniature of her."

"Soon after this," continued the lawyer, "a son was born, and was christened Francis Hood after his mother. Mrs. Porter now added the duties of a nurse to her other activities and the small household went on as before until the black day when, as we know, Edward Hume was killed by a fall from his horse. The shock nearly ended his wife's life, but Mrs. Porter nursed her through the long illness that followed. After some months, the widow with her small son and faithful friend moved to a small flat in London."

"Why did she not come forward then, when I was searching the whole world for my daughter-in-law?" whispered Lady Hume brokenly.

"She was determined to hide from her husband's people. The mere mention of them excited her so terribly that Mrs. Porter feared that she would lose her reason entirely. They remained in London until Mrs. Edward's death and then Mrs. Porter and the boy Francis went to Devonshire."

"She did not stay there long," Francis said. "She and Uncle did not hit it off. I remember the day she left and how lost I felt without her. She seemed the last link with mother—Poor Porty, how she cried when she went away!"

"I think that proves it," said Mr. Dutton with a self-satisfied air.

"Francis!" cried Lady Hume. "You won't hold out now—you—you—"

Francis bent down and took her two hands in his, holding them tightly.

"My dear," he said rather incoherently. "It was only that it seemed too good to be true. You know I'm glad —terribly glad."

Mr. Dutton blew his nose and followed Charles out of the room leaving Lady Hume and her newly-found grandson together.

There was a customer waiting in the shop to speak to Charles so Mr. Dutton was left to his own devices. He had decided to wait as there were several important points to be settled before further steps could be taken. It was unfortunate that the lawyer had no interest in old furniture for he had a long while to wait and the time passed very slowly. Pring provided him with a catalogue of a forthcoming sale at Christie's and, having done his best for Dutton's entertainment, returned to his lathe and settled down to work.

After a cursory glance at the catalogue, Mr. Dutton put it down and wandered to the window, but Trump Street provided little better in the way of entertainment. A few message boys dawdled along, basket on arm or hung on the railings chaffing the servant girls in the areas. A couple of stray dogs chased each other until they were tired. An occasional taxi rolled past, avoiding the busier streets so as not to get into a block.

At last when Mr. Dutton had reached the limit of his patience, he heard steps on the stair and Lady Hume came in, leaning on her grandson's arm. She looked very frail and white but there was a glad light in her eyes.

"I did not know that you were waiting," she cried in surprise.

"I would like a few words with Mr. Hume," replied the lawyer in a business-like manner.

It was a moment before Francis realised what he meant, it seemed so strange to be called Hume,

"I must see Lady Hume back to the hotel first," Francis said.

"You'll do no such thing," the old lady replied tartly. "I am perfectly able to go alone, or Mr. Dennistoun can take me. Don't worry Francis with business tonight," she added to Mr. Dutton.

Charles was only too pleased to act as her escort, he had visions of shooting on the moors which appealed to him vastly—and besides he really liked Lady Hume and was amused at her wit.

They went off together in high humour.

"Now sir," said Mr. Dutton. "If you can spare me a few moments it will be to our mutual advantage."

Francis eyed the man with interest. He sat down on the corner of a table and offered Mr. Dutton a cigarette.

"Well, Lord Hume," said the lawyer when he had lit up. "I hope you are as strong as you look for you've got some work before you."

Francis felt as if he were dreaming.

"You seem to have—accepted me very easily," he said, a trifle incoherently.

For a moment Mr. Dutton was embarrassed, then he replied, "If you could only see yourself—"

"You go entirely upon my resemblance to the Humes?"

"It isn't only outward resemblance," the lawyer said, trying to justify himself. "You are—I can only describe it by using the expression "a chip off the block," and yet methinks the chip is bigger than the block. There is something about you that Edward lacked—a strength, a purpose in life. Edward was an idle young man, as an army officer could be in those days. He cared for nothing but hunting and shooting. Although he was a big man he was always in the first flight—there was plenty of money in those days, plenty of money and he mounted himself well. He was a fine shot too, a fine shot. Herbert was more studious, he cared for the estate and was a good son, but Edward was the favourite."

"I have a cousin, haven't I?" Francis asked, a trifle whimsically. He still felt as if the whole thing were a dream from which he might awake at any moment.

Mr. Dutton smiled. "You have a cousin, the present owner of the property. He is Herbert's son. I think you will like him."

"Does he manage the estate."

"Nominally he does, but he is a delicate man, practically a cripple and the place is really run by Lady Hume. Now, nobody admires that lady more than I do, but she is getting old and things are sliding. I am hoping that you will be able to do something. Quite frankly the estate is in a bad way, farms have been sold and others mortgaged. We need a strong hand."

Francis laughed. "All that I know about land would fit into the shell of a walnut."

"You can learn," replied Mr. Dutton comfortably.

CHAPTER 11
Welcome Home

A WEEK LATER Francis boarded the Scotch express *en route* for Eaglefold. He had induced Sir Addison to give him three weeks holiday without much difficulty. As a matter of fact Francis had become such a valuable assistant that his chief was anxious at all costs to retain his services. Francis had no intention of sacrificing his career as a surgeon, he was too deeply interested in it for that, but he had promised Mr. Dutton to take an interest in the estate of Eaglefold and to do what he could to unravel the tangle of affairs, and he felt that he had enough energy for both.

The last week had proved beyond doubt that Francis was the legitimate heir to the estate, the records of the marriage had been found and an interview with Mrs. Porter had put the seal on the facts. She was the same "Porty" even to the starched apron and the gold brooch. She declared that she would have known Francis anywhere.

Francis settled himself comfortably in the corner of a Third Class carriage and prepared to enjoy the journey. He was filled with excitement at the prospect of "going home". It would be pleasant to see Lady Hume again. She had returned to Eaglefold last week to explain matters to Ernest—Francis had missed her.

To complete his satisfaction a friendly letter from his

cousin had arrived that very morning assuring him of a hearty welcome at his father's home. Everything was *couleur de rose*—but stay, there was one thing which had not come right. In all the excitement of the past weeks Emily had not been far from Francis' thoughts. Even the knowledge that she was soon to be the wife of another man did not dim her image. The stigma of his namelessness was gone and he felt nearer to her—this barrier was down. If this had been her objection to him he did not blame her, for he himself had feared the tricks of heredity. What wonder that Emily had hesitated to link herself for life to the unknown. If this had been her objection to him it was now gone and he was at liberty to approach her again. But was it?

"She loved me—I am sure she loved me," Francis said to himself. "And if I know anything of Emily, she is not fickle." How then was he to account for this new lover of hers, this Sir Joseph Leate who was so suitable in every way?

It was all such a tangle, he could not see his way through it, try as he would.

The drumming of the wheels of the train kept pace with his thoughts, London was left behind and the country, smiling in its green beauty spread itself before him. Francis knew that it was a fine hunting country; for the first time he deliberately tried to realise the personality of the father who had loved hunting and followed it even to his death. It had seemed a poor kind of life to Francis, a purposeless kind of death, but now he was not so sure. To own a horse, to feel the living creature pulsing between one's knees. Francis had never even owned a dog, and now—

"It's a fine country, sir."

Francis looked up and met a pair of twinkling grey eyes. They belonged to a thin brown-faced man, the only other occupant of the compartment.

"A fine hunting country," Francis said impulsively, putting his thoughts into words.

"Hunting is a fine sport," said the man with the brown face. "I've been all over the world and I still find an English fox-hunt one of the best sports going. Have you done much of it yourself sir, may I ask?"

"Never," Francis replied.

"Ah. You take my tip and have a run with one of these Shire packs. There's something fascinating about it— builds men, too, of the right English breed."

They said no more but the mere fact of voicing his thought made it more real to Francis, he began to feel definitely that he belonged. Belonged to Britain. His ancestors had owned their small part of her for generations.

It was late when at last he arrived at Eaglefold, the soft Scottish twilight lay like a blessing upon the countryside. Francis could feel his heart thumping against his ribs as he stepped out on to the little grey platform and handed his bag to the solitary porter. The air was clear and thin, it went to his head like wine and filled him with a queer novel feeling of exhilaration.

It was evident that the story of his coming had been circulated in the village. The stationmaster came out of his office to have a look at Francis and to wish him a fine evening and two men in a signal box were hanging out of the windows to get a glimpse of the new heir.

Lady Hume had come to the station to meet him. She was waiting for him, seated very upright in an old Renault which had seen its best days. To Francis there was something pathetic about the old car, it spoke of bygone glories now departed. He felt a dozen pairs of eyes were upon him as he crossed the station yard.

"Welcome home, dear boy," said Lady Hume, leaning forward and giving him her hands.

Francis never knew what answer he made to the greeting—it had moved him to the depths of his being. The next thing he was conscious of was the swift motion of the car as it rolled powerfully along the narrow road. They passed through a small clean village with bright gardens and then through country lanes towards the hills. Presently Lady Hume called to the chauffeur to stop and pointing westward she showed Francis the first glimpse of his new home.

Eaglefold Castle had been built in the 18th century, it was a compact building of grey stone with a tower at each corner. The roof was of blue slate, thoroughly weathered by the winter snows. A fold in the sloping hills cradled the old place, pine woods sheltered it on one side from the prevailing wind, a burn half lost in a deep corrie crooned Eaglefold to sleep.

Francis looked at it for a long time and his heart swelled within him, it seemed in some mysterious way familiar to him and already dear.

Lady Hume, watching his face, was satisfied with what she found there. She lay back with a little sigh of relief and did not disturb him.

Nearer acquaintance with Eaglefold Castle served to deepen the feeling of familiarity rather than to destroy it. The big square hall panelled in oak with a few faded rugs upon its stone floor, the wide staircase leading to a gallery from which the bedrooms opened, all seemed to have played a large part in Francis' life at some un-remembered period. It was all as it should be; he would not have altered a stone in the thick walls. Dim portraits of dead and gone Humes looked down from the walls interspersed with strange weapons and trophies of the chase.

Ernest was waiting in the hall to receive his new cousin. He came forward with a friendly greeting and the two shook hands heartily.

Francis saw a tall thin man with grey hair and a face which had borne suffering nobly. He looked older than his years but his hand clasp was virile as that of a young man. Several old retainers came forward eagerly and Francis shook hands with them all; he was uplifted by the feeling that they had accepted him so naturally and cordially as one of the family.

"There's no doubt about who you are, sir," said the old butler, looking up at the red-haired man with something like affection in his eyes.

Ernest laughed. "I expect my cousin is tired of hearing that," he said in a deep soft voice.

Francis shook his head. "You don't know how splendid

it is to feel that I belong—somewhere," he said a trifle incoherently.

They went into the library together, followed by their grandmother.

CHAPTER 12
Choosing Loneliness

SUMMER came to Longmeadows bringing little change to the inmates of the small house. Things drifted quietly. Josephine grew and waxed fat in the soft Devon air; she lay out most of the day in the golden sunshine and gurgled with sheer happiness. Her chief pleasure consisted of her meals and her warm bath in which there floated a profusion of ducks and green frogs and gold fish. Her troubles were few and soon comforted.

Emily was writing hard, she rode with Sir Joseph and walked with Helen or sat in the garden and played with the baby. It was one of those calm periods which come amidst the storms of life and have a fictitious aspect of permanency.

Where a younger man would have been impatient and anxious to put his fate to the test, Sir Joseph was content to wait, taking the good things given him by the gods without asking for more. He saw Emily most days, and filled the remainder of his time with his usual quiet country occupations.

Helen worked in her garden amongst the flowers—she too was happy, for her house and her heart were full of those she loved. It seemed to her that Emily and Sir Joseph were drifting towards each other almost unconsciously. Perhaps that was the best way for love to come, surely it made for permanency. If there was no young rapture about their relations with each other, there was a quiet sound friendship befitting sensible folk.

How much longer this state of affairs might have lasted, and what it would have led to, it is difficult to say had not the gods of chance decided to take a hand in the game.

One afternoon, when Sir Joseph rode over to Longmeadows he found the little household in an unusual state of confusion. Kitty met him at the door with a troubled face.

"Oh, sir, Miss Dennistoun is going north tonight. Her father is ill."

"Going north—tonight," repeated Sir Joseph stupidly. He felt as if a cold hand had touched his heart. Life without Emily, whole days without seeing her, without even the hope of seeing her tomorrow!

"May I see Miss Dennistoun for a few minutes?" he asked quietly.

Kitty nodded.

"I will tell her that you are here, sir," she said and flitted away to find her mistress.

It was Helen Roe that came to him first and found him striding up and down the little morning-room more like a young lover of twenty-five than a sixty year old baronet.

"Is this necessary, Helen?" he asked, turning a face to her which was full of trouble and bewilderment.

"I'm afraid it is," she replied. "Emily being Emily I see no way out of it."

"What do you mean? The man practically turned her out of his house, didn't he?"

"Practically," she admitted.

"Then why need she return?"

"He's ill you see—it would be just like him to die, he has a genius for doing uncomfortable things."

"Surely that is his own affair," the words were rapped out in a manner quite unlike Sir Joseph's usual suave tones.

Helen could hardly help smiling, although she, too, was distressed at this sudden breaking up of their peaceful time.

"Not entirely," she said thoughtfully. "You see if Mr. Dennistoun took it into his head to die and Emily had not gone to him, he would remain a shadow on her life for always. A shadow which would increase in pathos. Emily, being Emily, would immediately forget all his faults, which are many, and canonise his virtues which are few. I'm afraid there is no way out of it, my friend."

"Emily is determined upon it?" he asked.

"Absolutely. She is a saint with a duty complex and I know of no more obstinate breed."

"Helen, I can't bear it."

Helen looked at him pitifully.

"It's hateful," she said, "but perhaps she will come back —*if you ask her.*"

They looked at each other in a significant silence.

"Perhaps," he said at last. "And yet—I don't know. She has always been perfect to me, perfect in friendliness, but she has never—nothing she has ever said or done has encouraged me to hope for more. I would rather have been sure, but I can't let her go—like this."

"I will send her to you," Helen said. "She is upstairs packing."

Emily did not keep him waiting, she came down at once. She was pale and quiet. It seemed to Sir Joseph's sensitive consciousness that she had already started on her journey—she had gone from him in spirit if not in flesh. It was not a propitious moment for his proposal but, as he had said to Helen, he could not let her go from him with his love undeclared.

"Emily, must you go?"

"I must," she replied, giving him her hand. "Dr. Dingwall has wired for me. Father had a stroke yesterday, he is very ill."

"Couldn't somebody else go?"

"There is no one else."

He was still holding her hand and she made no attempt to withdraw it from him. It seemed to Sir Joseph that she did not realise that he still held it—there was no electric current of sympathy between them.

"Emily, how am I to let you go? Do you know what you have become to me in these last months—"

Emily withdrew her hand then, and the soft colour rose in her cheeks.

"My dear", he continued gently, "if I let you go now—will you come back to me? For I find that I cannot get on without you. Come back to me and make me happy. I know that I am too old for you but I have so much love to give you, so much sympathy and understanding—surely that can make up for youth. Emily, don't punish me for being born too soon."

"Age doesn't matter," Emily replied. "It isn't that."

Sir Joseph had once more taken her hand and again she let him hold it, she was so sorry for him, so unhappy at having to hurt him. For now that the time had come, she knew definitely to the very fibre of her being that she could never marry any one except Francis Hood.

"Give me hope," he said, looking down at the small white hand which trembled in his. "I was wrong to speak to you now when you are troubled and so unhappy. It was selfish of me. I could not bear you to go away from me without asking you to come back. Emily dear, I don't ask for love if you can't give it to me, only your dear friendship and companionship for always. We could be so happy together—travel would be twice as interesting with you to share the pleasure, and home would be a real home, not merely a bare barrack as it is now."

Bright tears swam in Emily's eyes as she raised them to his. "I want your friendship," she said faintly, "but I can't marry you."

"Think of it," said Sir Joseph earnestly. "There is no hurry."

"It would not be kind of me to let you hope," Emily replied. "Oh my dear friend, how I hate to hurt you like this but it is no use—no use."

"Is there somebody else that you love?" he asked her gently.

Emily nodded.

"I shall never marry. I was in love once—with a dream. I have tried to put it all out of my heart but—I cannot—it is there for always."

"Dreams are insubstantial things," Sir Joseph told her. "We must live our lives. If it is only a dream-man that is keeping you away from me I shall go on hoping, Emily. Hoping that the dream will fade. Dear, I shall be very content if you will give me second best."

Emily could not speak. She felt that she was being foolish in refusing the love of this good kind man and yet her decision was unalterable. After a few moments Sir Joseph began to speak of other things—of her journey and the arrangements that she had made for her comfort, but there was an estrangement between them which neither could surmount and very soon he took his departure.

Helen Roe asked no questions. She knew from Emily's face that things had not gone well but she knew her Emily too thoroughly to think that she could put matters right by interference. She was disappointed, but not unduly, for she was optimistic by nature and she hoped that she might yet live to see Emily became the wife of her old friend.

"You will come back to me, won't you?" she said as she kissed Emily goodbye. "And meantime I shall have Kitty to talk to about you—and darling Josephine. You know Emily, that child is simply wonderful, I must tell you what she did this morning—"

CHAPTER 13
Laura Becomes Articulate

WHEN EMILY reached Borriston Hall she found none of the difficulties and unpleasantness which her imagination had conjured up. The servants were all delighted to see her again, and the two nurses welcomed her quite naturally. Mr. Dennistoun was too ill to worry with explanations. The stroke had affected his speech—he lay very quiet in his bed and only his eyes seemed alive. But Emily thought she saw a gleam of something like pleasure in these same restless eyes when she went into his room or sat beside his bed. She fell into her old place with an ease that surprised herself, it seemed as if she had never been away.

The only person who made any allusion to the cloud which had hung over her hasty departure from her home, was Dr. Dingwall. He had often puzzled over it and now he could not resist the temptation to ask Emily what had happened.

The doctor was such an old friend that Emily found it quite easy to tell him the truth about Kitty and the advent of Josephine.

"Well, well," said the doctor. "You could not turn the lassie away, I mind her well, a wiselike creature. Miss Roe will like having her, and the baby will be a great interest. You'll be staying here, Emily?"

"I suppose so," she said doubtfully. "Do you think—"

"Oh, he'll get better of this shock," said Dr. Dingwall cheerfully, "though I'm not saying he'll ever be himself again. Of course it was his own fault—the break with you and Charles—but these kind of excitements are the worst thing for a full blooded man of his age—the worst thing."

"You think that caused his—his illness."

Doctor Dingwall sensed the anxiety in Emily's voice and answered tactfully.

"Hoots and havers. If he'd not been working himself into a fury about that he'd have been working himself into a fury about some other thing. It's just the nature of the man. By the way Emily, I met a friend of yours in High Street this morning. She said she would be coming to see you—Mistress Murdoch."

"Laura!" cried Emily. A faint flush rose in her cheeks; she had not seen Laura since—since that night—

"Aye, that's the lady, Laura Murdoch. They live in a very uncomfortable house the other side of the bay. As a matter of fact they've just got back from London and she was giving me a very good account of Charles which pleased me not a little."

"Did she see Charles in London?"

"She did that—visited his shop and found it full of customers. You did a good deed there, Emily, setting him up in business. It's made a man of the lad."

"It was splendid being able to do it," Emily said, flushing at his praise which was all the sweeter because she knew it to be true. "I consider my money well invested."

"And so it is," he replied thoughtfully. "I have often thought that stocks and shares were soul-less things, I should like fine if my own small savings were invested in something I could see."

The doctor's words brought Laura vividly before Emily's eyes, and having nothing better to do, she set off that afternoon to walk to *La Boiselle*. It was a fine afternoon, not too hot, and a breeze from the sea ruffled through the bent grass till the silvery spikes glimmered in the sunlight. The sea was deeply blue and the small white waves danced joyfully on the shore.

At first Emily's heart was heavy, for the place reminded her too forcibly of Francis for her peace, but she tried to think of Charles and his happiness and in doing so managed to relegate her own sad thoughts to the background of her mind. The sea breeze and the swift motion of her walk helped her, so that by the time she arrived at the Murdochs' bungalow she felt tolerably cheerful.

The bell was still broken. It hung dejectedly from its nail but the sight which would have horrified Emily at Borriston Hall or at Longmeadows merely brought a little smile to her lips. She lifted the latch and went in quietly.

The studio was deserted save for a black kitten which walked across the floor and rubbed itself against Emily's foot. She picked it up and stood for a moment looking round her.

It was all so familiar—just as she remembered it, even to the dust on the gate-legged table and the thin sprinkling of blown sand on the polished floor. Then the kitchen door opened and Laura came out with a tea-tray in her hands.

"Emily!" she said happily.

She put the tray down and held out her hands.

Emily felt the same peaceful pleasure that Laura's presence always gave her, she was glad that she had come. They sat down on the window seat together and began to talk of all that had happened since their last meeting. It was very quiet and peaceful.

Francis' masterpiece still hung over the fireplace—the glade of trees with the golden sunshine glancing through the branches. Presently a little silence fell between these two who had usually so much to say to each other. Laura was seeking for words. It was obvious to her that Emily was not engaged to the man in Devonshire of whom Charles had spoken, surely then, it would not be wrong to put in a word for Francis. She would be doing no harm to anyone in mentioning his name.

"I suppose you have heard about Francis," she said at last.

"I saw about it in the papers," replied Emily, trying to speak naturally. "I am glad for his sake that he has found his relations."

"Does it make any difference—any difference to *you?*" asked Laura in a queer forced voice.

Emily looked at her friend in surprise.

"How could it make any difference to me?"

There was silence then for a moment, and then Laura took her courage in both hands.

"I thought—I thought perhaps that it troubled you, his lack of family. I thought that was why you sent him away."

It was out now, the secret was a secret no longer and the two friends were gazing at each other, half frightened at the revelation which was upon them. It was not necessary for Emily to say "I did not send him away," for Laura could read the truth in her sensitive face.

"Emily!" she cried, shaken for once out of her shyness and diffidence. "There has been some dreadful mistake—Oh, how can it have happened? Oh, my dear, if only I had not been such a coward, I could have put this right long ago."

"What do you mean?"

"Francis is breaking his heart for you."

"But I don't understand," Emily said, her voice husky with the emotion roused by Laura's words. "He was going away with Alice—didn't you know? Father found them at Pennybrigg Station and brought her home. And then the next day he went south with her—Mademoiselle Jacquot saw them—and he took her picture—took her picture with him. I couldn't understand it," Emily went on brokenly, "because he said he would explain everything and then—this happened."

Laura hid her face in her hands. She felt as if all the strength had ebbed out of her body leaving it limp and flaccid. Emily did not know. She had not seen the flirtation between Harry and Alice which had been so patent to everyone else. She was utterly in the dark as to what had occurred, and she, Laura, must enlighten her, however much it cost. Emily deserved the whole truth—what did it matter if the telling of it were pain.

Fortunately for them both, the crucial nature of the situation had startled Laura out of her self-consciousness. Words came to her who was usually wordless.

She began at the very beginning with the arrival of Alice at Port Andrew and Harry's infatuation for the pretty creature.

"Of course the painting of Alice's picture was just an excuse for—for other things. It was finished long before the dance. Harry is like that but—but he always comes back, he can't do without me, you see."

"Oh Laura, my dear! How blind I was! And yet I thought you looked tired and ill the night of the dance."

Emily rose and walked up and down the room, twisting her handkerchief, a puzzled frown on her brows.

"Then it was *Harry,*" she said. "But how was Francis at Pennybrigg? I was waiting for him on the sandhills—he had promised to meet me there."

"He went after them," Laura said. "I told him that they had gone and he put on his Burberry and ran all the way to the station. I don't know what he did or said—Francis never told me—but somehow he persuaded them not to —not to go—"

"I see," Emily said slowly. "That was why he could not come of course, but what happened then? Why didn't he come back and explain?"

"Sir Addison wired for him—the wire came while he was at the station, it was urgent, he simply had to go. You know what these big men are—frightfully easily offended."

"But the picture!" cried Emily. "He took her picture with him. Surely that was strange unless he was—was fond of her."

"I asked him to take it," Laura said in a low voice. She felt that, however painful it was, she was bound to tell Emily everything.

"You asked him to take it?"

"Yes, I simply could not bear to see it standing there on the easel after what had happened. I know it was foolish of me but—but she was so pretty. Harry had come back to me and I had forgiven him, I wanted to forget it all. I wanted nothing to remind us of her."

"So Francis took it."

"He didn't want it. He asked what he was to do with it and I told him to burn it. Perhaps he has done so, I don't know."

"Ivette Jacquot saw him off and she said that they went together and that he had said things to her—"

"Oh my dear!" cried Laura. "You can't go by what Ivette says! She and Francis were always sparring with each other. He was probably pulling her leg or she may have misunderstood him altogether. She often takes up things quite wrongly, for her knowledge of English is not very sound."

"Don't you think that Francis would have tried to see me that night—if he had cared?" Emily asked in a voice, which, despite all that she could do, trembled a little.

"He did," replied Laura. "He went over to Borriston Hall and met Mr. Dennistoun on the terrace. Your father was very angry and upset and would not listen to a word."

"Are you sure of that?"

"Quite sure. Francis came back very crestfallen. I have never seen him so depressed. He sat down after we had gone to bed and wrote to you. He was writing here all night sitting at that table, for I got up twice and the light was still on. He went out in the early morning and delivered the letter himself at Borriston Hall."

"I never got that letter," Emily said in a quiet small voice.

"Emily! and you thought—you thought he had gone with Alice. How you must have suffered!"

The sympathy was too much for Emily. She hid her face and the next moment Laura's arms were round her and she was weeping against that comfortable shoulder.

It was some little time before either of them spoke. Tears did not come easily to Emily and she found it difficult to control a storm which had been pent up for so long. Presently however, she found her voice enough to whisper,

"Tell me—all about—him."

When at last Emily tore herself away, it was very late; the sun was setting over the sea in a blaze of glory as she walked home across the sands.

Laura stood at the gate for a long time till the sunset faded and the light was withdrawn from the land. Only the sea retained its brightness and glimmered whitely in the gathering gloom.

Laura was puzzled. How was she to help those two

friends of hers, these two dear people whose lives had been separated by such an unfortunate series of misunderstandings. She was wise enough in the ways of the world (very wise in her quiet fashion) to see that the situation was difficult in the extreme.

On the one hand was Francis, convinced that Emily had received his letter and had refused to take the risk of tying herself to a nameless man. On the other was Emily waiting for him to come to her. So far it was simple, the complication was in the change of circumstances, *for Francis was no longer a nameless man.*

How to convince Francis beyond all doubt that his letter had miscarried? Here was the crux of the situation. Where could the letter have disappeared between the time when Francis had laid it on the hall table and Emily had descended from her room?

Laura racked her brains but could find no solution to the mystery. She herself had believed Emily's bare word, there had never been a doubt in her mind, but then she did not love Emily with that queer passion of man for woman. She could judge dispassionately and without prejudice. There must be no blundering now, for a blunder at this point might spoil everything and, at the very least leave a cloud the size of a man's hand upon two lives. Francis must be convinced that Emily had not received his letter. Not for one single moment must he imagine that his change of position had influenced her decision.

Laura knew that doubts, if once harboured in the mind, are apt to return at the wrong moment with their insidious whisperings—there must be no doubts. That night she lay awake making one plan after another and rejecting them all.

At breakfast Harry found her distrait and unsympathetic about his latest masterpiece.

"What *is* the matter with you?" he said at last.

"I didn't sleep well," she replied truthfully.

"Good Heavens, Laura don't *you* begin to have nerves."

She shook her head and began to put away the breakfast dishes.

"You are in a devil of a hurry, surely," Harry grumbled.

"I promised to go over to Emily this morning," she explained, smiling down at him. Harry was such a child, she loved him even when he was fractious and irritable. These two were well matched in spite of their apparent disparity in age and temperament. He needed a mother's tenderness, a mother's care and understanding, and a beneficent providence had given him Laura.

"Off you go then, I'll wash up," Harry said, his bad temper vanishing as swiftly and with as little reason as it had come. Laura stooped and kissed him, then she seized her hat and went out of the door putting it on.

"Bet you Emily isn't up yet," he called after her.

CHAPTER 14
Truth

LAURA WAITED for a few moments in the dull little morning room at Borriston Hall until her friend appeared. She had decided to offer to go and see Francis herself and tell him exactly what had happened. It seemed to Laura the only possible way out of the impasse. She stood by the window looking out on the formal walled garden and tried to make up sentences to say to Francis.

"Look here Francis, Emily never got that letter of yours—" No, that sounded too dogmatic. "Look here Francis, I was talking to Emily the other day—" Oh, it was hopeless! The tears had risen to her eyes and she was flicking them away when the door opened and Emily came in already dressed to go out, she had a navy blue coat and skirt of heavy silk and a small black straw hat. She looked very pretty, Laura noticed, her eyes were shining and her cheeks were faintly pink.

"How good of you to come!" she said with sincere affection in her tone.

"I've been thinking about you and Francis," said Laura. "I do want to put things right—"

Emily stopped her with a little gesture of negation.

"Laura," she said quickly, "I know you've been thinking how to help me. It is dear of you but nobody can do that."

"Don't you think I might go and see Francis and explain how all the misunderstandings have arisen?" Laura suggested.

"No, my dear. Thank you all the same."

"But surely there must be some way out of the tangle."

"There is," replied Emily with a nervous little laugh. "But it is so simple that at first I did not see it. Yesterday I could see *no* way out, but in the night, suddenly, it all seemed easy and clear."

"It seems very difficult to me."

"I know, and it did to me, too. We are too civilised, Laura, too bound by convention and false pride and—and fear. We have to go back if we are to find the right path, for the right path is always straight and very simple. We have to become as a little child."

Laura thought for a moment.

"Perhaps you are right," she said slowly. "But where is the straight path amongst all the tangles and lies? What would a child do, Emily?"

Emily answered her with shining eyes.

"A child would go straight to a person it loved and tell him all about it, never doubting that it would be believed, cherished—forgiven, if need be."

"And you—"

"I am going over to Eaglefold today."

Laura did not answer just at once, it seemed so cruel to damp that happiness which shone in Emily's eyes. Then she said gently,

"Emily, of course you are much cleverer than I am but have you thought what Francis may think? You see Francis was quite sure in his own mind that the reason you did not answer his letter was because you were afraid to face his unknown parentage. He was dreadfully morbid about it—perhaps because of his being a doctor."

"I have thought of all that," Emily replied, "and yesterday it seemed impossible to do anything. I made all sorts of plans, *schemes* to convey the information to Francis but they were all—unworthy, I rejected them all. There seemed nothing I could do. But now I realise that I was thinking of my pride and of my own importance—I was not thinking of—him."

"It is right to think of your pride."

"Sometimes it is," she allowed. "But in this case I should be wronging Francis if I supposed for a moment that he would not believe me, absolutely. I should be wronging myself if I adopted any scheme which was not quite straightforward. Truth is the strong thing and the truth is that I would have married Francis joyfully and proudly if his parents had been criminals. But Laura, my dear, there was no risk, his parents must have been—all right—or how could they have produced Francis?"

Laura nodded. It was her own theory which she had expounded to the red-haired man long ago on that night of the dinner party at Borriston Hall.

"You see, don't you Laura?" Emily continued. "It did not matter to me when he had no relations, so why should I pretend that the mere fact of his relations having turned up makes any difference? It doesn't—it hasn't changed my feelings for him and I should be doing him less than justice if I thought for a moment that it would change his —his feeling for me. Francis' birth is nothing to me—he, himself is everything—"

She stopped then, a trifle ashamed of her outburst and began to draw on her motoring gloves. Laura was half convinced by her friend's logic, but the meeting between these two still seemed to her fraught with danger.

"Let me go to Eaglefold and explain everything to Francis," she said again.

"Thank you, my dear," Emily said, "but there have been too many people between us already. We should never have misunderstood each other if we had met. I would rather have this out with him face to face. There is another reason," she added in a lower tone. "Another reason why I must see him unexpectedly, before he has time to think—to prepare—"

"You mean—"

"If he has changed," Emily said, "if he has changed to me, I shall know at once."

Laura said no more then, she followed her friend to the door where Mr. Dennistoun's long grey car was waiting with the chauffeur in attendance. She watched Emily get into the back seat and then quite suddenly she leaned on the side of the car and spoke softly so that the man should not hear.

"Are you sure that you are wise, dear Emily?"

Emily looked into her friend's eyes, they were very soft with love for her and misty with trouble.

"I am quite sure," she said. "You see I had a—a sort of vision in the night. It was not a dream, because I was wide awake at the time—"

That was all, there was no time for more, the car started forward and rolled off down the avenue. Emily turned and smiled at Laura.

The explanation though far from complete, was comforting, Laura walked back to *La Boiselle* with an easier mind. Although visions in the night were hardly in her line, she was too broadminded to deny them to her friends.

When they had cleared the small town and swung on to the broad main road, Emily leaned forward and spoke to the chauffeur.

"Duff, you looked it out on the map?"

"Yes, Miss. I make it about eighty miles as near as makes no odds. There's a hotel at Wymington where we can stop for lunch."

"Thank you," Emily said. She leaned back after that and gave her thoughts free rein. Was it possible that she would be seeing Francis again in a few hours time? She had made little of her fears and her anxieties when she spoke to Laura but they were very present in her mind, only her sheer strength of will was carrying her through, that, and the knowledge that she was fighting for her happiness, and for his.

When the car stopped at Wymington, she got out and went into the dining-room. It was very empty, and for this she felt thankful. It was almost impossible to eat but she made a pretence of doing so for the sake of appearances. Emily was so conventional that, whatever happened, she would not own, even to herself that she could eat no lunch. At a reasonable interval she reappeared on the doorstep and found the admirable Duff waiting for her with the car.

"Have you found out where it is?" she asked him.

"Yes, Miss, about five miles from here."

They left the high road and turned towards the hills. Heather, purple as Tyrian dye, clothed the countryside with its luxuriant growth. It even encroached upon the narrow carriageway and caught at the wheels as they rolled past. Here and there a dark splash of pine-woods or the flash of a silver burn varied the monotony.

It was so wild and beautiful that, despite her preoccupation, Emily was stirred, and the poet in her rose to the surface. She lay back with the hill breeze in her face and her thoughts found peace. It was so long since she had seen the hills. England was beautiful—a land of gardens and small, safe fields with their red and white cows and little snug cottages—but it was not soul-stirring like this.

" 'Mine own beloved land,' " Emily quoted softly.

The car swept over a high bridge and turned in at a tumbledown gateway. The drive, which led through a pinewood, was full of holes and deep ruts, some of which had been filled with raw metal. These evidences of neglect or poverty seemed rather pathetic to Emily, she had a sudden sense of personal shame. "Poor Eaglefold, you are ashamed of your rags," she said softly.

A tall man in an old Inverness Cloak was coming out of the front door as the car drove up. He raised his cap with a courtly gesture and asked if he could be of any assistance.

"I would like to see Mr. Francis Hume," replied Emily rather shyly.

The tall man smiled and in a moment it seemed that

Francis looked out of his eyes. And yet it was not exactly a likeness to Francis that she saw, it was more as if the same spirit dwelt in this man and looked out of his eyes. It was more than a resemblance of form—or rather it was not a resemblance of form at all for Ernest Hume had inherited his mother's features—it was a resemblance of spirit, of personality.

"Come in, won't you?" said the tall man in a friendly way which yet had a touch of old-fashioned courtesy and dignity. "I will send for Francis, he is up the glen with the dogs, I think."

Emily followed him into the house; he led her into the library which faced the garden. It was a pleasant room, shabby and comfortable, full of afternoon sunlight. Over the fire-place there hung a portrait of a young man in the uniform of a cavalry officer.

Emily gazed at it in amazement.

"It is Francis!"

"It is his father," replied Mr. Hume. He was watching Emily's sensitive face and an idea struck him.

"Would you care to walk up the glen and meet Francis?" he suggested. "You can't miss him because there is only the one path. I would offer to come with you but I am not a good walker—"

Emily jumped at the plan. She felt too restless to sit still and wait for Francis and she was anxious to see him alone. She *must* see him alone, it was unthinkable that there should be witnesses of their meeting. Mr. Hume's plan chimed with her mood. A few moments later she was walking quickly along the stony footpath which led in a zig-zag line to the hills.

Ernest Hume watched the sturdy yet graceful figure for a few moments without moving from the window, he was so absorbed that he did not hear his grandmother come into the room.

"Who was that?" she asked, putting her hand on his arm.

He turned to her with a smile. "Someone to see Francis."

"It looked like a lady."

"It is a lady."

"And you sent her up the glen by herself to look for him—"

"She will find him."

"Ernest, it was scarcely courteous. I should like to have seen her—"

"You will see her, Grandmother," Ernest replied. "You will see a great deal of her in the future."

"What do you mean?" she asked, and then added swiftly, "Are you sure? What makes you think so?"

He laughed but did not answer. He and his grandmother understood one another perfectly, there was never any need to answer unless one liked.

"Ernest," she said, "what is she like? Who is she? What is her name?"

He laughed again but this time answered, numbering her questions and marking them off on his thin fingers.

"One—she is a dear. Two—I don't know. Three—I never asked."

"Oh well!" said Lady Hume resignedly. "He wouldn't be

a Hume if he were not a fool over women."

Meantime Emily had found the path and was on her way up the glen. She had no idea what she was going to say when she saw Francis although she had gone over the meeting with him a hundred times in her imagination. Now that she was so near her desire, the courage which had sustained her began to ebb. Would he be different because of his changed prospects, would he believe her story?

She stopped on the path and looked back. There was still time to fly, to find the car and be well on her way home before she was missed. She had told nobody her name so he would never know that she had come.

"Francis," she whispered. "Oh Francis, what shall I do? What will you say to me?"

There was a pile of boulders by the edge of the path, round, like giant pebbles. Emily sat down on one of these and looked back the way she had come. The rutty path, scored with storm-water, zig-zagged down the glen till it disappeared into the fringe of trees which surrounded Eaglefold Castle.

It was beautiful, far more lovely than Emily had imagined. How could she make Francis believe that it was nothing to her?

She was shaken by sudden panic, her heart beat unevenly and the landscape swam before her eyes. Her one idea was flight, but for the moment her strength had deserted her.

She leaned her head upon her hands.

"Can I help you in any way?"

The question startled Emily for she had heard nobody approach. She looked up and found herself face to face with Francis himself.

"Emily! You!" he cried in amazement.

He ran forward eagerly and took her hands.

"Are you real?" he whispered, gazing into the face which had haunted his dreams.

There was a light in his eyes which told Emily all that she wanted to know, told her more surely than a thousand words of endearment that she was still precious to him. She was tempted to yield to his arms and leave explanations to the future, he was so strong and she was unutterably weary.

And then suddenly her pride came to her aid, there was something she must know before she and Francis could come together. She drew on some deep reserve of strength that she did not know she possessed and held herself back from him.

"Francis, I have come all the way to ask you something—just one question."

"What is that?" he demanded.

"Did you—did you write a letter to me? You told Laura that you had done so—is it true? For God's sake answer."

"It is true."

"I never got it," she said faintly.

Francis looked down into her upturned face for a few moments without speaking. She bore his scrutiny bravely for she felt that he deserved that much. She could not help the tears which filled her eyes until they brimmed like pools in flood-time but through the film her soul shone clear and steady. Just for a moment an unworthy doubt had entered Francis' mind but now it had fled for ever. He was gazing into her soul; she was deliberately uncovering it for him.

"They said—you would not believe me," she said at last. "But, oh Francis, you must believe. How could you think, how could you have thought I would not have answered if you had written—"

"My poor darling," he said. "What a cad I must have seemed—to go away and leave you—"

She swayed a little for the strain had been terrible. Francis caught her in his arms and held her. She did not faint but only leaned against him as if all her strength had come to an end.

"My darling," he whispered. "My dear love."

To his virile strength she seemed fragile, delicate as a flower, yet he realised that she was full of courage to come to him honestly and openly. It would have been easier to write, but Emily was not made for easy paths. Her faith in his love seemed marvellous to him, filling him with a proud humility.

"Emily," he said at last.

She understood, and, lifting her head, gave him her lips as straightforwardly as a child.

All about them the heather bloomed, a purple carpet spread over the sunlit hills; below them lay Eaglefold, cradled amongst its ancient trees; above them in the azure sky a lark sang of love and happiness, hovering on outstretched wings.